Eve
Eversz, Robert.
Killing paparazzi

 W9-CIB-168

$ 23.95

Praise for Shooting Elvis

'Eversz's novel reads like *The Catcher in the Rye*
with high explosives'
Daily Telegraph

'A thriller with complex characterization,
a streak of misanthropic wit, a bleak world-weariness,
and no easy answers . . . *Shooting Elvis* is that rare creature,
a Generation X novel that skips the lifestyle accessories
and goes to the heart of the malaise'
Scotsman

'Good fun'
The Times

'Pulp fiction run amok'
Time Out

'A groovy little debut, and no mistake'
Melody Maker

'Best Humorous Crime Novel, 1996:
Wild, wicked and off the wall . . . Fast, frightening
and very, very funny'
Val McDermid

'It's amazing what a new writer can do with
the old routines. In his first work of crime fiction,
Shooting Elvis, Robert M. Eversz took the hard-boiled
formula for a terrorist-on-the-lam thriller and worked it
into a feverishly hip satire of the Hollywood zeitgeist . . .
With his slick style and cheeky cynicism, he is already
an expert at setting heads to spinning'
New York Times

Killing Paparazzi

Also by Robert M. Eversz

Shooting Elvis

Gypsy Hearts

Robert M. Eversz

Killing Paparazzi

St. Martin's Minotaur
New York

www.minotaurbooks.com

ISBN 0-312-28902-2

First published in Great Britain by Macmillan
An imprint of Macmillan Publishers Ltd

First St. Martin's Minotaur Edition: January 2002

10 9 8 7 6 5 4 3 2 1

This book is dedicated

in memoriam to my mother,

who as a young woman could

out-ride, out-shoot and out-fight

most men in their prime.

To photograph people is to violate them, by seeing them as they never see themselves, by having knowledge of them they can never have; it turns people into objects that can be symbolically possessed. Just as the camera is a sublimation of the gun, to photograph someone is a sublimated murder . . .

– Susan Sontag

1

The horn sounds before dawn when you're paroled, as it does every morning. You stand at the bars for prisoner count and when the hundred bolts on your block fire back you step out of your cell and walk in silent two-by-two down a concrete corridor to the same breakfast you've eaten for the last year, two years, twenty years, however long you've been resident. But it's not like any other morning, you see that on the face of every inmate you meet. You don't belong any more. You're not one of them. You're out. Some touch you for luck when the officers aren't watching. Some whisper, See you back here soon, bitch.

The previous day you reported to work detail. On parole day, they shunt you aside with one or two others getting out the same time. You settle your account at the canteen. They give you a box with the clothes you wore into the joint or something your family – if you have any – brought for you to wear on the day of your release. You remove the prison overalls and put on your street clothes. You sign papers. Even five years out of style you start to feel the blood flow through your veins. If you haven't been rehabilitated to walking death, you feel a little like you again. Over a scarred counter they hand out whatever money you saved working at twenty-five cents an hour. You sign more papers. They fingerprint you one last time and check your prints against the prints on file to make sure they're releasing the right inmate. At every step in the process you stop before steel bars and wait for the buzz and thunk of the lock springing back. It's a sound you know like your own cough in the night. Last of all they cut the prisoner identification number from your wrist. The number is embedded in a thin plastic bracelet and it goes into a file reserved for your return. Through the last set of steel bars and down sunlit stairs an exit sign flickers green above an open door. You're out.

I was the first inmate released from California Institute for Women that morning. The San Gabriel mountains rimmed the northern horizon, snow-dusted peaks glinting white and gold under a sun that rolled like a bright yellow marble up the blue bowl of winter sky. Across the road Bandini Mountain steamed under the first rays of sun. Though I hadn't seen it for five years, I hadn't forgotten the sight or smell. No inmate could. Six days a week, blue overalled workers shovelled its perpetually expanding base into a fertilizer factory. Bandini Mountain measured over a mile in length and rose so high snow might have capped the peak if not for the heat generated by the horse, cow and human faeces that formed its mass. The stench penetrated concrete, steel and the deepest dreams. Behind the razor wire, everything smelled like shit: the air, the food, the inmates, the officers – even the warden, a well-meaning soul imprisoned as much as anyone by the smell, could never completely wash the odour of excrement from her hair.

The Sergeant-at-Arms opened the rear door of the police cruiser that was to take me to the bus station twelve miles down the road. I crawled into the caged compartment and shut the door behind me. I didn't fool myself into thinking I was free. The wire mesh that screened me from the driver was just another set of bars. Nobody released on parole is free. The chain might be longer but the State still owned me. The Sergeant-at-Arms started the engine and accelerated past Bandini Mountain. I moved my lips in a voiceless goodbye to five years of doing the same thing every day the same way. Five years of a concrete and steel room with a squat toilet in the corner. Five years of never being alone, not to shower, to urinate, or defecate. Five years of lock-ups and head-counts six times a day. Five years of being watched everywhere, always. Five years of no dogs, no cats, no birds, no children, no men. Five years of no touching. Five years of imposed silences and arbitrary punishments. Five years of a flashlight beamed up my rectum and vagina. Five years of humiliation, five years of fear. Fear of solitary, fear of emptiness, fear of time. Five years leaking into my veins like formaldehyde to a walking corpse.

I ceased being the responsibility of the California Institute for Women the moment my foot hit the bottom step of the Greyhound bus. The driver took a long look at me as I leaped on board. He'd been driving a bus so long his butt sagged over the edges of the seat.

He said, 'Welcome back to the free world, honey.'

I grew up watching the fights on television. My dad was a big fight fan. He'd sit me down next to him on the couch and between rounds send me into the kitchen for beer. My favourite part was the introduction, when the referee explains legal versus illegal types of mayhem while the two fighters try to take each other down with bad-ass eyes. That was the stare my parole officer gave me when I walked into her office. The terms of my parole required me to check in with a parole officer upon release. She was the hundred-and-forty-pound ball at the end of my chain. She looked my age plus five years, a thin-lipped blonde with chisel-marks around the eyes. Muscle flexed at the corners of her jaw and corded down her neck. Her body had the cut look of sculpted stone. She could have cracked walnuts between the biceps and forearms showing below the sleeves of her white cotton blouse. Nothing about the woman appeared soft. Even her wash-and-wear hairstyle had a muscular curl to it. We were in the same weight class and I was in the best shape of my life but it was no contest. My jail face was still on. Don't talk back. Don't smile. Don't grimace. Don't stare someone down who can stick you in the hole or give you a hard time.

'So which one are you going to be, Miss Baker?'

'I beg your pardon?'

'Are you a loser?' Her blue steel glance made one smooth

incision from my pelvis to forehead. 'Or someone who can straighten out her life?'

She wanted me to think about that one. I didn't worry about going back to the criminal life because I'd never been in it. Before my arrest I'd photographed babies for a living. I wore knee-length white skirts and pink sweaters and painted my nails to match. I never did drugs or broke the law. I was a good girl. Then everything went wrong and I discovered my goodness was a façade carefully constructed over something so dark and twisted it frightened people.

I said, 'Only time on the outside can judge that.'

She dipped her shoulder, yanked back a drawer and flipped a thin manila file onto the desktop. 'Just about everybody who comes to this office swears they're going to stay clean and the ones who swear the loudest are usually the first to fall.' She flicked through the file page by page, spending half a minute on one, a few seconds on the next. 'You just might be the rare parolee with a healthy attitude. Then again, you might be clever at conning people.' She stuck me with an inquisitor's smile and went, 'Hmmmm?'

Nothing I could say to that. She was the professional, the one who did this for a living. I was a first-timer along for the ride.

'Most of the people assigned to me are just marking time before they're bounced back to prison. That's where they belong. They're losers. I might sympathize with them. I might even like them. But when the time comes, I'll punch their ticket back without a second thought. Don't expect me to treat you any differently.'

'No ma'am.'

She lifted a No. 2 pencil from a chipped white coffee cup and drew a parolee release form toward her elbow. On the wall behind her head hung a framed diploma from USC.

She'd received her bachelor degree in psychology. Other than that diploma and the chipped coffee cup, her office was stripped of any evidence of a life. Considering the quality of her clientele, I didn't wonder why. It would take just one convicted murderer to comment 'Nice family' to pull every photograph off the desk.

'Do you have a job lined up?'

'I thought I'd try to find work as a photographer.'

I watched her write 'Photographer, no steady employment' in a box marked 'Means of Support'.

'What about your place of residence? Where do you plan to live?'

'With my husband.'

She began to write it but stopped mid-word and set the pencil down.

'What husband? I didn't see any mention of a husband in your file.'

'That's because I don't have one yet.'

'Are you overly optimistic or have you actually met somebody?'

She thought she was being funny.

'We have hotel reservations tonight in Las Vegas.'

'What's the rush?'

'Anything wrong with me wanting to get married?'

The muscle above her jaw jumped. The workout she gave it daily built and defined it like a triceps. 'There's little I can do to prevent it, let me put it that way. He have a criminal record, your fiancé?'

'Not that I know of.'

'How did you meet him?'

'Through my cellmate.'

She flipped open my file again and rifled through the pages. 'Rose Selavy, that cellmate?'

'They're cousins.'

'Your ex-cellmate Rose is a hooker and drug addict.'

'Was,' I said. 'There's not so much opportunity in prison.'

'What does he do, this guy you want to marry?'

'He's a photographer.' I laid out the information without comment, knowing that was the beauty of the arrangement. We were in the same business. That was how Rose thought of getting us together in the first place. Her cousin was English. He needed a green card. I needed money. She'd never met her cousin but they used the same lawyer, Harry Bendel. I never questioned the illegality of marrying him. Bendel had made the arrangements. I didn't even know what my husband-to-be looked like.

My parole officer picked up the pencil again and tapped it gum-side down, each tap premeditated like the squeeze of a trigger. 'Forgive me for being blunt, but why does he want to marry you?'

'You don't think I'm attractive?'

'Look in the yellow pages under escort services. A hundred places will sell you attractive for a lot less than a wedding ring.'

'He knows my work. Five years ago he saw photographs of mine in an art gallery and fell in love. He thinks I have talent. He wants to help me. And I hope to hell he wants to jump my bones.'

She thought she could judge whether or not I lied by my eyes. Law-enforcement officials like to observe the eyes of suspects for traces of truth or deception. My eyes had a naturally honest shine. I fooled everybody, including myself. I'd lived a lie until my first crime at age twenty-three. I'd always been a good liar, even when I thought I was telling the truth.

My parole officer reached into her top desk drawer and

slipped out a form stamped with the state seal of California. 'I hope you're not being clever. No matter how clever you are you'll screw-up and I'll know it. Criminals are screw ups by nature. Sooner or later you all end up behind bars.' She filled out the form with the dates and locations and signed it. 'This is your travel permit. You need it to cross the state line. Check in with the Las Vegas Police Department when you arrive. They like to know when felons come to town.'

I said, 'Yes ma'am, I will,' knowing I wouldn't. I didn't expect any trouble. Despite my time in prison, I never thought of myself as a criminal. Maybe that was because I never really regretted the acts that imprisoned me.

Run-off from a storm the night before swept newspapers, lawn clippings, dog droppings and shredded cardboard into the storm drain at Pico Boulevard and from there out to the fish in Santa Monica Bay. Toward the pier, black smoke piped from a swarm of bulldozers pushing sand into a line of defence against the next tantrum from El Niño. I waded through fifty yards of beach sand and sat at the sea's faltering edge, where the waves beat themselves into a line of beige foam. For the first time in five years, no one watched me. When I worked up the courage I stripped to my underwear and sprinted into the Pacific. I'd been dreaming of that moment for five years. I dived through the first wave and swam furiously until my body temperature rose to fight the December chill. Past the wave break I trod water in a slow half-circle. The coast curled from Point Dume to Palos Verdes like the tail of a beast backed into a great blue wilderness. I felt almost peaceful.

At my arrest I'd worn eight silver earrings and a dagger nose-stud. All but three of those piercings had fused to scar tissue during my time in the Institute. The jewellery stripped from me at my booking lay sealed in a zip-lock baggie with keys to a car I no longer owned and an apartment I no longer rented. Not much of what I once was still fit what I'd become. I jabbed two rings into the lobe of my right ear and the dagger stud into the left and stored the rest in the side pocket of a leather jacket I'd just bought, along with white jeans, a stretch velvet v-neck and black Converse All Stars, at a retro-fashion shop near the beach. The jacket looked like the last person to wear it had been hit by a truck. I sympathized. I tossed my jail rags into the first trash-can I came to. I felt more free than I had in a long time.

At a row of vending machines I bought a fresh newspaper and walked into the Firehouse Café to wait for my prospective husband to show. I propped the newspaper against a sugar shaker on a table by the window and scanned the headlines. Political scandals, wars and fires raged around the world. In five years nothing much had changed. When a waitress stopped by to fill my coffee cup I ordered bacon and eggs sunny side up with hash browns and a side of ham, another side of pancakes and a glass of orange juice.

The guy at the next table asked, 'You know what my mother always said to me about food?' He sat splay-legged, black jeans tucked over Beatle boots, one long leg curled under the table and the other sticking into the aisle like an accident waiting to happen. A wise guy. While he looked at me he spun an empty coffee cup with one hand, caught it, and spun it again, grinning like he thought he was really something. His smile was contagious. It had been so long since a man smiled at me I'd forgotten how dangerous it could be.

'No,' I said.

'Never eat anything bigger than your head.'

I could tell from his accent that he wasn't from California. I asked, 'You know what my mom always said to me about food?'

He wagged his head. I let out a belch. It took him a moment to get the joke but then he thought it was pretty funny. He had a peculiar laugh, high pitched and percussive, like a dog with a stepped-on tail. I couldn't help but want to laugh along with him, even if I didn't.

'No, that's not true. My mom is a lady. She always told me, "Mary Alice, mind your manners." It's not her fault I turned out how I did.'

He snapped the wobbling coffee cup from the table and the pinpoint focus of his eyes diffused as though he was suddenly unsure he wanted to be talking to me. I looked like the woman he was supposed to meet but the name threw him. 'Is that your name? Mary Alice?'

'Was then. Now, just strangers call me that.'

I dug into the hash browns and eggs the waitress laid on the table. He went back to spinning the coffee cup and watching me. Soft brown hair tumbled down his forehead and over his ears. His hairstyle and square black plastic glasses seemed cut from the sixties, as did the silver pendant that hung down the front of his black T-shirt. Like a lot of people into retro, maybe he unconsciously wanted to look like his parents.

'Those who know you, what name do they use?'

'Nina. Nina Zero.'

He sprang to his feet and introduced himself as Gabriel Burns, my prospective husband. I wiped the bacon grease off my hand and when I extended it he flipped the wrist palm down to kiss my fingers at the knuckle. Nobody had ever done that to me before. I wasn't sure I liked it.

'This is just business, right?'

He slid into the chair across the table and though he did not speak, his mischievous grin communicated plenty. He brought the empty coffee cup to his lips and stared at me over the rim. The hands wrapping the cup were broad at the palm and the fingers long but small-knuckled. In form, they matched the width of his shoulders and the angular tapering of his torso to the limbs below. The sudden desire to feel those hands on my back reminded me how long it had been since I'd had a man.

I said, 'I don't want us to get started here with the wrong ideas.'

'We don't have to be so grim, do we? If we can't giggle over something so silly as getting married in Las Vegas, what's the point?'

'Let me see your hand.'

He held it out for me palm up. His veins ran like blue ink beneath parchment coloured skin. I flipped his hand and kissed the back of it, like he'd kissed mine. He laughed at that. He liked to laugh at a lot of things. I asked, 'You brought the money? That's not a problem?'

'Will you take a cheque?'

'Sure I'll take the check. Then I'll pay and go and you can find somebody else to marry in Vegas.'

'Joke, darling, joke. Where did you lose your sense of humour?'

I could see it pass across his face that he'd forgotten I'd just been released from prison and that was as good a place as any to lose a sense of humour or to have it stolen or beaten out of you.

'Harry Bendel told me two thousand. Is that right?'

'That's right. Cash.'

He snatched a strip of bacon from my plate, asked with his eyes if he could eat it and when I nodded he said we had a deal.

4

Mid-way between the towns of Littlerock and Llano the Englishman tossed me the keys to his Mustang. The Pear-blossom is a double-barrelled shotgun highway – two lanes shooting fast as buckshot through a flat stretch of scrub desert. I kicked the accelerator hard enough to crack verte-brae. The desert soared to distant mountains rippling in clear winter light. A car, a man, a clear winter day in the desert. This was paradise, I thought.

My hubby-to-be pointed his lens across the desert floor toward the granite slopes of the Sierra Nevadas. 'I can never get my mind around the distances in America. How far away is that mountain range? Twenty miles? A hundred?'

'About fifty.'

He let the camera hang on its neck-strap and stared out the windshield. 'I feel like a pygmy out here under so much sky.'

From his bag he retrieved a 28-millimetre fixed lens and swapped it with the telephoto.

I watched his image like a movie on the silver screen of the rear-view mirror, pleased by his English parchment skin, so thin I could trace the route of blue veins at his throat. 'What do you like to shoot most, people or objects?'

'Both. People who are objects.'

'You mean, like Edward Weston or Robert Mapplethorpe,

studies of people that resemble objects in like, their approach to the beauty of the human form?'

He looked at me like a monkey had just spoken to him in French. 'Not that at all, but don't think for a moment I don't understand what you just said, even if I'm surprised to hear you say it.'

'Surprised by what? That I'm not an idiot?'

'Not every ex-con is conversant in the iconic figures of twentieth-century photography.'

'You know a lot of ex-cons?'

'Ex-cons, no. Icons, yes. I photograph people whose physical images are a commodity consumed around the world like a bottle of Coca-Cola.'

'If you mean celebrities, why don't you just say celebrities?'

'It's more fun when you have to work a little to get it.'

'To get what? That you're a paparazzi?'

'Paparazzo, singular. Most people just call me "princess killer".'

He pointed his lens out the window and photographed a giant lobster crawling out of the desert, one of a line of monsters marching toward Las Vegas. Just out of Victorville half-naked showgirls strut from roadside billboards and money rains into pots advertising one casino or another but as the drive grinds on and the stomach grumbles the billboards appeal to baser instincts. About a hundred miles from the state line giant shellfish and cuts of meat rear out of the bleak landscape like an advancing army, each clutching an 'All You Can Eat for $7.95' sticker in the shape of a buzz-saw blade.

At the Last Vegas county courthouse we stood in a roped-off line for an hour, paid $35 to a bouffant Betty in a loud sweater, and got our no-blood-test, no-waiting-period, no-criminal-record-check, no-embarrassing-theology or second-thoughts-allowed wedding licence. You could marry a dog in Las Vegas and as long as you paid the licensing fee no one would care unless you and the dog were the same sex. At the curb of the courthouse steps we asked a tuxedoed blond polishing a limousine where we could go to get married and he told us we could do it in any of the casinos or one of a couple dozen wedding chapels. The best one depended on our needs and how much money we wanted to pay. The place down the street would marry us for $25 if the minister was sober enough to stand.

'Can we get Elvis?' Gabe asked. 'I heard we could get Elvis to marry us in Las Vegas.'

'That's true, we got the world's only ordained Elvis imper-sonator.' The driver admitted this with some pride, as though every town wanted one. 'But Elvis is booked days in advance. You gotta wait if you want Elvis.' He scratched his cheek and appeared to give the matter some thought. 'If you can afford a hundred dollars or more, the most elegant chapel in town is here.' He backed away from the door and pointed to a magnetic slap-on sign advertising 'A Special Memory Wed-ding Chapel™'. He even offered to give us a free ride out, no commitment to stay and marry if we didn't like the place.

When I saw the old-fashioned clapboard steeple of the New England chapel rising from a dry as dirt cinderblock housing tract, I realized we couldn't have picked any better than 'A Special Memory Wedding Chapel' given a month of research. Inside the chapel pine needles and roses perfumed the air. A red carpet rolled down the aisle between padded oak pews and, with dark-stained beams arching over the altar, Las Vegas seemed two thousand miles away. The bride even had her own dressing-room and special entrance down a set of steps to the aisle. With only two steps in the set the bride's entrance might have been short on drama but I appreciated the thought that had gone into putting it there. A nice woman from Australia gave us a tour of the place and listed our marriage options. We picked the 'Memorable Memory' package at $199 and got artificial candlelight, an organist, three roses for me and a rose boutonniere for Gabe, nine photographs from a professional wedding photographer and a souvenir scroll of our marriage vows.

The problem with two photographers marrying each other is that the number of cameras is greater than the possible subjects and when the vows are read the bride and groom are more likely to be trying to photograph the event than participate in it. I shot with a disposable cardboard camera bought at a drugstore. Going up against Gabe's motor-driven Nikon I was seriously out-gunned but at least armed. I'd take his photograph, he'd take mine, then we'd both run over to get one of the organist. Then the part came when Gabe was supposed to put a ring on my finger, but he didn't have a ring, he had this silver amulet attached to a leather strap, something he said he picked up once while on assignment in Papua New Guinea, a circular disc engraved with the markings of the prehistoric Papua New Guinean calendar. The hole in the middle was just big enough to fit my finger so I told him to pretend it was a ring and then it was kiss the bride time. We were both shy about that, hesitating and almost missing each other's lips but when our lips did meet it was like they never wanted to separate. His breath was warm and sweet and there was this special smell about him that went to my head like a shot of whiskey.

When the photographer stepped forward to take one of our nine official wedding pictures, Gabriel lifted me into the air and told him to go ahead and shoot and then he slung me around his back. I screamed with laughter and that's the photograph I thought I'd like best, Gabriel looking straight at the camera with me riding piggyback laughing at him, both of us shocked to be suddenly crazy about each other.

The orange glow on the horizon as we left the chapel wasn't from the setting sun but the fused incandescence of a million lights wired into the mile-long cluster of casinos that formed the fabled strip of Las Vegas. We set our course by the casino lights and walked. The first stars punched through a neon blue sky to wash the landscape of cinderblock homes, chain-link fencing and dead grass with twilight the colour of zinc. In the desert even ugliness takes on a particular kind of beauty. I put my arm through his and when I did his body leaned into mine with a kind of surrender.

'Time to take care of business,' I said.

'Can I pay by credit card?'

This time I laughed and that pleased him. He dipped his hand into the inside pocket of his creased leather trench coat for a white envelope that looked and felt about twenty bills thick. 'I got a fabulous deal on hundreds from my local counterfeiter. If you'd like, we can stop under the street light to count them.'

'I trust you.' I put the envelope in the left flap pocket of my leather jacket.

'You really shouldn't. I'm a scoundrel and a cheat and you shouldn't believe anything I tell you because it's likely to be a lie, particularly if it's the least bit funny.'

I thought he was joking so I smiled. This look passed across his face like he wanted to kiss me and not as part of any fake ceremony. I was all for him giving it a go but he hesitated and the moment passed. That might have been the beginning and end of our sexual relationship if not for the jogger who came upon us between street lights, the kind of regular Joe in mismatched sweatshirt and sweatpants who turns his baseball cap backwards. I didn't pay any notice to him until he pulled up and said, 'Let go of her, you prick.' I didn't wait for him to let go of me; I released his arm and stepped back. With two grand in my pocket I couldn't be certain Gabe wasn't trying to scam me. That's how doing time influenced my thinking. In my head I heard, *Pay off the bitch and get your man to stick her up at gunpoint.* I'd just spent five years with people who pulled that kind of stunt for a living. But the jogger grabbed Gabe's shoulder and spun him like I wasn't even there. I'd been around enough fights to understand that the aggressor has all the advantages; most often the fight is over before the assailed understands she's even in a fight.

I said, 'Hey mister, leave us alone, we've done nothing to you.'

Gabe stepped aside like he wanted no part of it. He said, 'I'm not about to – ' but didn't get to finish what he was trying to say before the jogger grabbed his neck and threw him down. Gabe lay flat on his back as though he couldn't understand how he got there. The first moments in a fight are critical. It isn't so much the punch as the counterpunch that tips the winner. Gabe's idea of a counterpunch was to shout, 'What are you doing? You're bloody nuts!'

The jogger fumbled at the ankle hem of his sweatpants and straightened with a folding combat knife between his thumb and forefinger. He smiled like he was enjoying himself. The carbon-steel blade was dark as asphalt. At night you'd see the fist hurtling toward your chest but not the blade. Gabe tried to scramble to his feet but the jogger kicked his legs out from under him. He turned his back to me and flicked the blade forward like he wanted to cut, not kill. He didn't consider me much of a threat. I was only a girl. What I knew what I could do. I shucked my leather jacket and could I do?

threw it over his head, then kicked him just below that thing all women are supposed to envy and I tell you he suddenly wasn't so happy he had it. His knees knocked together and he bent over at the waist. I kicked the side of his knee and he went down but he wouldn't let go of the knife so I aimed for his kidney. It wasn't so much fun. I don't care what my reputation is, I don't like hurting people. The jogger wasn't a quitter but after I kicked him in the head a couple times he didn't have any fight left and when he curled into a shell I grabbed my jacket from the ground and we both ran. We didn't know if anybody else would come after us and even though we won the fight we were still scared. When we reached the safety of lights we caught our breath on the curb.

'Who was that guy?' I asked.

'Never saw him before in my life.'

I looked at him like, who are you trying to fool?

'No, really! A complete stranger.' He lowered his head and I dropped mine until just our foreheads were touching.

I said, 'Pretty scary, huh?'

'I haven't been so frightened since my big brother locked me in the closet with the girl next door.'

'How old were you?'

When he said 'Twenty-seven' we both laughed and it felt like the fear left us with each exhalation of breath. Whatever his deficiencies as a fighter his wits hadn't left him. Then he kissed me a good long kiss right there on the curb and I knew it could lead to only one thing.

5

'Will that be one bed or two?' The registrar at Bally's Casino wore a friendly smile and name badge that read Cathy.

I said, 'One bed. If we don't get along he can sleep on the floor.'

Her friendly smile didn't waver a bit. People in corporate customer-service jobs rarely understand when you joke with them. But then, it wasn't really a joke. I didn't like the wild way my heart raced at a hundred and twenty beats a minute and then skidded all four chambers down to no beats at all. Half the time I couldn't breathe fast enough and the other half I felt drugged.

On the casino floor below, roulette wheels clattered, slot machines shrieked out the big winners and everywhere hummed the machinery of dreams. Two hours earlier the sun had set but inside the casino the lights blared as brightly as they had at noon or at midnight or at any time since the power switch had been thrown. Next to Hollywood, which exists only in the imagination, Las Vegas is the most surreal city in America. I'd just survived five years of cold-steel reality. I loved the twenty-four-hour artificial dream-time of six-foot showgirls, $7.95 all-you-can-eat buffets and million-dollar slots and most of all I loved the idea that in another day or two almost everyone would vanish into lives that had no connection to the place.

'No matter what happens tonight, we're still free,' Gabe said when we rode the elevator up to the room. 'Even though we're married, we have no obligation to each other except to be truthful.'

Free. I loved the sound of the word so much I didn't consider what he meant by it. I watched him bounce from the bed to the window, where he drew back the curtains to a view of carnival lights below. It had been so long since I'd made love to a man that I didn't know what to do, what to say, how to move. I wasn't courting a man so much as disaster.

Then before I could stop or even slow it down we were in each other's arms and I'm lying to you because I didn't want to stop or slow it down, I wanted it here and now. I ached inside from emptiness and longing. We held each other so fiercely that in moving toward the bed we tripped over the armchair and nearly sprawled to the floor. He slid his hands underneath my v-neck sweater and wrestled with the twin hooks of my bra, vanquishing them upon the third assault. I stripped off his black cotton T-shirt and flung it arm over arm across the room. His chest was thin and smooth as a young boy's. He gasped and then laughed when I took my teeth to it. Gabe was ticklish in body as well as mind and he most naturally inhabited a zone between the erotic and the amused. I'm not a woman of much experience but, compared to the limited number of men I'd known, Gabe was not an accomplished lover. He was the funniest man I'd ever sacked and did not lack enthusiasm for the act itself even if he had the endurance and technique of a hundred-metre sprinter; ten seconds after the gun sounded he'd take his victory lap and head for the showers. He wasn't intentionally inconsiderate of my pleasures, just fast and at the end of his run, too exhausted to help me across the finish line. His humour made him fun to be around despite this but a laugh is not a substitute for an orgasm.

Gabe differed most from other men I'd known in his ability to talk, sometimes for hours about absolutely nothing, and this kept us in bed together as much as the sex. We talked mostly about our childhoods and families – typical new-lover stuff. I told him I was the youngest child of a machinist and a woman who had worked a series of retail jobs throughout her life, most recently at K-Mart. I didn't tell him any of the bad stuff about my family. I didn't tell him that I hadn't seen or talked to my sister since my sixteenth birthday, wasn't even sure she was still alive. That my brother Ray was the only one of five children who stuck around, either out of loyalty to Mom or because he was too weak to make his own life. That my dad thought I was a devil-child and was proud to say so whenever he could. Maybe I was guilty of projecting a false history of myself, but I didn't like to talk about the violence and hatred that coursed through my family like a disease. 'What about you?' I asked.

'One brother, Nigel. Absolutely mad about football. Arsenal's greatest fans, we were. As kids we were close as cleats on a football boot. He's too respectable for football now. A barrister, very solid sort, wears the wig in the Queen's court. Not like me at all.'

'Yeah? And what are you like?'

'A complete rotter. Haven't told the straight truth about anything for twenty-two years and counting. Every time I try, the silver spoon gets in my way. My family is frightfully UMC you know.'

'What's that?'

'Upper middle class.'

'Does that make you a Lord or something?'

'God, no. Grandfather had the rotten luck to be illegiti-
mate. Father's never got over it. Tries to compensate all the
time. Dresses in tweeds, speaks as though he has a mouth
full of marbles. What a bore. But dear mother had a wild
streak in her youth. My middle name is Keith because she
was so daft about the Rolling Stones she shagged my name-
sake once. She's respectable now so let's not mention it to
anyone and certainly not to father, but she's the one I take
after.'

'How does Rose fit into the family picture?'

'Who?'

'Rose Selavy, you know, your cousin.'

'I don't have a cousin named Rose – whatever.'

'Of course you do. My cellmate. The one who set this up.'

'That's just a figure of speech, you know, "Our American
cousins". The marriage was arranged through my lawyer,
Harry Bendel.'

That was when the clock struck midnight and my grand
coach of a romance began to turn into a pumpkin. That Rose
had lied shouldn't have surprised me. A junkie prostitute
can't be expected to tell the truth when money can be made
with a lie. Maybe the lawyer had offered a finder's fee. No
harm done, except that I'd just married a man who wasn't
exactly who I thought he was. Most brides have a similar
experience.

When we rode the elevator down to the casino I asked
him why he needed a green card. I didn't get an answer. The
moment the elevator doors opened he sprang toward the
nearest blackjack table. Sometimes people are too tied up in
their own thoughts to listen to you and sometimes they just
don't want to answer. I tossed a five-dollar bill on to the box
next to his and split two tens. Gabe drew a three and a two
with the dealer showing four. I tried again. 'Do you need one

to work, or do you have some hidden desire to become an American?'

'God, no! I'd just as soon be Australian.' He asked the dealer for a card. The dealer tossed him a king. Gabe glanced up at me.

'Stay,' I advised.

He hit, drew an eight and busted.

'Bloody luck.'

'The way you play, luck's got nothing to do with it.'

The dealer hit a face card on fourteen and busted. The hand exposed the red plastic marker at the end of the decks and we waited while the dealer loaded a new shoe.

'I'm not drunk enough to play. Hell, I'm not drunk at all. Nobody has any luck stone sober. Want a beer?' He glanced around for a cocktail waitress but instead of calling for a beer shouted, 'Bloody wanker!' Before the epithet cleared his lips he sprang from the table. As we were surrounded by Mid-westerners who had no idea what a wanker was, much less a bloody one, his curse didn't attract much attention. Even his sprint through the blackjack tables didn't draw more than a few glances from faces hypnotized by the click of cards. Well ahead of Gabe, past the roulette wheels and breaching the sharp-elbowed grandmother section of slot machines, I spotted a bird's-nest of bare skull and hair bobbing rapidly above the crowd. I pulled our chips from the table and chased after, partly out of loyalty to Gabe, who might need my help if he actually caught the guy, and partly to learn what the hell was going on.

Gabe was little better at running than he was at fighting. I caught sight of him through the wall of glass doors at Bally's entrance, so badly winded he bent at the waist to rest his palms on his thighs. Whoever he had been chasing was long gone. The figure had been too tall to be the one who had attacked us outside the chapel yet Gabe clearly knew him. I didn't see a need to let him know I followed and retreated to the blackjack tables.

'Your partner, he have friends in town?' The dealer's eyes were a faded blue, as though left too long in the sun, and her face had tanned to the colour of leather. By the pale band of skin on her ring finger I could tell she had her share of man troubles.

She dealt me an ace-ten blackjack so I answered, 'Who knows? Whatever goes on in the little minds of men is a mystery to me.'

She paid me three for two and dealt me two face cards. 'Men. Can't live with 'em, can't shoot 'em.'

'Sure you can. You just go to jail if you do.'

I played through my string of cards until five losing hands in a row proved the deck ran against me. I tipped the dealer ten of the two hundred I carried away and found Gabe at the nearest roulette table, tossing chips at random boxes. His system didn't make any sense but then neither did Gabe half the time, which I thought to be one of the secrets to his charm, something it had just occurred to me to distrust.

'Who did you just chase out of here?'

'The scalp collector.'

'Who?'

The steel ball shot around the rim of the wheel, bounced like a wild hubcap and wobbled into the number seventeen slot, about the only bet he hadn't covered. The dealer raked his chips from the table with the air of a bored bankteller.

'A bloody thief, worse than this wheel. He must have followed us all the way from Los Angeles.'

I began to fear I'd just married a guy who had more troubles than I did. 'Why would he want to do that?'

'Lack of imagination. I'm on a hot streak at the moment and as a result he's been following me around. He's a poacher. Probably thinks I'm in Vegas to shoot a big celeb.'

'He's a competitor?'

'In his wildest fantasies.' He tossed the last of his chips on seventeen, a bet he liked because nobody else would think of betting on the previous winning number.

'I know I'm a little late saying this, but the kind of marriage we have would be a violation of my parole if anybody was able to prove it.'

He could see I wasn't going to let the subject drop. 'I have a Type One visa. I can photograph and report here as much as I like.'

'I thought the whole idea of a green card was so you could work.'

'I'm already working. I need insurance. What would happen if someone convinced an immigration officer to yank my visa the next time I enter the country?'

'Why would somebody do that?'

'Because I caught him with his knickers down, shagging a hooker in his Ferrari, and published the resulting photograph in newspapers around the world.'

'You really did that?'

'Just an example.'

'So the guy that attacked us, maybe he didn't come from nowhere?'

The dealer called an end to betting and made his toss. Gabe watched the steel ball race against the spin of the wheel. 'He's nothing. I don't worry about thugs. The person who sent him, he's the one who scares me.'

'You know who sent him?'

The ball hit the 00 slot and stuck.

'No. But most of the people angry with me earn twenty million dollars a picture and that much money can buy the ability to make a lot of trouble.'

Mid-way down the mountain to the San Fernando Valley Gabe looked at me in a funny way from the passenger seat and admitted, 'You're really a lovely girl but you know the time we spent in Vegas was more than a little unreal.'

'Yeah?' I said, not getting it. I'd been talking about what we could do when we got back to LA.

'I've had a great time with you, but we have to look at the situation realistically.'

'What situation?'

'Our situation.'

'What about "our situation"?'

'We can't continue this same relationship back in the city.'

'You mean, we can't pretend we have anything more than a strictly legal agreement?'

Gabe looked like a man long underwater coming up for air. He said, 'You understand exactly what I'm saying.'

My right foot – the one on the accelerator – acquired a sudden and uncontrollable weight problem. The Mustang lunged forward. 'You're saying this has been nothing more than a weekend of vigorous sport fucking?'

I could see it in his eyes, the terror that I was not going to be reasonable, I was not going to be a sport about it. He said, 'Oh dear. I thought you knew.'

The RPM gauge climbed so far into the red the needle began to bleed. Beyond the windshield, the landscape blurred. 'Knew what? That you wanted a whore?'

'I didn't say that. I did not say that. I just want to look at the situation realistically.'

With its light frame, 6-cylinder engine and 200-plus horsepower, I figured the Mustang could go pretty fast and it did, even if it handled with all the sureness of a hang glider in a hurricane. The speedometer claimed the car would do 140 mph but I couldn't get it over 135. Then the freeway sloped downhill and I did what I'd secretly wanted to do since getting behind the wheel: pinned the speedometer. 'If I'm going to be a whore, then at two grand at least I'm not a cheap whore!'

'You're angry!' He had to shout above the engine and wind noise to hear his own voice.

'I'm not angry! When I'm angry I shoot people! Now I'm merely annoyed!'

'We have two relationships here! You have two thousand dollars and I have a document for my green card! That's the legal relationship! I think you're smart and sexy and so bloody crazy you'll kill us both! That's our personal relationship!'

Men become reasonable when they want to squirm out of something, as though lack of reason explains the mistake of having seemed to care about you. Maybe I lightened my foot on the accelerator but it wasn't because I believed him. I didn't want a couple of traffic tickets to add to my troubles. When I pulled into the Department of Motor Vehicles lot in Santa Monica he said, 'I had a great time this weekend, I'd very much like to see you again, not just about the legal matters, but just to see you again. Do you understand?'

I understood too well. 'Your terms are not my terms. You think if you say the right words I'll sleep with you again without wanting anything more out of it, but I won't.'

The truth shocked him. He tried a sad look.

I slammed the door on it.

People break up all the time. I didn't have anything to complain about. I was free. I had over two thousand dollars in my pocket and after standing in line for an hour, taking the test and getting my photograph taken, I possessed a valid driver's licence. I took it to a used car lot on Santa Monica Boulevard and bought a 1976 Cadillac Eldorado with 170,000 miles on it. Nothing matters more in Los Angeles than the car you drive and the Caddy was a stylish monster, a gas-guzzling, road-hogging, middle-finger-extended statement on four wheels. So what if I didn't have enough money to pay rent after the purchase? The trunk was bigger than some apartments and the back seat alone could sleep a family of four.

I keyed the ignition and drove north, through the San Fernando Valley and over the pass to the town that I hadn't so much grown up in as been stunted by. It was a small town that had stopped being small because people who worked in Los Angeles fell in love with the fresh air and big houses and country lifestyle and moved there in such numbers that the air wasn't so fresh any more and most of the country-side was hidden beneath vast sprawls of tract homes. Part of the American dream is finding something you love and then destroying it.

I pulled into the parking lot of the new K-Mart Mom worked at, didn't go inside but stayed in my car, radio on, watching the entrance. She came out a couple hours later, looking smaller than I'd remembered, more frail. She'd had me at the end of a run of five children. In another year

K-Mart would fire her and call it retirement. I stepped out of the Cadillac, smiled and waved. I had in my mind this photograph she'd taken of me when I was about ten. In the photograph, my bony red knees poke out beneath a green corduroy jumper. I wear white sandals and oversized white sunglasses. My lips open to a gap-toothed smile. I wave at the camera, my arm bent at the elbow to a crescent shape. I look not just happy but innocent.

Mom had come out of K-Mart with a younger woman who shared her same home-permanent hairstyle and owlish glasses. You could tell from the red and white K-Mart blouses they worked together. They looked like mother and daughter. When Mom saw me she turned to the woman and very clearly said goodbye. The woman got into a primer-grey Toyota Corolla one row over. Before pulling away she looked at me like she guessed who I was. I didn't blame Mom for not introducing us. It would have been too complicated to explain how somebody who did the things I was convicted of could be her daughter.

Mom took my arm, said, 'Well, look at you,' then, 'I just can't get used to that hair, Mary Alice, no matter what.'

I wanted to hug her but we weren't a hugging family so I just stroked her arm and tried not to let her see how shocked I was. She'd come to visit me twice at the Institute but the circumstances were so strained that I hadn't really noticed the changes. It wasn't just the age lines webbing across her cheeks, the wattle of loose skin at her throat, the increasing curvature of her spine, the shortness of her steps or the seeming precariousness of her balance; she seemed less certain of being, her eyes opaque as if she had already begun her retreat to the void. I couldn't reconcile the figure standing before me with the young and vital woman of my childhood. My mother had become old.

'I knew you were getting out soon, but I'm sorry, honey, I didn't know when to expect you.'

Code. I'd written her the date of my release and promised to see her soon after that. But we'd made no appointment. 'Don't worry Mom. I just drove up to say hi.'

'I have to get home, fix dinner . . .' She didn't finish the sentence. She didn't have to. I knew. Home was off limits.

I said, 'Good to see you.'

Mom said, 'Sure is.'

Her grip on my arm loosened. She looked toward her car. I knew she didn't feel comfortable with me. She had her own problems reconciling images, of understanding how her sweet blonde child had become a black-haired virago who, the last time she'd seen her father, had held a gun to his temple and threatened to blow his head off.

I said, 'Next time, can I ask you to do me a favour?'

She didn't say yes or no, just cocked her head to the side.

'Could you bring some of the stuff I left in my apartment? I could really use some clothes, 'specially my jeans and tennis shoes.'

Mom looked stricken. 'Your dad cleaned out your apartment after you were, after you were, after . . .'

'After I was arrested,' I said.

'Yes. And I'm afraid he gave everything to the Salvation Army.'

'My camera?' I asked. I had left it at the house that night, the night I had been arrested. 'Did he give that away too?'

Mom snapped open the purse on her arm. 'No. He took your camera to his workbench in the garage. Then he . . .' Mom lost track of what she was saying, her mind down with her fingers.

I asked, 'What did he do to my camera?'

'He took a hammer to it.' She laughed, small and nervous,

and plucked out a wallet. Her voice turned to sing-song. 'You know your father.' She slipped a twenty from her wallet. 'I felt that wasn't right. I saved some money but I didn't bring it with me.'

She meant to give me that twenty-dollar bill. It horrified me. I put on the cheeriest smile I could, told her I'd just got a big assignment from one of the glossy magazines and swept my arm across the vast expanse of El Dorado. 'You can see they gave me a lot of money up front. I got more than enough left to buy a camera, I needed to get another one anyway.'

I leaned in through the window to grab the cardboard instamatic from the front seat. The moment Mom saw it she stepped back. 'Now honey, I just got off work and I look a fright.' But I insisted, just a snapshot for my wall when I had one to put something on. I put one arm around her, held the camera out facing us, told her to smile, laughed like I was having fun and snapped.

'I'll be back to see you again soon as I can,' I promised.

'I look forward to it,' she answered.

We both lied.

7

Two days later I sobered up enough to look for work. I don't know what had gotten into me. I'd parked my car across from a church a couple blocks from the beach in Santa Monica's Ocean Park, stepped into a bar on Main Street and didn't stumble out until 2 a.m. closing time. From a homey with a pit-bull on the Venice Beach Boardwalk I'd bought a used Nikon F3 with a 28–85 mm zoom lens, no questions asked. After that I lost track of events, woke up on the sand thirty hours later with plum-sized bruises on my arm and knuckles scraped raw. I couldn't remember hitting anybody. Under my leather jacket I still clutched the Nikon. The last of my Las Vegas money had been given away, spent or stolen except for a twenty-dollar bill hidden in my shoe. A cheap bathing suit took most of that and after I washed up in the open air showers at the beach I spent the last of it on breakfast and the paper.

I needed work but didn't qualify for any of the jobs listed in the classifieds. My only work experience had been taking pictures of toddlers and infants and I didn't think I could go back to that. I walked up and down Main Street looking for Help Wanted signs but didn't see any. At a dozen stores I asked to fill out an application but when I admitted that I'd spent the last five years in prison they couldn't get me out the door fast enough. Nobody wanted someone a little down

on her luck. I was feeling pretty low about myself. I didn't
mind starting at the bottom. I would have felt happy being
tall enough to reach up to the bottom.

My stomach began to eat its lining after sunset. Hunger is
a problem solver. You can have a million troubles but if you
don't eat, hunger is the only one that matters.

Across the street a steady procession of Mercedes, BMWs
and Porsches rolled up to a restaurant's valet parking. White
block letters spelled out a nouvelle cuisine name on the
awning. Nobody stopped me when I walked through the
glass doors and stood near the bar area to the right. I didn't
sit anywhere, just stood around like I was waiting for somebody. The faces at the bar and across the partition in the
dining-room had that airbrushed quality of having emerged
from a television set. Everybody was young or played themselves ten years younger. You could hear the jangle of
platinum credit cards with each step. Even those who dressed
informally – and LA is the informal dress capital of the world
– wore their jeans, bomber jackets and baseball caps with the
carefully studied intent of costume design. Most galling of all
each of them drove cars worth more money than I'd ever
made in my life.

When I worked up the courage I backed to a bar table
vacated by a party of four and jammed bread sticks into my
pockets a fistful at a time. I didn't get more than two steps
out the front door before I heard someone shouting at me
from behind. I took off running. The bread sticks might have
been worth less than a quarter but people have been arrested
for less and theft was a violation of my parole. The shouts
kept up for about fifty yards and stopped just before I veered
onto a street that would take me over a parking fence and
out to the beach. What stopped me from jumping the fence
was my name. It had been the last word called out before

whoever chased me pulled up lame. I eased an eye around the corner of the building to observe him. From the shabby look of his jeans, windbreaker and tennis shoes he didn't work in the restaurant and didn't have the money to patronize it. He walked with a winded gait, clutching his hand to his ribs to cover the stitch the run had given him. I didn't recognize him at that distance but maybe I'd met him while I'd been drunk and just didn't remember. He had some size to him but most of it was out front where he could see it hanging over his belt. I couldn't see the gain in waiting to hear him out but curiosity wouldn't let me do the smart thing and disappear.

The breath still wheezed heavy in his lungs when he passed the corner of the building and saw me munching on a bread stick. He swiped at the sweat on his forehead with the back of his hand, asked, 'Why were you running so fast?'

'None of your damn business.' I didn't mean to be vulgar, just firm.

'That's the way to answer.' He turned his shoulder to cough up some lung. 'Personally, I can't understand why Californians are so nice all the time, have a nice day this and have a nice day that, I have a hard enough time not slapping the prissy bastards around to remember to be polite.' He pulled a pack of Winstons from the pocket of his red and black windbreaker. 'Name's Frank. From Chicago originally. Smoke?'

'What do you want, Frank?'

'You mean other than a cold case of beer and a hot babe?' He sucked a cigarette out of the pack and lit it with a silver Zippo. 'Can't say I want much of anything. I thought I recognized you in the bar, and now that we're up close and personal, I'm sure I recognize you. Nina Zero, right? The babe who blew up LAX.' He pronounced it 'ellayex'. Los Angeles International Airport.

'Not the whole airport. Just one terminal.' I turned and walked. The past didn't interest me.

'Hey, hey, stop a minute,' he called.

I didn't even slow down.

'Why don't you lemme buy you a hamburger?' He kept a respectable distance off my elbow, pluming smoke like an old Chevy burning oil. 'Yeh, a hamburger and fries washed down by a cold beer would taste real good right now. That ritzy joint we just came outta, that's business to me, I don't actually eat there.'

'What do you mean, business?'

He dug into his windbreaker and handed me a card that read staff writer for *Scandal Times*.

'A tabloid writer.' I said it like I wanted to spit. The regular papers had been sensational enough but the tabloids went wild at my arrest. One of the scribes had been inspired to pen a poem: Mary had a little gun / Whose sight would take your breath, / Because wherever Mary went / She shot a man to death.

'You've got nerve chasing me after all that crap you wrote.'

'I'm from Chicago. People from Chicago got a lot of nerve. But I didn't cover your story then. I just read about it.'

'The story's over. Now I just want to live like everybody else.'

'You get hungry like everybody else too. C'mon, lemme buy you a hamburger. If you've gone Californian, the same place serves rabbit sprouts on whole wheat bread so damn whole you'll be picking the husks out of your teeth.'

My hunger was greater than my pride. I let him lead me

across the street to the back table of a restaurant where the smell of frying beef fat was thick enough to clog an artery. He had to be looking for a 'Whatever happened to . . .' kind of story but I didn't have to tell him anything. Like every other casual dining joint in Santa Monica the menu included a list of salads and sandwiches with Italian-sounding names but most of the customers we passed were there for the red meat. Frank didn't bother to crack the menu and the waitress didn't need to listen to his order to know it wouldn't be the Dolphin Safe Tuna Sandwich. She took the order down by memory and wrote times two when I ordered the same. 'This is the only honest restaurant for miles around but even here you've got to put up with a bunch of crap on the menu,' Frank complained. 'Personally, I don't understand this obsession with dietary health. Don't these people know when the next big one comes we're all going to the bottom of the sea? What difference will it make then what your cholesterol level is?'

I slipped my camera out of its case and looked it over. The colour film had advanced a dozen frames but I couldn't remember shooting anything. The camera was so hot homey had worn gloves when he'd sold it to me.

'Yeh, yeh, you were some kinda photo nut, weren't you?'

'Still am.' I put the viewfinder to my eye and took a good look at the guy across the table from me. His face was pale and fleshy and I would have thought him soft if not for his eyes, which inhabited his flesh like a stranger. The sag to his cheeks and the dull droop of his mouth belied the bright aggression of eyes that did not so much look at something as slash it. The shabby clothing and unfashionable shape were undoubtedly useful to his work. Nobody would pay much attention to him or believe him capable of writing the stories he did. He could hang around at will and if they didn't get a good look at his eyes they'd probably feel a little sorry for him. Just another fat-boy loser. Then he'd write something sharp enough to cut their throats. When he glanced at me out the corner of his eyes and tipped the beer to his lips I wanted to burn that look into the emulsion but the restaurant was too dark and the film too slow. I needed a fast black-and-white film stock with diamond-sized grain to match the feeling I had about the things I saw through the lens. Colour didn't express my emotions the way a grey scale did. I opened the camera back and tossed the film.

'That what you're doing now?' He tried to sound guy-to-guy casual. 'Trying to make it as a photographer?'

I didn't see any advantage in answering a direct question from a tabloid writer. If I answered one question, he'd just ask another and a day or two later I'd see my name in the newspaper. I capped the lens and dug into the basket of bread the waitress slid onto the table to go with our beers.

'You can make good money with that camera if you're aggressive enough and know where to use it.'

'How's that?' My mouth was full of bread. The words came out gummed together, like 'howzat'.

'Take the publication I work for, it pays good money for certain kinds of pictures.'

'You mean like the ones taken of me when I was arrested?'

'Yeh, but someone like you only comes around once a year. Celebrities, that's the bread-and-butter work. Preferably drunk or stoned or humping the maid in the back of a convertible, but that's just the bias of our publication. The star can be picking his nose if he's hot enough.'

'Lack of aggression isn't one of my problems,' I said.

'Yeh, but you gotta know where, that's the key. Like tonight, a tip came in that Spielberg had a table at that place down the street. Turned out it was *Sidney* Spielburg, the Marina Del Rey orthodontist, but you get the point. Contacts are vital to the business. It's important to know people.'

The way he was looking at me, he meant to be one of those people important for me to know. I had thought he wanted to write about me but his eyes suggested I was date material. I didn't want to tell him I was married to somebody in the business. Right then, Gabe was the last person I'd contact for a favour. But his advice got me to thinking about people I did know who might help set me up. Then the cheeseburgers arrived accompanied by a golden nest of fries and I didn't think about anything else except the taste of the food going down.

Frank was one of those guys who could take a bite at the beginning of a sentence, chew through the middle and lunge for another bite without so much as a comma to separate mouthfuls. He said he'd moved out to the West Coast six years earlier and after a short stint with a local alternative paper moved on to the tabloid press, which he thought contained the most radical writing in America. The alternative newspapers had sold out to a radical chic consumerism as bourgeois as mainstream culture but the tabloid press he thought a great medium for ridiculing the American obsessions with wealth and fame. Sure, nobody took the tabloids seriously but that was the point; no matter how many magazines and newspapers representing the so-called 'serious' press ran elevated profiles of this or that snot-nosed actor or brat musician the tabloids drove them back to the gutter by exposing how trivial and ugly their lives really were. Being from Chicago gave him an edge in the business because the culture there was clear-eyed and tough. People from Chicago had a lot of attitude. If Chicago ever declared war on Los Angeles it would be like a battle between hog butchers and beauticians. A meat cleaver versus a blow dryer. Wholesale slaughter.

'Got a pen?' I asked.

He'd been talking so long my voice startled him. He unclipped the ball-point from the neck ring of his T-shirt. On a clean napkin I wrote 'IOU $20', signed and shot it across the table.

'Hey, you don't have to pay me back for dinner, my treat.' He flicked the note back to me.

'I hadn't planned to. That's for the twenty bucks you're going to loan me.' I folded the napkin and pinned the corner beneath his bottle of Rolling Rock. 'I'm good for it. And I wouldn't ask you except I'm a little short of friends right now.'

'Yeh, OK, I understand.' He dipped his fingers into a dun-coloured wallet and gave me this piece-of-pie-left-out-on-the-counter-so-he-might-as-well-grab-it-while-no-one-was-looking look. He asked, 'You available?'

'You mean for work?'

'I mean for dating.'

'You don't need the trouble. Trust me.'

I thought that might create some bad feelings between us but just the opposite, when we said goodbye on the street he said the way I acted I could be from Chicago, which I think was his idea of a compliment.

8

When I first met Cass she was making a documentary about alien abduction conspiracies from an artist's loft in downtown LA. During the brief interval between the incident at the airport and my arrest, I'd gone underground in the centre of the city's thriving arts community. Cass had been my roommate. She chain-smoked then and experimented with various pharmaceuticals which she claimed put her on the same wavelength as the aliens, though, to her disappointment, never in direct contact. They hovered just at the corner of her vision but the moment she turned her head they vanished. She went everywhere with a video camera grafted to her eye in the hope of capturing one on tape but they always eluded her. When she met me she shot a short documentary of my scrape with the law which went to the Sundance Film Festival and from there she hit the big time with a concept for a reality-based television programme based on the activities of the County Coroner, titled *Meat Wagon.*

Since then Cass had moved to a suite of offices around the corner from 20th Century Fox Studios. The building was typical of the Taco Bell-ranch house school of Southern California architecture: the same single-storey wood-frame style of construction housed most of the city's fast-food franchises and strip malls as well as production companies.

The name on the office door – Alpha Centauri Productions – was the same as the one that had graced the door to her loft, though the plaque had changed from hand-lettered cardboard to embossed bronze.

'Ms Mitchel thought you'd like to see an episode of our current show,' the receptionist said when I told her I had an appointment. She led me to a screening-room, pulled a video tape off a rack next to the big screen television and fed it into the VCR. The thirty-second promo before the episode announced *Meat Wagon* as a show with maximum visceral impact. Visceral impact was right. Viscera was all over the screen. The opening sequence faded up from black to the red and blue lights of a police cruiser flashing over gunshot victims on a street in South Central. Cops spooled out crime scene tape to hold back bystanders and voyeurs. No narration or music disturbed the documentary images and natural sound. The screen cut to a guy driving his car and talking about the rigours of his job as a forensic pathologist. A couple of shots later he was knee-deep in dead bodies, joking with homicide detectives while he probed massive gunshot wounds.

When the episode ended the receptionist led me back to the lobby. Cass sat on the corner of the reception desk, swinging her left Prado pump an inch above the carpet while she spoke on the phone. 'What did you think of the show?' she whispered, hand cupped over the speaking part.

'Great television,' I answered.

'Yes, yes,' she said, speaking both to me and the person on the other end of the line. Thankfully she didn't get the oxymoron. She dressed stylishly down in jeans, satin windbreaker and a baseball cap that read girl-power, but even dressing down was a big step up from the Cass I'd known. Beneath the baseball cap her hair was styled in a Dutch-boy bob and her lips were sticked scarlet. At thirty-something Cass had discovered make-up. Skin formerly bumped and ridged by blemishes, wrinkles and the activities of thought were brushed smooth of imperfections and character. No matter how artfully applied, cosmetics couldn't conceal the natural bulge of her eyes. Cass was a thin woman, all sharp-angled bone, but her eyes belonged to someone twice her size. The expression of her face at rest was that of a cartoon character with its paw under a steamroller.

While she spoke on the land-line her cell phone rang and with the expert timing of a trapeze artist she let go of one conversation to grab the other. With a kick of her pump she scooted off the corner of the desk, pantomimed to the receptionist her intention to eat and curled a finger to indicate I should follow. She spoke into the phone about Nielson ratings and audience shares while she led me out of the building and down the street to a courtyard cafe with sunlit tables shaded by huge canvas umbrellas. *Meat Wagon* was almost a hit, she told the caller, ranking second in its time slot. The Nielson ratings weren't astronomical but they were getting great audience share numbers. 'My accountant,' she confided.

When the hostess came up to seat us Cass's cell phone rang again with the production manager telling her that the camera package they had reserved for that night had developed colour balance problems. Cass talked over the problem of fixing it or finding another while we looked at the menu and when the waiter came over she pointed to what she wanted. The waiter nodded like he was used to taking orders that way. After she disconnected I started to say something but she glanced at her watch and held up her right index finger. The cell phone rang again.

'One of the top producers in the business,' she whispered.

While she talked she plucked a sterling silver box the size of a pack of cigarettes from her purse and spilled onto the table a dozen vitamins, minerals and immunity enhancers of various shapes and colours which she swallowed, one by one, between sentences. I gathered from Cass's half of the conversation that she and this producer had pitched a couple of studio suits an idea for a feature film and now speculated how it had gone. The food came mid-conversation and Cass cradled the phone between her shoulder and ear so she could better cut her poached chicken to eat and talk at the same time. After that call ended Cass said she was sorry it was impossible, she knew, but she had to make one phone call, just one, and then I'd have her undivided attention. That was a follow-up call to a development exec. She stroked him so thoroughly it sounded like phone sex.

I thought Cass might ask me something personal about the rough course of my life and what it was like to be free again but she was so happy to share the details of her success that she never quite got around to asking how I was. The production was going on call that night, which meant the crew would be assembled and waiting for news about any homicides appropriate for a national television audience. An upper-class death on the Westside of LA would be good, she said, particularly if the death was from mysterious or violent causes. This was not to say she would ignore a really juicy gang killing, like some little kid getting AK-47ed in gang crossfire, but mostly she wanted to move the show through the different ethnic groups and socio-economic classes to demonstrate that death was the great leveller. *Meat Wagon* had a higher philosophical purpose than to titillate audiences with blood and guts, despite what some critics alleged.

I guess I looked like the kind of person who needed lunch

bought for her because the waiter discreetly slid the bill next to Cass's elbow. She handed him a platinum coloured credit card without bothering to check the addition. 'Wonderful to spend time with you again,' she said. 'I can't get over how you really haven't changed a bit!'

'I've spent the last five years in prison, of course I've changed.'

Cass looked at me then and not just in my general direction. When not obsessed with herself she had a remarkable capacity to observe others and intuit what she called their 'personal issues'. 'You're bitter,' she said.

'I'm an ex-con without a job, I'm not only bitter, I'm desperate.'

'I really wish I had a spot for you on the production staff but I'd have to fire somebody else to get you on.'

'I'm not asking you for a job.'

'When the going gets tough, the tough get going.'

'I'm not looking for advice either.'

The waiter brushed by in a flash of white to leave the bill folder on the edge of the table. Although I couldn't say Cass had ever been completely present during our lunch now she wanted only to be gone. She signed the slip and scooted her chair back in one motion.

'I wouldn't mind a favour, though.'

'Anything I can do.'

'Let me take photographs at your next crime scene.'

'Can't do that. Can't betray the trust the police and coroner place in me. Could put the whole show in danger. Wouldn't be fair to the people working for me.'

'I thought we were friends. Have you sold out completely?'

'I didn't sell out. I bought in.'

'You owe me the favour.'

'I owed you lunch,' she said, springing for the door. 'And I just paid for it.'

In a town like Hollywood friendship doesn't go nearly as far as betrayal. After sunset I settled into a parking spot across the street from her production office. I had a sack of burgers and coffee, the radio and a wide-mouth pee jar to keep me company. I knew how to wait. Boredom meant nothing to me. It wasn't like I had anything more important to do. The coffee kept me awake until three in the morning, when Cass and two burly men lugged boxes of equipment out to a van and sped onto the empty streets. *Meat Wagon* emblazoned the sides and back of the van in red. It wasn't difficult to follow. At Sunset Boulevard, the van turned east. When a police cruiser blasted by at a speed to blow off my doors I swung around the van and gave chase through Bel Air and into Beverly Hills. That time of night, we were all going to the same place.

9

The cruiser swerved into the driveway of a top-ten icon of the Southern California good life, a pink and palm-treed hotel where movie stars and European royalty mingled with the merely wealthy. In deference to the sleep of the rich, the cop extinguished his bubble-gum lights at the top of the drive and joined a line of parked emergency vehicles missing only a fire truck. I followed the cruiser until a flash of green uniform in my headlights braced out his hands to stop me. I started to sweat because I was poor and driving a beat-up old car, even if it was a Cadillac. The uniform would take one look at me and know I wasn't the type of person who stayed in that kind of hotel. I hit the button that made the window roll down and, before he could get a word out, said I had missed the last flight out of San Diego and had to drive up, sorry if I had to wake somebody to check in.

'Do you have a reservation?'

I told him somebody at Warner Brothers Records made it for me but I wasn't sure what name it was under. You get all kinds in Los Angeles; people who look ragged enough to be living in their cars can be rock stars worth millions. He glanced around inside the Caddy interior then handed me a parking stub. 'Welcome to Beverly Hills. Please leave your keys in the car.'

The headlights from the van dusted my shoulders in white light as I got out of the car carrying my duffel bag. That I was too poor to buy a professional camera case proved my good fortune because even if he was just a parking valet I think his job was to keep out the media. He and two other green-jackets converged upon Cass's van before the lights dimmed and from the sound of their voices I don't think they offered valet parking. Hotel security looked to be a bigger obstacle than the cops. I counted six green-jackets standing in the lobby and not one of them carried a tray of canapés. It was a hell of a lobby, all soft peaches, greens and natural burl wood done up Art Deco. They could have roped it off and charged an entrance fee. To the rich it probably wasn't anything out of the ordinary.

The green-jacket at the front desk couldn't find my reservation and we went back and forth about whether some mistake had been made until he got around to telling me he had rooms available, even a few in the budget category of $300 a night. I snapped Cass's platinum card onto the counter. After lunch it had somehow slipped into my pocket. I hadn't meant to take it but after I'd picked it up from the table I'd forgotten to give it back and considering how our lunch ended I wasn't going to return it personally. Technically, I was committing credit card fraud but in the unlikely event she reported it stolen it wouldn't show up on the system yet. Cheque kiting, credit card fraud and other fiscal scams had been the third most common profession among the sisters at the Institute, behind prostitution and drug dealing. Sure, my teachers had all been nailed by the law but I'd learned a lot about what someone could get away with nine times out of ten. I asked for a high floor at the back of the hotel, where I figured I could see the cause of the commotion, then followed a sleepy bellman who held my bag between two gloved fingers at some distance from his body. I asked him why all the cops.

'Big rock group down in the Presidential Bungalow. Made a little too much noise earlier this evening.'

'What's the name of the group?'

He said he heard it was somebody called Death Row, then opened the door to my room and showed me how to work the drapes and lights as if I couldn't figure it out myself. I knew Death Row's music because an ex-boyfriend once drove me crazy listening to it. They had a hit a half-dozen years back named 'Faceful of Cherry Pie' and then one just out titled 'Taste the Juice'. Both were big with the head-banger crowd. I tipped the bellman my last five bucks even though he made a lot more money than I did. He pocketed the bill without a word, like it was on the low end of acceptable.

From the corner of the balcony I could see something was going on at one of the twenty or so private bungalows hidden among the palm trees four floors below. With my elbows braced on the railing I maxed the zoom lens. The bungalow's interior lights burned brightly and beneath a canopy of trees outdoor lights illuminated what looked like a back patio. Paramedics and police hustled up and down the bungalow's front steps. At ASA 400 the film was fast enough to make an exposure but at that distance and angle the image wouldn't sell for a dime.

From the balcony I marked out where I could stand to watch the one green-jacket I needed to evade and when he wandered a little too far from his post I slipped down the path that led behind the bungalow with the lights. The hotel grounds were immaculately swept so I didn't worry about stepping on dry leaves when I veered off the path and crept through the hibiscus to a lone oak tree by the back fence.

After two failed jumps at the lowest limb I found a knothole to boost me up and I clawed from there to a branch that hung over the fence.

The tableau that appeared before me was too unexpected to understand at first glimpse. Somebody had hooked a photoflood to a bougainvillea branch, spilling a harsh glare across the paving stones. The balding dome of a crouched man glinted in the light as he crept hands and knees to lift something with tweezers and drop it into a zip-lock baggie. Two plainclothes cops in light leather jackets stood backlit in the rear doorway, drinking coffee out of paper cups. A photo tech with a 35mm camera and a good-sized zoom lens walked carefully around a hot tub, taking photos of four long-haired, multiple-tattooed men and two young women who sprawled naked along the rim like they had been flash frozen in the middle of having a really good time. Through the picture window to the right of the rear door two women, wrapped in towels, talked to a potbellied man who recorded their answers in a notebook. An extension cord ran from the corner of that window to a small amplifier near the hot tub, then a different cord stretched from the amplifier to a guitar strapped around the neck of one of the rockers. Sure, it's easy to figure out what happened now but at the time I couldn't figure if they'd sexed themselves to death, been victims of a mass overdose or some deadly cocktail of the two, even if I did realize I had six dead bodies in front of my lens and four of them could be considered famous.

The photoflood provided more than enough illumination to shoot. After I fired off the first half-dozen frames, one of the cops in the doorway looked sharply in my direction and stepped around the technician working on his hands and knees. I waited until the fence obscured his line of sight and dropped ten feet into a dead run. The squawk of a walkie-talkie on the path ahead warned me to slip behind a palm tree just before one of the green-jackets sprinted past. I didn't see anyone else on the way back to my room except a half-deaf septuagenarian jogger coming out of the elevator for his five a.m. run.

'Early bird gets the worm!' he shouted.

'Already got mine!' I shouted back.

The Scandal Times

Exclusive photo by Nina Zero (more photos on page 2).

DEATH ROW ELECTROCUTION

ROCK GROUP FRIED IN HOT-TUB MISHAP

By Frank Adams

Chief Los Angeles Correspondent

BEVERLY HILLS – Top guitarist Nick "Hot Licks" O'Leary was fried out his mind when, after an electrifying performance Friday night at the Fabulous Forum, he decided to repeat for members of the band and select "guests" the scorching guitar solo from the group's hit single, *Taste the Juice.*

The heavy metal group returned to their private bungalow at an exclusive Beverly Hills hotel just past 1 a.m. in a partying mood. According to earwitness reports, the group proceeded to party hearty in the bungalow's private hot tub until 2:30 a.m., when a completely nude O'Leary plugged his electric guitar into a portable amplifier. Encouraged by the other three members of the group and four female admirers, also completely nude, O'Leary repeated his trademark solo, complete with split-legged stage leaps. The noise awakened guests and alerted hotel management, but ended abruptly at 2:35 a.m., when O'Leary slipped on the wet pavement and plunged guitar first into the hot tub.

Arriving paramedics found the only two survivors of the incident, twin sisters Dawn and Fawn Miller, trying to resuscitate band members with room service coffee, reportedly unaware that the group had been electrocuted. Paramedics declared six dead at the scene. In addition to O'Leary, the victims include death Row drummer Thug Moron, bass guitarist Slug Moron (no relation), lead singer Iks and two women whose identities are being withheld pending notification of relatives.

SPIELBURG LOVE TRYST

VENICE – Top dentist Sidney Spielburg

10

Just before dawn I rang the back-door buzzer to a one-man photo agency run out of a media services building in Santa Monica, wired from a cup of coffee to go and the proof sheet I'd collected from an all-night developer in Hollywood. The guy who answered the door had the vampire glow of someone who dropped into his casket at dawn. In contrast to his black beard and matching turtleneck the whiteness of his skin nearly blinded. Frank told me the guy's name was Lester and he was looking for new talent. I told him I'd taken some photographs of a famous rock group I'd seen at a hotel in Beverly Hills.

'What group?'

'Death Row.'

I could tell from his non-reaction that he hadn't heard what happened. Few people had. The only other photographer on the scene worked for the Beverly Hills Police Department and as far as I knew he wasn't selling. 'Can't move it,' Lester said. 'A group like that, the only action is the heavy metal mags. They don't buy a lot of candids and when they do they pay some of the lowest rates in the business.'

'These might be a little different.'

'Any babes? A good-looking babe hanging around the neck of a rocker, I might be able to do something with that.'

'Sure, babes are part of it. Nudity too.'

'Might be worth a hundred bucks then.' He invited me into an office so cluttered with telecommunications and photographic gear that the only free floor-space was a narrow aisle down the centre of the room. Black-and-white photographs of various celebrities papered the walls, from Elizabeth Taylor on the arm of one of her many husbands to Sean Penn looking like he was about to smash the photographer's lens. Freshly printed eight-by-tens hung pinned to a cork board over his desk. Most depicted the back of a famous head, a bodyguard's hand stretched toward the lens or a third-rate celeb vamping shamelessly for the camera. 'The catch of the night,' he explained. 'Some nights you get lobster, other nights you get flounder.'

When I set the proof sheet under the lamp on the light table Lester's eyes darted straight to it. From the back pocket of his black jeans he drew a bronchial inhaler and without taking his eyes from the proof sheet plugged it between his lips and gave himself two quick blasts. After scanning the basic content he bent over the light table with a magnifying loop to examine specific images. He stood no higher than my chin when he straightened and to stand that tall he needed the boost of black combat boots.

'Incredible,' he pronounced. 'Were you a guest of the hotel?'

'No.'

'How did you know to be there?'

'Had a hunch.'

'None of my business, you're right.' He took a white grease pencil from the light table and circled several of the images. 'You ever work through an agency before?'

'Never.'

'I'm gonna tell you the way it works and it works only one way and the only way to avoid a later misunderstanding is to listen clearly now. Understand?' Before I could respond he flew into the next sentence like he'd spiked his bronchial inhaler with amphetamines. 'When you take a picture you think can be sold to any media you bring it to me. Not to anybody else. I don't care if it's going in the Rotarian Club Newsletter, it goes through me. If the image has no immediate news value it goes into the stock file to be used when a publication needs it as filler.' His eyes took on a funny gleam as he paced the length of the aisle and back and back again, twirling a yellow No. 2 pencil between his fingers like the baton of a drum major. 'If the photographs are very hot – and the ones you've brought are scalding – I'll go to the trouble and expense of calling editors and art directors to pitch them. I bear all expenses involved in this and in return I take 40 per cent. I do not take less. When the publication makes out the cheque, they do so to my agency. I then write a cheque to you for 60 per cent of the amount. If someone cuts a cheque with your name on it, we send it back and tell them to issue a new one. That keeps the record books straight and the tax man happy. Are we agreed?'

'Something you should know first.' I'd been rejected so many times I braced myself for it. 'A week ago I was released from prison. Right now I'm on parole.'

The pencil jammed between his fingers and skidded to the floor. 'What did you do?'

'Shot somebody.'

'Good.'

'Good?'

'Weak sisters never last in the business. You mind if I call you Shooter?'

'No.'

'It'll be our joke. Shooter. Get it?' He cocked his thumb back and flexed his forefinger. 'Bang!'

The Death Row photographs ran in most major newspapers in the US and even some papers in Europe and Australia. I made enough on the rights not to worry about money for a couple of months and a reputation for being in the right place at the right time. I didn't think about the tragedy that had resulted in my good fortune. They were already dead when I got there. I just helped to advertise the wake.

The advance on my first cheque as a paparazza bought me a lease on a studio apartment a half-block from the beach, two floors up a four-storey building populated by drug dealers, petty burglars and a few romantics like myself who thought living by the boardwalk in Venice Beach would be inspirational. My needs were simple. Fruit crates scavenged from the dumpster of a local market doubled as bookshelves and bureau. At a discount store I bought a small futon, one glass, one mug, one set of silverware, one plate and one bowl. I didn't expect company.

Lester gave me my first formal assignment a couple days later, the premiere of what he called the *Gone With the Wind* of disaster flicks at the Mann Chinese Theater in Hollywood. I was anxious to do a good job for him, got there five hours early to stake out a spot. A half-dozen photographers already milled behind a roped-off area in front of the theatre's red pagoda façade, each toting a camera that looked big enough to blow up a tank. Bus-loads of tourists measured their feet and hands against the concrete prints of dead movie stars and yelped with the pleasure in Swedish, Japanese, Portuguese, German and the flat accents of Kansas. When I approached the moulds for Bette Davis I too stopped, knelt and palmed her hand print, dumb as any tourist from anywhere and happy I was not yet so cynical that it didn't thrill me. When I realized her modern counterparts would hate me for how I was about to make my living I moved on.

To the side of the entrance a young woman sat at a card table. Her tag identified her as the press coordinator. She checked my name from a list, handed me a blue tag that read Photo Press and pointed to the ropes. 'The pen is over there. Wander around as much as you like, but after six don't go past the barrier.' She let the command hang in the air for a couple seconds before she added, 'Please.'

I pinned the tag to my shirt. 'The pen?'

She looked at me like I was brain damaged. 'The area behind the ropes is the pen, where the other photographers are.'

I thanked her and walked away thinking, Great, I get out of one pen to start a profession that lands me in another one. I ducked beneath the ropes and set my duffel bag in the corner nearest the curb. A moment later a frizzy-haired photographer walked over and said the spot I stood on was reserved. He was somewhere in his forties, had that flash-bulb-glazed look of someone who watches too much pornography. The photographs of famous celebrities hung from his camera strap like scalps. I figured that was why Gabe called him the scalp collector. I wanted to extend some courtesy to my new colleagues so I moved over a notch. I couldn't stand there either, he said, that was somebody else's spot. I asked him where I could stand. He pointed at the fan's bleachers across the red carpet and laughed, raucous as a crow.

I aimed my camera at him and shot. That shut him up.

He said, 'I'm serious. That spot's reserved. You can't work there.'

I could see right away there wasn't all that much difference between pens. In prison I learned that you can't take any shit, not ever, because if you do, they'll just keep giving it to you for the rest of your time. I pulled the camera strap off my neck, zipped the camera in my duffel bag and set the bag at my feet. 'Do you get any special pride out of being an asshole, or is it like a birth defect, something you can't control?' I said it loud enough for everybody to hear.

He flushed from his receding hairline down. 'Look lady, there's a pecking order here.'

'And you're the chief pecker?'

He was smart enough to see in my balled fists and flat stare a willingness to escalate the conflict. He called me a bitch but he was backpedalling when he said it. Nobody talked to me after that but I didn't mind. Photographers trickled beneath the ropes in ones and twos until it was job enough holding my spot amid the pushing and shoving of the new arrivals jostling for an angle. Most of the photographers knew each other and gossiped back and forth about who got beat up lately. Bodyguards and actors beat on paparazzi all the time, they said. The way it sounded to me, they wanted to avoid getting beaten up by bodyguards but didn't mind when hit by actors because they usually got a picture and big news story out of it. With bodyguards all they got was a broken rib.

When the lead limousine rolled in front of the theatre the photographers in the rear surged forward to wedge themselves into the front line against the ropes. An arm hooked around my waist to jerk me back and a bearded burly man in a bush hat and combat vest thrust forward to take my spot. I yelled at him but across the aisle three hundred fans were screaming themselves pink and my protest didn't attract much attention. I unpinned the identity tag from my shirt. The point was about two inches long. I jammed it knuckle deep into the guy's shorts. He let out a jumping howl, got tangled up in the rope and flopped on to the red carpet at the feet of an octogenarian actress strolling up the aisle. A security guard arm-locked him from behind and I thought that would be the end of it except the press coordinator darted over ready to hook me too.

'The big baboon tripped,' a voice behind me said.

Her eyes addled to a soft gaze and with a dizzy nodding smile she fled back to her corner. I glanced back to find my husband grinning down at me. It shouldn't have surprised me that other women found him as irresistible as I thought him impossible. 'No thanks needed,' he said. 'You're short. He's tall. It's easier to shoot over you.'

The limousines rolled to the carpet, the attendants dipped and swung open the big black doors to a gowned and heeled or crisply trousered leg, and after a dramatic pause a face made famous by pretending to be someone else ascended to the adulation of fans and the brilliant photo-flash of the paparazzi. When a blonde kid who looked about seventeen stepped out with his mom it was like St Elmo's fire swept the scene. Cameras clicked out a barrage of photo-flash and across the carpet the fans screamed with teenage love-anguish. He waved and smiled at the cameras, jaunted over to the fans to sign a few autographs, causing at least three dead faint-aways, and when he turned his back to enter the theatre the motorized rewinds in the pen sounded considerably louder than the next limousine to pull up to the curb. As I straightened from my shooter's crouch a hand grabbed my waist. I'd been pushed and grabbed all I could take for one day and rammed my elbow into ribs I realized too late belonged to Gabe. 'Sorry, thought you were someone else,' I said.

Gabe winced and put one hand to his side. 'Right, if you knew it was me you would have hit harder.'

I couldn't help smiling because he was half right. He took that as encouragement and said, 'Come on, let's have a jar together.'

I glanced around the pen. The fans on the opposite side of the carpet were holding true but the photographers had lost interest. Some rewound film, packed lenses and cameras, and some just walked away.

'A jar of what?'

'Ale for me, I always like to go for a jar after I drop off my film.'

I was about to tell him not a chance but then he ran his thumb and forefinger along my ear. Involuntary delight shuddered down my back. I had great memories of the time we spent together whenever it slipped my mind that I didn't want to have anything to do with him again. I bit down hard and smoothed the hair standing straight up on my arms. I was angry that he had touched me, angrier still that my body electrified when he did, but angriest most of all that I said yes.

The Formosa Café had been a Hollywood haunt since the 1930s, when the Oriental theme of the place evoked almost as much mystery and romance as the celebrities and deal-makers who wandered over from the adjacent Hollywood Studios lot for their two-martini lunches. Like so much of Hollywood, the theme of the place didn't extend beyond the façade, which had been painted Honk Kong red to fool the blind drunk into thinking the joint looked like a pagoda. One step past the front door, the Orient dissolved into a shrine to celebrity. Behind the bar and above the horseshoe booths hung a photo gallery of Hollywood film and television stars from the 1950s and 60s, some still famous and others no more than a face not even the bartender could pin a name to. The bar itself was black with red vinyl padding at the edges, easy on the elbows and helpful to those with a sudden need to rest their forehead on something soft. The hostess who came to greet me was of the same vintage as the stars on the wall. Save for the conspicuous lack of tobacco smoke, it could have been 1965.

Gabe handed me a beer when I walked up and introduced the other paparazzo in the booth as Hank Vulkovitch. With pockmarked cheeks and a hook nose, he was ugly as a cartoon villain but his deep-set black eyes glittered with humour and an intelligence that seemed two steps ahead of

everybody else. He grinned at me like we were old pals.
Right away I liked him. He reached out with his free hand
and we shook.

'Nice to meet you, Hank.'

'Most people call me Vulch.' He had a deep voice and a
slow, pleased smile.

'Short for Vulkovitch?'

'Vulture, short for vulture,' Gabe said.

'Why vulture?'

He turned his face profile. 'The beak.'

'Bloody hell, it's the helicopters.'

He flashed a chorus line of capped teeth set incongruously
in a B-picture face. Even those feeding off the famous were
pleased with their own small celebrity.

'Vulch was one of the first to shoot from a chopper. And
to use parabolic microphones, cell phone intercepts and electronic tracking systems. If he can get to a car on the studio
lot, he can track it anywhere.'

'Tech has its uses but like I was telling Gabe nothing beats
legwork and creative determination. I saw your Death Row
photographs. Hell, everybody did. How did you hear about
it? Nothing went over the police channels and the staff at
BHH is notoriously hush-hush.'

'Just got lucky while cruising Sunset. Saw the lights and
went to check it out.'

He didn't believe me, but then, I didn't expect him to. He
dropped a ten and stood to go. Like most paparazzi he was
tall. It gave them an advantage in crowds, but as most actors
are short, the resulting perspective never balanced to my eye.
'I'm tracking a very major star involved in a torrid affair with
his podiatrist. I'd tell you who but you two jackals would just
steal it from me.'

'I wouldn't steal it. I'm an honest girl,' I said.

He laughed at that. 'We're all honest. It's just that none of us can be trusted. Never tell another photographer what you're working on, not even a friend, because you'll lose both the exclusive and the friend.' Before he left he punched Gabe on the shoulder and said, 'You're luckier than you deserve, bud.'

I asked, 'Why are you so lucky?'

'I told him we were married. Do you mind?'

'Yeah, I mind.'

He shrugged like maybe that was important to him, and maybe not. 'When I saw your byline this morning I knew I'd see you again.'

I rubbed at the ring of condensation left by my beer on the table. 'We're both in the same business. Bound to happen.' I downed the beer and ordered whiskey from a passing waitress. Some nights just aren't meant to be taken with sobriety.

'I'm sure I put my foot in the pie but I still don't understand what made you so angry. Las Vegas was the most fun I've had since coming to the States.'

'You expecting a visit from the immigration authorities, need me to play wifey for you, is that why you're making so nice?'

'You have a lot of attitude.'

'I know, and most of it bad.'

'I don't need anything. I just happen to have missed you.'

I didn't want to go into it. I wanted to enjoy a few drinks with him and who knows what might happen after. I wanted to hear him talk and watch his lips when he smiled. But I didn't want him to con me. You can't miss something you never had. I said, 'Whatever. What are you working on now?'

'A story.'

'What kind of story?'

'A story about greed.'

'Great idea. Wish I'd thought of that.'

'I've burned out as a photographer.'

'I thought you were doing pretty good.'

'You've seen how brutal the business is.'

'You mean the fact that we act like jackals?'

'We serve the public,' he asserted. 'The public wants to see gashed throats and ripped entrails. If we're jackals, we're jackals in public service.'

'It's just a pay-cheque. No reason to get hung up about it.'

'Don't get me started on the money.'

'The money is good.'

'The money is a pittance compared to the sums celebrities make. Five, ten, twenty million a picture, unbelievable amounts of money for two to three months of half-talented work. The bastards think fame and wealth put them above the very same public that elevate them. They believe themselves entitled to live like bratty little gods. And along come the paparazzi, the dark side of that public craving, demanding more than carefully crafted fictions, clamouring for bones, blood and the viscera of the soul.'

Strong passion in a man is both attractive and frightening; attractive because strong opinions can be evidence of strong character and frightening because the guy can turn out to be a crank. 'Maybe it's not that complicated,' I said. 'Maybe we're just taking pictures of famous people.'

'It's more complicated than either of us know. Celebrity is a Faustian bargain and paparazzi the hounds from hell.'

I let out a howl like I was a demon dog and Gabe thought that was funny so he howled too. And that should have been it, right, two pros talking shop and getting silly over a couple of drinks. I have a habit of drinking too much when there's something I know I shouldn't do but want to do anyway. And Gabe was an attractive drinker; the more he drank the more handsome he looked, with his flushed porcelain skin and green eyes dancing like the devil. Or maybe I only thought so because the more I drank the lower my standards dropped.

When a couple of whiskeys later he mentioned some papers from immigration had come in the mail and did I mind coming over to look at them I was disappointed but not surprised. He had to want something. I didn't figure him going to the trouble of drinking with me unless he had some pay-off in mind, my signature or sex or maybe both. Not that I didn't trust him, but he seemed the kind of guy who always had a secret agenda hidden behind his ulterior motive.

His apartment wasn't bad on the outside, one of four in a pre-war Spanish two blocks south of Melrose, but when he opened the door I saw right away he wasn't the kind of guy I wanted to live with; from the shirts, socks and pants strewn on the floor it looked like a small army had been vaporized. Gabe had the decency to be embarrassed. I waited safely behind while he kicked, plucked and tossed a clear path into the living-room.

'Coffee?' he asked.

'Not if the kitchen looks as bad as this.'

He took that for yes and left me with an envelope from the Immigration and Naturalization Service. I swept a pair of tennis shoes off the only chair in the room and sat down to read the forms but the words staggered across the page like little drunks and when I did catch one it wouldn't hold still long enough for me to focus down on it. I decided to freshen up and got out of the chair to wash my face with cold water. The only towel in the bathroom was on the floor. I dried my hands with toilet paper. The best thing would be to sober up, sign the papers and go before I had some fun I'd later regret. On my way back to the living-room I saw a half-open door and pushed it open. The only photograph in the room hung above the bed. That he'd hung that particular photograph at all surprised me more than any of the other surprising things Gabe had done.

I leaned against the kitchen door and watched him put together a plate of cheese and crackers. He glanced up once, asked, 'Find everything you need?' and buried his head in the refrigerator. When he emerged he noticed I hadn't moved. He set down the knife, turned to me like maybe he had done something wrong to deserve such close scrutiny and asked, 'What is it?'

I went up to him, put my hand on his chest, brushed my lips across his cheek, his eyes, his mouth. He stood as still as a deer encountered in the forest. 'You're a hard one to understand,' he whispered. 'I know,' I said. And then he kissed me all passionate and I kissed him back with an angry tenderness. It didn't have to mean anything. I didn't want a serious relationship. I just needed somebody who would return my call the next morning. I took him by the hand, led him to the bedroom and we fell together to the bed below an eight-by-ten taken when Gabe and I had been married. In the shot, I'm riding Gabe piggyback, framing his face with my hands and resting my chin on the top of his head. I'm looking straight into the camera with a serious expression on my face that makes me look like I'm about seven years old. I couldn't remember ever looking so young. Gabe is smiling up at me like he's the happiest man in the world.

Pictures lie, I told myself. Pictures lie all the time.

I woke before dawn. Gabe sat on the edge of the bed, fingering something in the circle of light around his hands.

I sat up, drank half the glass of water on the night stand and asked what time it was.

'Three.'

Beneath the light he held the amulet from Papua New Guinea he'd given to me on the day we were married. 'I'm surprised you still wear it,' he said.

'If women threw out everything given to them by their ex-boyfriends, the country would need a dozen new land-fills.'

He fastened the clasp around my neck and gently laid the amulet between my breasts. 'If anything should happen to me, look closely at this and remember. Then smash it against the wall and forget you ever met me.'

That sounded pretty weird. I got out of bed, started looking for my clothes. 'Why do I get the feeling that you're not telling me something here? Are you expecting trouble?'

'Not at all. If I did, I'd simply leave the country.' He pointed to the far corner of the room. 'Your socks are over there. But why are you leaving? Stay for breakfast.'

I kissed him on the forehead and put on my shoes. 'Thanks for the invitation but I don't do sleep-overs. If you want to spend the night with me, you'll have to do it at my place.'

'Name the night and I'll be there.'

'What are you doing this weekend?'

'Working on the story. This weekend isn't good for me.'

'Fine, we'll call each other next week.' Why did he say name the night if he didn't mean it? I drove home slowly enough to pass for sober. It was one thing to be emotionally unavailable but something else to be deceptive and I didn't know if Gabe was just hard to get or playing some game with me. He wanted me to think he put special value on the time we'd spent in Vegas to fool me into coming over to sign his immigration forms. If he knew I was coming over to sign the forms, he'd prepare. He'd anticipate my anger and lack of trust. He'd frame our wedding photograph and put it on the wall above his bed, knowing I'd consider that photograph proof of his feelings.

The bastard set me up and shot me down like a clay pigeon.

If Southern California's reigning literary form is the screen-play, its favourite category of non-fiction is the self-help book. The bookstore near my apartment contained a section the size of fiction devoted solely to self-improvement guides. I spent the morning thumbing though titles like *The Conscious Heart: Seven Soul-Choices that Create Your Relationship Destiny;* and *When Things Fall Apart: Heart Advice for Difficult Times;* and then a book with a title almost longer than the book itself, *Men are from Mars, Women Are from Venus: A Practical Guide for Improving Communication and Getting What You Want in Your Relationships.* Each author claimed to have a secret formula for self-fulfilment: within weeks readers could heal family wounds a quarter-century in the making, find the ideal part-ner and in some cases shed excess pounds at the same time. With so many books to guide them, Californians had to be the most self-improved people on earth. I bought a half-dozen of the most promising titles and read through the afternoon, scribbling notes in the margin when I thought something applied to my situation, reading and re-reading key passages in a furious attempt to learn how to be normal again.

Gabe called the next afternoon. I was home when he called. I let the answering machine pick up. I understood Gabe wasn't the problem. The moment I began to trust someone I panicked. I was the problem. I figured to return the call after the weekend, when I didn't have to compete with the story he was writing.

At sunset I packed a cell phone into my camera bag, jumped into the Caddy and cruised toward West Hollywood, the mid-point between Beverly Hills and Hollywood proper and my central launching point. Whenever I spotted a newsstand I pulled over to chat up the attendant. Celebutants are media junkies, known to drop by the local newsstand a couple times every week to check the magazines for proof of their celebrity. You read the publications, I'd say to the attendant, you know who's hot, you ever see anybody like that come to the stand? Most earned minimum wage. They were happy to make an extra buck. The same with busboys and waitresses. A good tip rated a C-note. When a call from an informant came in I chased it down, Thomas Brothers Guide spread open on the seat to map the fastest route. Half the job was racing around town to catch somebody walking away from a newsstand or restaurant and the other half waiting around for the phone to ring. I answered a half-dozen or more calls a night, some legitimate tips and some cranks, but I never expected to hear from Cass late on Saturday night, particularly not with the news that she had something to share with me. I hadn't spoken to her since our lunch together but she couldn't have missed my exclusive on the Death Row photographs.

'I've got a floater up here in Lake Hollywood,' she announced. 'Beat, stabbed, strangled and then dumped in the lake. You want it?'

'I thought you'd be angry at me.'

'Yesterday I was angry. Today I need you.'

People were killed so often in Los Angeles a body wasn't news. I'd learned a lot in a few days. 'Unless there's some hook, I don't see how I can sell it.'

'The show is the hook. We'll pay you our standard still photographer's fee and if you can sell something to the tabs you can keep the commission.'

That sounded like a good deal to me. I drove up Beechwood Canyon and then wound through the maze of hillside streets to Lake Hollywood Drive. At the top of the lake police lights flashed red and blue amid a stand of eucalyptus trees. Despite the romantic name Lake Hollywood was purely utilitarian. It wasn't even a lake. Surrounded by an eight-foot chain-link fence, it served as a reservoir of fresh water for the city below. Because people drank from it the city wouldn't allow anyone near enough to spit. Still, the reservoir and surrounding hillsides were among the last open public spaces in a heavily developed city. A Department of Water and Power access road that ran just outside the chain link fence made it a popular destination for joggers, strollers and the occasional killer with a dead body to dump.

I parked the Caddy and slung the camera gear across my shoulder, watched by two uniforms whose job was to stand at the entrance to the access road and keep the curious at bay. When I told them I was there to shoot publicity stills for *Meat Wagon* the older of the two advised me to watch my step, clicked on a torch-sized flashlight and led me down the path toward a circle of lights at the edge of the lake. 'We cleared the site but you should exercise caution and good judgement. Don't touch anything you don't absolutely have to and if you so much as pick your nose put the goods in your pocket. Don't drop anything – and that means nothing – on to the ground. But you've done this a hundred times so I don't have to tell you.'

'Actually, this is my first time.'

He stopped, cupped the bright end of the flashlight in his

fingers and lit my face with the pink glow of his flesh. 'You're a virgin?'

'Figuratively speaking, yes.'

'Whatever you do, don't barf at the crime scene. Get as far away as you can before you let it heave. And don't barf into the lake or some lady in Beverly Hills will have it running out her faucet in the morning.'

Twenty yards past the coroner's wagon a gate blocked the path where it curved down to the lake. When the gate squeaked open Cass waved me over. She stood between a video cameraman and a sound recordist in a fringe of light at the edge of the water. Four portable photofloods focused the light white-hot on the lab coat of a balding pathologist who crouched over a semi-nude male, casket ready on the grass. I put the camera to my eye and zoomed to telephoto. Thick black glasses distorted the eyes of the pathologist, who worked with such concentration I could have mistaken him for feasting. On the opposite side of the circle of light two men conferred, lips to ear, one dapper in a mid-calf trench coat the colour of fog and the other in jeans and a tan windbreaker. The smell of law drifted from them strong as meat; homicide cops probably.

The pathologist called that he was ready for camera. His teeth gleamed in the bright lights. He removed his glasses for the filming and without them his eyes didn't line up straight; the right one hung lower and drifted off to the side of his face like a stray marble. Cass instructed me to wait at the edge of the lake until the videotaping had finished. She stood just behind and to the right of the camera while the sound man kneeled on the grass to the flanking side. I couldn't see much but I heard well enough. The pathologist snapped on a fresh pair of latex gloves and manipulated the joints, detailing his observations while he worked. His voice sounded like his sinuses had been corked.

Based on the body's temperature and the warmth of the lake, he estimated the time of death at between 24 and 30 hours before the body had been found. The victim was a Caucasian male, between 25 and 35 years of age, approximately 175 pounds in weight and 6 foot in height. A preliminary examination of the teeth indicated dental work of a kind not commonly practised in the United States. A canister of 35 mm film had been found between the tongue and larynx but minimal abrading of local tissues indicated that it had been placed behind the tongue post-mortem. He would have to check the lung tissue to be certain but the absence of froth in the mouth and nose when the chest was compressed suggested that death had not been caused by drowning. The depth and chafing of the ligature marks on his wrists and ankles implied he had been bound while still alive. Cuts on the palms of both hands and forearms – classic defence wounds – suggested that the victim had struggled with his assailant. At some point in his ordeal, he had been stabbed in the chest, shoulder and stomach. Though none of these wounds alone may have been fatal the combined trauma and resulting loss of blood was a potential cause of death. This was just the preliminary examination. A full autopsy and laboratory analysis would yield much richer information.

'Cut!' Cass called out. 'Brilliantly done!'

The pathologist beamed.

Cass waved me over to take the stills. I'd seen dead bodies before. I was pretty sure that as long as I kept my eye to the lens the corpse of someone I didn't know wasn't going to bother me. Then I got my first clear look at the face. After twenty-four hours in the lake the flesh had distorted to a mask of swollen indignation. Both eyes were dulled to dead glass. Abrasions reddened the skin at the forehead and cheeks, and a wedge of flesh hung from a gash at the left brow. The sacs beneath the eyes were bruised black. The face had swollen first from a terrible beating and later with the gases of decomposition. But the face hadn't swollen beyond recognition. It meant something to me. Something so terrible and real I was afraid that if I pulled the camera away the lens would take my eyes and I would go blind with the memory.

'Can you identify this man?' asked a voice behind me. The voice was gentle but hard.

'Yes,' I said.

'His name?' The tone was respectful and professional; the tone was merciless. The voice would not tell me that people did not kill, that the sky at night was not black.

'Gabriel Burns.'

'How well did you know him?'

'I knew him.'

The camera dangled by its strap around my neck. I stared at the ground. The grass lay bent and twisted from the tramp of cops, individual spears struggling upright to glint in the white hot light. A wallet-sized photograph, rippled by moisture, appeared between my eyes and the ground.

'Is this a photo of you and Mr Burns?' the voice asked.

'Yes.'

'Where was it taken?'

'Las Vegas.'

'What were you doing in Las Vegas with Mr Burns?'

'Getting married.'

The photograph drifted away again. The voice conferred with another somewhere behind me. The grass looked like a jungle seen from miles above. I wanted to get closer. I dropped to my hands and knees. I wanted to push my way through the blades of grass and hide in the riotous green.

'What's she doing?' A different voice this time. 'Get down low, get down on the grass with her.'

The lens of a video camera descended to my field of vision. In the front element of the lens I saw myself reflected, staring into the camera.

'Ma'am? Are you all right, ma'am?'

I sprang forward to grab the lens. People yelled at me. Too late. When I felt the lens mount snap, I let go. Then I sat back on the grass again. Strong hands gripped my arms, my shoulders, my neck. I did not resist.

13

The room they put me in contained a table, two chairs, a door and a hidden microphone. I'd been in rooms like it before. Overhead, the acoustical tile ceiling sagged on a tired metal frame and below my feet a stained carpet curled at the corners. The furniture had been worn to splinters by others and when of no further use or comfort consigned here. The detective guided me to a chair, gave me a cup of coffee and said he'd be back to talk in a few minutes. Too many years of sitting had crushed the seat's padding to a hard bowl and the coffee tasted like it had been scraped off the sidewalk. I moved to the chair facing the door. The detective wouldn't be in a hurry to talk to me. He'd have lots of work to do before he was ready for that. Reading my extensive criminal record would entertain him for some time. I didn't mind being alone. Sitting inside a small room for hours gives you time to think. I had a lot to think about. I had to be careful what I said. He could give me trouble, I knew that, even if I hadn't done anything wrong. My record gave him the right and leverage to push my face in the dirt.

The death of an Englishman in Los Angeles – even one so brutally murdered – would normally rate back page-news in a city where dirt naps are handed out like candy at Halloween. The detectives who'd brought me in would be digging the ground on a half-dozen cases. They couldn't go hard and deep on each one. But the cops would be working under television lights on this one. They would dig deep and hard and if they thought I was dirty they'd bury me with the corpse.

'Another cup of coffee?' The detective shouldered through the door with a file and a chipped brown mug. A black moustache perched above his lips like the wings of a well-trained bird. I hadn't really looked at him before. Two hours alone had sobered the shock out of me. I took notice of him then. At four in the morning he looked like he'd just stepped out of a clothes-press; his charcoal-grey slacks, sport coat and white dress-shirt hung on his frame not just unwrinkled but neatly creased. Deep lines scored his forehead as though in counterpoint to the smoothness of his clothes. He wore his gelled hair swept back and furrowed by a big-toothed comb. When he unbuttoned his sport coat to sit he flashed a detective badge worn at his belt like a phallic symbol. His moustache dipped into the coffee mug and the thin mouth beneath it twisted to a grimace. 'About this time of night we're scraping the bottom of the pot, but hey, it costs two bucks less than Starbucks, so you can't argue about the price.'

I said, 'No thank you, sir.'

'Call me Keith, Keith Harker.' He wanted me to relax, forget where I was for a moment, look at him as a human being, trust him. I'd talked to enough cops to know the guy was not my friend but some aren't your enemy the moment you step in the ring with them. He opened the manila file folder he'd brought into the room with the coffee. 'You have a very interesting record, Mrs Burns.' He drew out the word interesting to its full four syllables. 'You were a model citizen up until, what, age twenty-three?'

'I never got into trouble, no sir.'

'Not even a traffic ticket?'

'No sir.'

He shook his head, like, isn't that amazing, turned a page in his folder, then another page, and another. 'What the hell happened? Looks like some kinda crime spree, I see charges of – Jesus, this is a real laundry list – murder one, manslaughter, two counts of attempted murder, multiple counts of assault with a deadly weapon, grand theft, unlawful discharge of a firearm and possession of explosive materials.'

'I had a rough time,' I admitted.

'Murder one is certainly rough.'

'I was not convicted of first degree murder, sir.' I was not foolish enough to call him Keith.

'No. You were convicted of manslaughter and one count of assault with a deadly weapon.'

'Convicted, sentenced, imprisoned and released.'

'A model prisoner, according to the record.'

Not such a model prisoner. You can't be a model prisoner where I was and keep any pride. They just never caught me. 'I've rehabilitated myself, sir.'

He shut the file folder and nodded like he was trying to believe me. 'I'm happy to hear that. And I want you to rest assured that we're not here to put you on trial again. You've served your time and it's not in anybody's long-term interest to put you back in jail, if, as you say, you've rehabilitated yourself.'

That gave me reason to worry. Whenever somebody said they didn't want to do something bad to me I figured he'd already made up his mind to do exactly that. Harker fingered his coffee mug and focused his eyes a hundred yards behind my head. His glance dropped to the mug, then rose to me, then dropped back to the mug again. He looked like he had something he wanted to say but didn't know how to begin. It was a good look. I was sure he used it every day, maybe a couple of times a day, when he wanted someone to believe he wasn't exactly sure how to say what was on his mind. He said, 'I have to tell you I find it more than a little odd that just out of jail you married a foreigner, then didn't live with him and from what I know didn't even see him.'

I told him Gabriel and I had been introduced by a friend of mine in prison. We met on the day of my release and it was love at first sight. We drove to Las Vegas on a lark, got married, had a fantastic honeymoon, then argued, said some nasty things to each other and broke up. We'd seen each other again earlier in the week and hoped to get back together. If we were a couple of movie stars, nobody would think what we had done strange at all.

'How often did you do cocaine with your husband?'

'Excuse me?'

'Of course you did. Just out of jail, looking for a good time, he takes you to Vegas, you get married, you do a little blow, that what happened?'

I was too shocked to say anything.

'I'm not going to report this to your parole officer,' he lied. 'I just need to know if that's what happened.'

'No sir, that's not what happened.'

He gave me this very specific type of stare people in law enforcement employ, like if he stared hard enough I'd break down and confess everything. 'I'll let that one go. I'm not really interested in whether *you* did cocaine or not.' That was his way of saying he was doing me a favour, that he didn't believe me. 'How often did you see your husband doing cocaine?'

'Never, sir.'

'I don't have to remind you of the risks you take by lying to me?'

'I'm not lying.'

'Your husband was a coke-head. You're either lying or stupid.'

I didn't say anything to that.

'Let's be charitable and say you're just ignorant. Did you notice your husband take frequent trips to the bathroom, seem unusually excited or nervous?'

'He went to the bathroom all the time – sure, I noticed that – but most guys who drink a six-pack a day do that. And was he unusually excited? I don't know what's usual for him, but we made love four times in two days and that was excited enough for me.'

That pissed him off. 'I haven't called your parole officer yet. Have you kept in touch with her?'

'It's not a parole violation to have a dead husband, is it?'

'A green card marriage is a federal offence. That would violate the terms of your parole and slam you back in jail faster than you could pack your underwear, so don't get cute with me.'

I don't react well to men who threaten me. They remind me of my father. I said, 'If you want to ask me any more questions, start asking through my lawyer because I got nothing more to say to you.'

He gave me his hard stare. I stared back. Tougher people had interrogated me before, and for days, not hours.

'I've seen the wives of victims go into shock, I've seen them weep, I've seen them go wild with hysteria, but only the guilty ones show me hostility. Your husband is lying on a morgue slab right now, and you know, I don't think you care.'

'I stopped crying years ago. No point to it.'

'I'm supposed to believe it was true love?'

'I'm a healthy woman. I'd been locked up for five years. Try hormones.'

'So you hump your brains out a couple nights. You don't marry him.'

'I'm surprised you'd make such a suggestion. I'm a very moral girl.'

'Convicted of manslaughter and you have a problem with premarital sex?'

'Maybe I found Christ,' I said. 'I wouldn't be the first.'

'The story stinks and you know it.'

'Everybody's private life stinks a little bit, detective. I'd think you'd have noticed that by now.'

The morning sea curled smooth as rolling glass and splintered to shore in six-foot sheets. Beyond the wave break a wing-shaped formation of pelicans skimmed a foot above the surface of the sea, their ponderous bellies and heavy beaks acting as gravity's counterpoint to the aerodynamic lift of wings. I ran across the sand until my legs cramped to stone. Later that afternoon wind would chop the surface. The sea would look more violent then but the waves wouldn't swell any larger nor would the current pull more powerfully. With a stray piece of bottle glass I etched a three inch cut into my arm and washed the wound in saltwater. I didn't cry or grit my teeth. I felt nothing. My heart was shot full of Novocaine.

My parole officer waited outside my apartment building when I walked up the street. She stepped out of her car with a cup of Starbucks in hand. There was a store just down the street. There was a store just about everywhere, outlets multiplying like McDonald's franchises. 'I'm going to search your apartment,' she announced, no smile or nod of recognition. Her eyes were swollen with sleeplessness and anger. She didn't like being awakened at five in the morning, she didn't like one of her charges getting into trouble she didn't learn about first and that meant she didn't like me. And I was just one of a hundred cases she handled on top of what I guessed was a rotten personal life. At the head of the stairs I turned and made a meek effort at resistance.

'Do you have a search warrant?'

'I don't need one. I have the right to search your apartment whenever I want, as many times as I want. It's in your parole agreement. I suggest you read it.' Her lips tightened to a smug smile. She had been asked the same question a hundred times and knew there could be no argument. She had the power.

I unlocked the door and swung it open. Before stepping across the threshold she peered carefully inside. She might assume I lived alone but didn't take any chances. She nodded toward my arm.

'What happened?'

'I cut it. Down at the beach.'

She walked into the apartment and nosed around. 'Does anybody live or stay with you?'

I told her I lived alone.

'Then everything I find in here is yours, is that correct?'

I said what little there was, was mine.

She thumbed through the self-help books I'd bought and almost smiled at the titles. Maybe she had read some of them. Maybe she had her own problems. 'Bathroom?' She asked. The location was obvious. I pointed to the only other door in the apartment. She checked the toilet tank and rattled around the bathroom cabinet. I could hear her popping the tops of vitamin and aspirin containers. She came out of the bathroom with bandages and rubbing alcohol in the crook of her arm. At the sink, she poured a paper cup of tap water and passed it to me. 'Drink, then put your arm on the kitchen counter.'

I drank, returned the cup and laid my forearm bone-side

down. She probed for grains of sand and swabbed at the cut with cotton dipped in alcohol.

'You need stitches. I'll bandage it but you should see a doctor.'

I figured the wound would close with a scar. I didn't mind.

'This cut looks self-inflected. Is it?'

'What does it matter?'

'Another half-inch deeper would make it attempted suicide, is how it matters. That would be a serious parole violation.'

She didn't appreciate it when I laughed.

'Were you trying to do something like that, maybe working up the courage?' She pressed the wound edges together, applied gauze along the length and adhesive strips across the width of the cut. I didn't answer. I didn't know why I did it. I just did.

'What are these from?' She took my right wrist and examined the half-dozen red welts rising like a chain of volcanoes up my arm.

'Some guy burned me,' I said, 'with a cigarette.'

'You were kidnapped, wasn't that it?'

'That was it.'

The scars served me well. At my trial, I stood and showed my arm to the jurors. I walked on murder one. After they saw the scars, they didn't want to convict me, whether they believed I did it or not.

'Into the bathroom for your A and T.' She knew her way this time, opened the door and hooked her chin toward the toilet.

'My what?'

'Urine test. If you've done any drugs in the past week, they'll pop up on the lab report.'

'I was never arrested for doing drugs.'

'It's still a violation of your parole. You marry a doper, what do you expect? I warned you about this guy. They found enough coke on his body to choke a horse.' She handed me the same paper cup I'd drunk out of minutes before.

'You want me to pee into this?'

'That's right.'

'And you're going to stand there and watch me?'

A smile almost bent her rose-frost lips. She thought I was distressed because I'd been doing drugs. Maybe her job was so tough she had forgotten some people still like to have a little dignity. I peeled down my pants, squatted over the toilet and positioned the cup where I might catch something. For the past five years I'd peed in open view of the deputies but that didn't lessen the humiliation.

'You want to drink more water?'

'Same cup again? No thanks.'

We waited. I stared at my feet, examined the ring in the bathtub, whistled through my teeth.

'As long as it takes,' she said.

'I never saw Gabe do any drugs.'

'Did you see him at all? That's the question now. How much did he give you to marry him?'

'I saw him a couple days before he was killed. We were getting back together again. That's what I thought.'

'Then where's the ring?' She pointed at my ring finger. 'You didn't live with him, you don't wear his ring, how am I supposed to believe this was anything but a green card marriage?'

With my free hand I fished from beneath my shirt the circular pendant Gabe had given me. 'He never gave me a ring. He gave me this. He wasn't very conventional, you know?' I had begun with the idea of committing the crime of marrying him for money and ended, what? In love with him? I didn't know for sure that I didn't. Maybe I did. Warmth gushed over my hand. My parole officer dipped her hand into her bag and pulled out a small plastic vial with a screw top. When I had enough to slosh around I held out the cup. She unscrewed the cap and set the vial on the sink edge.

'You pour,' she ordered.

I set the cup down next to the vial. My face burned. She did this for a living, I told myself, I shouldn't feel shamed. I creased the cup, filled the vial, screwed on the top and washed it in soap and warm water. I said, 'Look, maybe Gabe and I started off with one kind of relationship and ended with another. Maybe it was just something fun to do at first but then it got more serious. Does that make sense to you?'

She wrote the date, my name and parole number on a sticker and affixed it to the vial. 'No. You either married him for money or you didn't. A homicide detective leaned on me very hard this morning. He thinks you're guilty of something, a green card marriage to start. He doesn't want me to COP you. And if I find any evidence at all that you've lied to me, I won't COP you.'

COP: Continued On Parole. Every parole officer had the power to recommend continued freedom or re-incarceration. She zipped my urine in her purse and didn't wait to be shown the way out the door.

15

The address my ex-cellmate Rose had given me for the lawyer who had arranged the green card marriage connected to a two-storey faux French chateau in Hancock Park, the final outpost of wealth and privilege separating the Westside of Los Angeles from the melting pot of poverty to the east. Like most of the city's enclaves for the moneyed, the residential streets were wide and quiet, save for the occasional whoosh of a Mercedes Benz or the distant buzz of Mexican gardeners mowing a lawn. Those lawns were, inevitably, like the houses themselves, big. In Hancock Park, anything under three thousand square feet was tear-down material. Water piped over the mountains from the Owens Valley coursed through automatic sprinklers and flowed into swimming pools, sustaining an almost tropical landscape rich in hibiscus and palm trees. The neighbourhood was lush in a way that only natural sun shining upon imported water, soil and plants tended by foreign labour can make a place.

The street sign in front of Harry Bendel's mini-manse prohibited parking, as did the sign across from it and the one down from that. All the signs up and down the block carried the same warning. Parking anywhere on the street was illegal. If you needed to park on the street, you didn't belong in the neighbourhood. I pulled into Harry's half-circle brick drive. Like all old cars the Caddy leaked considerable oil. That was going to be Harry's problem.

'Jesus! Harry, it's one of yours!' The woman who shouted this to the cavernous hall behind the front door was thin and blonde and from the smooth sheen of her face it looked like the most serious problem she had was an overstocked refrigerator. Her clothes were Sunday casual but had that crisp, out-of-the-box look. Some people have a talent for that, mostly people with money. She shut the door in my face. Though of solid oak the door wasn't strong enough to bar her voice. I heard the word 'unhappy', a long but muffled adjective preceding the word 'clients', and the emphatically voiced phrase, 'in my house!'

The door snapped open to the pink face and massive body of a fifty-something man who started life big and got bigger eating too much steak and playing weekend golf. His shoulders stretched to both sides of the door frame and the size of his chest was prodigious though his belly had some time ago overwhelmed it. His body might have been out of shape but his voice wasn't. 'I don't care what your problems are or how you got this address, never come to my house, ever. Are you absolutely clear on that?' I'd never met someone whose natural speaking voice could be described as stentorian. His was.

'One of your clients has been murdered,' I said.

'That is not a rare event. My clients are frequently murdered. That is the type of clientele I have. If you wish to discuss it with me, stop by my office tomorrow morning. I charge one hundred and fifty dollars an hour.'

I straight-armed the door before it closed. 'The client is my husband, the man you set me up with, Gabriel Burns.'

'The Englishman?'

'I'm Nina Zero. I roomed with your client, Rose Selavy.'

He nodded with his entire body, leading with the shoulders, and darted a glance over his shoulder. He looked like a big kid worried about what might catch him from behind. 'Go around to the side gate,' he whispered. 'I'll meet you there.'

When I crossed the lawn in front of the living-room window they were going jaw to jaw beside the sofa. His voice boomed out, 'She's not a drug addict, she's a widow for chrissake!' The thin blonde didn't flinch. I couldn't grasp her exact phrasing but the substance of her snarl and yap was clear. Maybe her smooth face was like the crispness of her clothes, a given attribute of class and completely unconnected to her inner being.

'Sorry I can't let you inside,' Harry apologized when he slid the bolt and opened the side gate. 'My wife has a hard and fast rule: no clients allowed at home.' He led me along the side of the house into the small piece of paradise found in the back yards of most California homeowners, though his was larger and considerably more paradisiacal than most. We sat in lawn chairs by the side of the pool, shaded by forty-foot palm trees. A hundred and fifty dollars an hour can buy a nice chunk of cloud. 'Nobody's contacted me about this,' he said. 'No reason they should, I suppose. I didn't know him that well, only performed the one small legal service which I suppose you know about.' He was just filling space, waiting for me to begin.

'They found him up in Lake Hollywood, beaten and stabbed to death.' The words ground together in my gut like stones.

Harry leaned forward, elbows on knees, and clutched his hands together. Though out of shape, he moved with an athletic grace that made me think he could act quickly if needed. 'Frankly, his death shocks me. Mr Burns wasn't a typical client. He was a fun guy, the last of my clients I'd expect to catch the scythe.'

'How was he not typical?'

'He wasn't a prostitute or a drug addict. Almost all of my cases involve so-called lifestyle crimes.'

'Then I don't get the connection, why he would come to you.'

Harry tilted back in his deck chair and gazed somewhere up among the palm trees. 'I met him in a bar. I had to pull some overtime for a case on the docket the following morning. But I didn't want to miss the 49er game – Monday Night Football you know – so I dropped by a local sports bar to catch the second half. Mr Burns was at the table next to me. He didn't understand a damn thing about the game. Whenever anybody kicked the ball for any reason he'd shout, "That's right, that's the way to do it!" ' Harry's smile faded with the realization that the memory was now his alone. He tilted the chair back down to all fours. 'Damn. I'm sorry to hear he's dead. But to be blunt, what do you care? His death absolves you of legal responsibility. Is that what you came to hear?'

'No. I came for personal reasons. I came to find out . . .' I couldn't finish the sentence. The thought splintered to the hundred things I didn't know, then crystallized into the one thing that perplexed me the most. 'Why me? Out of the million and a half single women in this city why did you choose me to marry him?' When his hands came up to calm me I realized I had stood and shouted at him. 'I'm sorry,' I said. 'There's just too many things about this I don't understand.' I knelt by the pool and splashed water on my face.

Harry watched as though he suddenly remembered I was an ex-con and could not be counted on to obey the laws of decorum or even those against physical violence. Or maybe he realized that if he didn't placate me I could tell the police how Gabe and I met. I wasn't an expert in the law but arranging a green card marriage had to be as illegal as participating in one.

'I'm not an immigration lawyer,' Harry admitted. 'I advised him straight away to go to a specialist but he said he already had one of those and didn't trust him. He wanted to go outside the circle. He was working on something he described as incendiary and feared an immigration lawyer could be extorted into betraying him.'

'Didn't that sound paranoid to you?'

'Paranoia is when you're snorting a dollar for every two dollars you deal and you think the FBI has planted a homing device up your ass. Mr Burns told me he'd been threatened with deportation, that somebody was investigating his life and asking a lot of questions that seemed directed to proving he was violating his work visa. Based on the type of photographs he took for a living, I'd say he was reasonably cautious, not paranoid.'

As it set, the sun reflected whole and clear at the deep end of the swimming pool. I didn't wonder whether Gabe had lied to me, but how often he lied to me. When we were attacked in Las Vegas he said he hadn't known the assailant but from what I had seen the assailant certainly knew him. A gust of wind rippled the surface of the pool. The sun bobbed precariously, split apart and warped to an orange smear. The image of a smile carved into flesh – the purplish line left on the skin by a stab wound – clicked before me like a slide. The man in Las Vegas had attacked us with a knife.

'Would you like a glass of water?' Harry knelt beside me, his hand on my shoulder.

I shook my head. The surface of the pool calmed to glass. The sun again became whole. Gabe hadn't loved me enough to leave me with the burden of his death. 'The cops told me they found coke on his body. Could he have been a dealer?'

'No.' His voice was terse and sure. 'I'm around these people all the time. Mr Burns was not of that ilk.'

'An addict?'

'In certain professions every Angeleno under the age of fifty has sniffed coke. It's a fact of life in the fast lane. He didn't seem like a heavy user those few occasions we met. But anybody can be a recreational user and only a lab technician with a urine sample would know.' He grunted and rubbed his right knee when he stood from the side of the pool and settled again in his deck chair. 'Do you want to know what I think?' The question was rhetorical. He was a lawyer, accustomed to giving advice and being paid well for it. 'Cops like to exaggerate when interviewing someone they think might be connected to the case. They wanted to throw a scare into you, nothing more. As a parolee, you'd be suspected of everything from supplying him with the coke to killing him.'

If their objective was to frighten me, they succeeded. I understood the situation. When my urine sample came back negative, they'd look for another pretext to revoke my parole. I had no rights. The burden of proof was on me. 'Rose told me Gabe was her cousin.'

A derisive Ha! boomed from his chest. 'Rose was not Mr Burns's cousin. Rose is my cousin.'

'Why would she lie to me?'

'She lies to everybody. Part of her charm. I asked her if she knew somebody. She named you. I do all her legal work pro bono. She lied to you because she owes me. When I mentioned you to Mr Burns he authorized me to go ahead and arrange it.'

'A green card marriage to an ex-con. Why?'

'He wasn't sure he could trust the people he knew. If word got around that he was looking, there were people who would turn him in. He wanted to marry a perfect stranger. But in your case specifically, the deciding factor was probably the money.'

He watched me while he twisted a massive gold football ring around his index finger, as though he weighed the impact of what he was about to say.

'What about the money?'

'The other girl I suggested wanted five grand. You settled for two.'

16

A few blocks outside the boundary of Hancock Park the interior of my car lit the colour of blood. When I pulled to the curb and hooked the transmission into park I laughed at how my hands trembled. Five years in the joint and I still lost my nerve when a cop pulled me over. Reflected in the side view mirror the door of an unmarked police car opened into traffic and the immaculately pressed figure of Detective Harker stepped out. I was careful to keep my hands on the steering wheel. I didn't want to give him an excuse to shoot me.

'May I see your driver's licence and registration, please?'

I handed the documents through the open window. 'Next time you want to talk to me, why don't you try my cell phone?'

He glanced at my licence for no more than a second. 'Step out of the car.'

His partner waited on the curb, a club-sized flashlight gripped like a knife to rake across the back seat. He wore the same tan windbreaker and blue jeans from the night at Lake Hollywood. The man looked more shopkeeper than law; his waist extended beyond the plane of his shoulders so that in profile his body had the shape of a split pear. His close-cropped black hair thinned at the crown of a wide, freckled face that bore no identifiable expression except dispassion. I'd never seen a black face look so blank.

'You were driving erratically.' Harker walked me around the trunk of the Caddy. When he brushed aside the tail of his sport coat to rest his hand on his hip I noticed he still wore the detective badge on his belt. 'How many drinks have you had this evening?'

'You're wasting your time. I haven't had a drink in days.'

'I distinctly smell alcohol on your breath. Close your eyes, lean your head back and touch the tip of your nose with your right index finger.'

I closed my eyes and did it, no sweat.

'You just failed the field sobriety test. Under California Consent Law you have no legal right to refuse a breath test.'

His partner opened the passenger door, crouched and worked the flashlight under the seat. The hairs of my forearm began to stand straight and pay attention. 'If you plant any drugs in my car, the urine test will show I'm clean. You can explain that contradiction to the judge.'

Harker gripped my arm at the biceps and steered me on to the curb. 'You didn't have a beer this afternoon? All it takes is one open beverage container to ship your ass back to prison.' He broke a disposable mouthpiece out of plastic, inserted it into a portable electronic box and held it up to my mouth. 'Blow,' he commanded. When the numbers read negative for alcohol his glance lifted over my shoulder and he slowly shook his head. I looked back. His partner nudged the passenger door shut. Had any alcohol registered on my breath, one of his pockets contained an open pint of something to get me busted, I had no doubt about that.

'I'd like to talk to you about my husband's murder.'

'Your husband? A green card arrangement between a coke-head and a murderess doesn't make a marriage.'

I dealt with a lot of misplaced aggression in prison. Soon enough you learn you can't get into a fight with everybody who's willing to fight with anybody. 'Somebody attacked us with a knife. In Vegas.'

Harker pulled out a notebook. 'Did you report it?'

It wasn't a question, the way he asked it, more of a challenge. My parole agreement required me to register with the Vegas police department. I hadn't. Gabe didn't think it would be worth the trouble. We hadn't reported anything. I said, 'No.'

'Were there any witnesses?'

'Me. I saw it happen. The guy was early thirties, about five foot ten, dirty blonde hair. '

'We'll keep our eye out for him.' Harker flipped his notebook shut without writing it down.

'It's a shame you can't sue a cop for malpractice.'

'The department has a phone number for citizen complaints. It's in the book.'

'The coke on his body was planted.'

'Oh, a conspiracy.' His arched eyebrow told me what he thought of that.

'He was working on a story that pissed off some people.'

'What's the story, who's the people?'

'I don't know yet.'

'I didn't think so.'

I felt stupid. That was how he wanted me to feel. 'I think somebody hired a private detective to get him deported.'

'And that's why he married you, isn't it? To get a green card. So he couldn't be deported.'

I couldn't say anything because he was right, even if he was right about the wrong thing. But to him, being right about one thing made him right about the other. He jabbed a forefinger into my shoulder. 'You haven't even thought about what you're gonna do with the body, have you?'

I didn't get what he meant. 'The body?'

'The body of your dead husband. Remember him? Most relatives like to claim the body. But you haven't asked me a single question about that. Did you forget about him?'

I hadn't thought I was responsible for his body and the expression on my face told him as much. I didn't even know how to get in contact with his family.

He jabbed my shoulder again. 'You still want to tell me this wasn't a green card marriage?'

The partner came up to Harker's side, wiping his hands on a white handkerchief. 'Your keys are in the trunk.'

'On the trunk?' I repeated, not quite catching him.

'I heard him say *in* the trunk.'

He strode toward the hood end of the curb.

I went after him.

'I need to get into my husband's apartment. As his widow, it's my right.'

He stopped dead still. His eyes looked hard and clear enough to stare into the sun. 'Convicted felons have no rights. The apartment is sealed. You can get access next week, in the unlikely event you're not back in stir.'

Harker stepped into the street.

I went after him again.

'Haven't you ever lost anyone you cared about?'

He turned on me so fast I didn't get my hands up in time to keep him from slapping me to the ground. I tried to get my feet under me but he grabbed the back of my head and rode my face into the gutter. 'Don't you ever talk to me about loss! You don't know a fucking thing about loss!'

Out of the corner of my eye a tan shape flitted between Harker and the night sky. The weight on my neck lifted. I twisted on to my back and coughed. The partner pinned Harker against the door of the cruiser. 'It's not worth it!' He shouted, again and again, his voice dropping with each repetition until his lips moved with a sound less than a whisper. When Harker nodded, twice and emphatically, his partner let him go. Not once did he look at me. He straightened his sport coat with great shrugs of his shoulder and jerked open the door.

The partner stared down at me like trash. He offered advice but no hand. 'You should watch your ass.'

I dragged myself out of the gutter. The partner may have locked my keys in the trunk but he hadn't locked the passenger door, either out of kindness or lack of imagination. I crawled on to the back seat and lay there, counting my heartbeat down, beat by beat, until it dropped below the speed of a frightened rabbit. Then I made a call. One good thing about spending time in prison, it gives you a lot of connections. It's like college in that way. You meet people you'll know for the rest of your very short life.

17

The headlights of a Jeep Cherokee woke me about an hour later, the time it had taken Brenda to drive into Los Angeles from Sierra Madre in the foothills of the San Gabriel Mountains. Though I was born and raised in California, Brenda was the only Native Californian I'd met, with three Chumash grandparents and one Mexican grandfather. She wasn't sure where she got her size and strength, but at 200 pounds she had enough of both nearly to break my ribs when she hugged me. There was always a lot of warmth between us. Though I was not a professional criminal like herself, the magnitude of my crimes commanded her respect. She'd been released two years earlier than I after serving eighteen months on a B and E – breaking and entering – charge. I'd heard she'd done well. Brenda was among the top lock-picks in Los Angeles.

'You're one 'a the few people I'd drive more than two minutes to see, *cariño*, but how could you be so dumb you lock your keys in the trunk?' She knelt to eyeball the lock.

'I was being hassled by the cops. It was their idea of a joke.'

Brenda unsnapped a leather case, clicked on a mini-flashlight and selected from a couple dozen picks, rakes and tension wrenches the sizes she figured would do the job the fastest. 'I thought you were gonna be a regular citizen when you got out. Why you being hassled by the cops?'

'Just the usual ex-con bullshit.'

Though a big woman, Brenda had delicate hands. She worked the lock quickly, thinking with her fingers. In another society she would have been a surgeon. She once told me that her great-great grandmothers had been medicine women and folk-healers. Born to poverty in an East LA neighbourhood with more convicted felons than San Quentin, she had learned early to operate on locks instead of people. She flipped the trunk lock in less than ten seconds.

Her flash spotlit the keys above the left wheel well. She picked them off the carpet and dangled the key ring from her forefinger. 'Any garage monkey could 'a popped the trunk for you, so you gonna tell me what you drag me out here for?'

'I'd like to buy a set of picks.'

Big Brenda had a face like her native land, wide and generous and browned by generations of sun; her earth-brown eyes carried timelessness in their gaze and her bone-white teeth flashes of mortality. 'So you *have* joined the life,' she mused.

'I'm still a citizen, at least trying to be.'

'Citizens don't need a set of picks.'

When I told her my husband had been murdered and the law wouldn't let me into his apartment she opened her arms and buried me in a hug. I accepted it long enough to be polite and broke free. I didn't want to be comforted. 'I'll pay you the going rate.'

'What you think you're gonna do with a set of picks?' She rocked back on her heels, looking at me in a critical way I didn't like.

'You gave me a few lessons, remember?'

In jail she had cut a set of picks from the baling steel that had wrapped a crate of foodstuffs. She had kept the picks hidden in her cell, not to use in any escape attempt, but to stay sharp for her return to the outside.

'A couple jail house lessons don't make you a pro, *cariño*. I'm not gonna give you a set of picks so you can go get yourself arrested.'

That was it. I'd never known Big Brenda to change her decision on anything once she stated it. I figured I'd break in through one of the windows.

'But tell you what I am gonna give you,' she added.

'What?'

'Me.'

The one good thing about California bars closing at two in the morning is that by three you can be pretty sure some drunk isn't going to stumble on to whatever illegal enterprise you got going. Los Angeles is such an early night town that we could have hit the apartment before midnight and not run much risk of getting caught but Brenda insisted on waiting until three, the safest hour for nobody-at-home break-ins. The Spanish fourplex in which Gabe had lived was dimly lit by a distant street light. Not a window on the entire street was lit from the inside. We didn't talk while climbing the stairs but neither did we take extra effort to be quiet. She knelt at the lock with a mini-flashlight gripped between her teeth. I stood behind, shielding her from the street, and after first unsticking the yellow police tape sealing the door rummaged through my duffel bag like I was drunk and looking for my keys.

The trunk was a toy compared to the serious metal on Gabe's door, a seven-pin dead bolt and key entry knob. She needed two picks, a tension wrench and a hook to work the dead bolt. Sweat began to break out on her forehead after the first minute. At two minutes she began to hum, very softly in the back of her throat. She cracked the dead bolt at three minutes and moved quickly to the knob-lock. Not a single car passed on the street below. The citizens were safe in their beds, those who had one. A homeless man pushed his shopping cart toward Melrose. He looked up at us once and moved on. Brenda took down the knob-lock in thirty seconds, pushed the door open and pulled me inside.

'Cell phone on and volume down?'

I double checked.

'One ring is a warning. Stop and listen. Don't answer, don't leave a record of the call. A second means get the hell out. Remember that?' She squeezed my arm. 'Wait for a third ring in case somebody else is calling you. I'll hang up on the second ring if *algo va mal*.' *Algo va mal*. If something goes wrong. She slipped out the door before I could thank her and I could no more hear her footsteps down the stairs than I could a cat's.

I breathed deeply the air of the enclosed room, wanting to smell Gabe, that special scent he had, but couldn't through the rancidness and dust. I clicked on the flashlight. Motes danced in the beam as it played over a rug torn to the corner floorboards, a scatter of books ripped from their bindings, a sofa gutted of stuffing like a burst pussy-willow. I trod carefully through the ruin to the kitchen, stopped at the threshold by the debris. Flour and sugar dusted the counters. Honey pooled from a broken jar on to the stove, narrowing to a congealed stream on its descent to the floor. Every box in the kitchen had been ripped open, emptied and tossed aside, every bag slit, every pot, pan and container pulled from its cupboard. The door to the refrigerator hung open like a wound, spilling soured entrails to the floor.

My first thoughts were of Harker. Rage and desperation had visited the apartment. Whoever had sacked the place had been confident of finding something which, eluding them, provoked a barbarian fury. Harker was the only person I knew carrying that much anger. I stepped over broken glass in the hallway and pushed on the door to the bedroom. The bed lay twisted upside down, mattress slit, cloth covering torn away from the bed springs. Pens, broken glass, rubber bands, lens cleaner and tissue lay scattered among the rubble beneath the night stand. I nudged open the door to the closet with my foot, ran my free hand over the shirt he'd worn our last night together. The objects of the dead are weighted with a living past. I took it off the rack and stuffed it in my duffel bag.

Gabe's pillow lay crushed under the bed. I pulled it out, leaned against the wall and held it to my face. His scent rose faintly from the cloth. I hadn't found an address book or letters from his family, nor a single canister of film or set of negatives. I still didn't know what he'd been working on before he died or how to contact his family. If Harker was investigating Gabe's death as drug related, confiscation of the photographs didn't make any sense. But then cops aren't scrupulously truthful to scum like me. He could have been lying. Or the apartment could have been searched for something else by someone who got here before the cops, just before or after murdering Gabe. The search seemed too violent and rushed to be carried out by homicide detectives, even raging ones. Cops empty the cereal boxes in the trash or sink, not on the floor.

A picture frame leaned against the wall. I propped it against my knee to study the image. The glass had splintered. It was the photograph taken at our marriage in Las Vegas, the one that had hung above his bed. Two glass shards had been thrust into the image, one through Gabe's heart and the other spearing mine. I set the photograph back against the wall.

At the sound of the cell phone I bounded across the wreckage to the sliding glass door in the back, flipped the latch and stepped out on to a balcony that overlooked a garden of orange trees, rose bushes and a postage-stamp lawn. I climbed the railing and at the second ring let go of the bottom rung. The third ring sounded on the flight down. I rolled to the side when I hit the grass and came up holding Gabe's pillow, not so stunned by the blow of earth that I didn't curse my stupidity; I'd jumped one ring too soon. The phone rang again. I reached into my bag and silenced it. A light clicked on behind the curtained window at ground level. I crawled behind a rose bush. A groggy face appeared in the pane of glass. With the light on behind, he wouldn't see far into the darkness. I crouched low and used the bush as cover to skirt around the side of the house. A couple of fences over, a slow-to-wake dog began to bark. The side gate was locked so I vaulted it. The phone began to ring again. I shackled my legs to a citizen's stroll, kept my head down and fumbled through the bag. Brenda's face jutted out the window of her Jeep Cherokee. I pulled the phone out of the bag and found the switch to turn it off. She dipped her head once and accelerated slowly away from the curb, her lights dimmed until well down the block.

On Brenda's instructions I'd left the Caddy open and the key in the ignition hidden by a towel thrown over the steering wheel. The engine turned first try. The front porch light ignited as I dropped the transmission into drive. In the rear-view mirror I watched a figure stumble toward the sidewalk. The distance made a reading of my plates impossible but Cadillacs are not anonymous vehicles. I didn't flick on the headlights until I reached Melrose. I glanced over at the cell phone and almost threw it out the window. Instead, I turned it back on. Immediately it began to ring.

'Payback time.' A voice, rough with smoke. Frank. 'You up for a little night shoot?'

I'd called him first with the Death Row story. He thought he owed me. 'This isn't a good time.'

'I heard about the Englishman. Sorry.'

'Whatever. I'm not really working now.'

'This is news, not work. You know Dave Schuman?'

I scanned the rear-view mirror for bubble gum lights or fast-moving police cruisers. It took me a moment to match the name with a face. 'The scalp collector,' I said. 'The guy who walks around with photographs of celebrities taped to his camera strap.'

'The scalp collector, right.' He barked a laugh. 'Only this time somebody collected his scalp. A half-hour ago they found his body in the trunk of a car parked on Ledgewood, just beneath the Hollywood Hills sign.'

A hundred yards from the crime scene my headlights picked up the white door and black city seal of a police car turned broadside in the street. A young patrolman slouched against the hood and sipped at a paper cup of coffee. Even a harmless cop like that, drinking coffee to stay warm and awake at the end of a long shift, unnerved me. I backed into a driveway to turn around. A thump on the rear fender put my foot to the brake. I thought I'd hit something. Frank put his face against the side window and his lips moved 'Ha-ha'. I powered the window down. He pointed to a red Civic down the block and said he found a couple of witnesses to interview.

As I angled to park on the street, the faces of two teenagers in the back seat flashed in my headlights. I set the Nikon for night shooting, loaded a fresh roll of Kodak and walked over. The roof light kicked in when Frank opened the door. Both boys were well-barbered whites with bloodshot eyes and flushed cheeks. They looked about seventeen, wore Patagonia windbreakers, Gap jeans and hundred-dollar Timberland hiking boots. When I introduced myself the blond one said, 'I'm Sean an' this is Randy.'

'What brought you guys up to the Hills tonight?'

'I've got an agent,' Randy claimed. 'We were up here looking at houses to buy if I get cast in this pilot I – '

'Bullshit,' Sean objected. 'We were just up at the Holly-wood sign, you know, just, like, you know – '

'Partying,' Frank prompted.

'Right,' Sean nodded.

'Wanna tell us what happened?'

'Right. Well, ahhhh – 'bout two in the morning we come down the hill, you know, an' it's like real late so nobody else is around, an' we're tired because we've been, you know, like really, really partying.'

Randy framed the air with his hands. 'Cut to this beat-to-shit Plymouth Fury, ugliest car in the known universe.'

'Right,' Sean nodded. 'An' we both look at each other like – '

'What's this car doing here?'

'We mean, like, this is celebrity turf – '

'Keanu Reeves lives just down the street. '

'Right, a million a house minimum, an' smack in the middle is the ugliest car you've ever seen. We're thinking – '

'It can't belong to someone in the neighbourhood.'

'It has to belong to somebody partying up in the hills.'

Randy framed the air with his hands. 'Cut to close up. The trunk.'

'It's open.'

'Not a lot, not like wide open.'

'But you could see it hadn't closed right.'

'We started thinking . . .'

'What if they left something in the trunk?'

'Like a case of beer.'

'We weren't going to, you know, rip them off,' Sean protested, waving his hands.

'We were just curious.'

'So Randy here – '

'Sean didn't want to touch it.'

'He looks around to see if anybody is watching an' – '

'I open the trunk.'

'An' he screams, I mean, like, really screams.'

'Wouldn't you? Expect a case of beer and you come face to face with some dead guy?'

'So I come up to look at what he's screaming about – '

'Sean here threw up in the curb.'

'I had the spins. I told you I had the spins before.'

'Those dead eyeballs gave you the spins real fast.'

'Tell him about the weird part,' Sean nudged.

'Right, the weird part. Once I got over the shock, I leaned in for a closer look – the guy was covered in blood and had these gashes all over his body like he'd been stabbed – '

'It was really gross.'

'Totally gross. And I see this stuff coming out of his mouth.'

'Film,' Sean said.

'But it had no pictures on it, like the stuff in the film cartridge before it gets developed.'

'It looked like somebody stuffed a roll of film down his throat.'

'That's exactly what it looked like,' Randy agreed.

'Did you see any ligature marks?' I asked.

'Huh?' Sean blinked.

'She means from ropes,' Randy explained.

'You mean, like, he'd been tied up?'

'I didn't see anything. He was wearing this Hawaiian shirt, you know, short sleeves.'

'Ugly too.'

Sean gulped the air in a sudden yawn. Randy fought it, but a second later, he too let out a yelp. The boys sat quietly for a moment, blinking. Frank scribbled on a notepad propped on the front seat.

'You won't write that bit about me, like, throwing up in the gutter?' Sean asked with an intense concern for his reputation.

'I think I can leave that detail out and keep the integrity of the story intact.' Frank reached into his pocket and handed two twenties across the seat. 'Once we get the photograph you can go home and read all about yourselves in tomorrow's *Scandal Times*.'

In the east, light blue ink seeped above the black outline of hills. I used the Caddy to double as the trunk in which the body was found and took some hokey shots of the boys 'discovering' the body, the kind of thing the editor and readers of *Scandal Times* lapped up. The boys left happily dreaming of fame. The nightmares would strike later, when they realized the body in the trunk one day could just as easily be them.

'How you coping?' Frank leaned against the fender of the Caddy as I rewound the film.

I tossed him the canister, shrugged. 'What do you think of this?'

'Not exactly the way the last one, your friend – what do I call him, anyway?'

'My husband,' I said, without thinking.

Frank looked to see if I was being ironic and seemed surprised when he saw I'd said it straight. 'Not exactly the way your husband caught it, but close enough.'

'The knife wounds sound the same. But Gabe was tied up before he was killed, and this guy wasn't.'

'I see what you're saying. If it was a serial killing, you'd expect the details to line up, right?'

'I don't know what I'm saying.' I had no doubt that Gabe's and the scalp collector's killer were one and the same but other than their line of work I couldn't see the connection. The scalp collector couldn't have been collaborating on the story. Gabe hated him. Maybe he had been murdered not for what he had been doing, but because of who he was. Like the scalp collector, I could be murdered by the same criteria. 'Why do you think it was him and not me or any one of a dozen other paparazzi?'

Frank thought it over while he shook out a Winston and lit it. 'You hear things. You don't know if they're true or not but it's weird that you even hear them.'

'What did you hear?'

'He was pulling blackmail schemes. Strictly small-time hustles. Five or ten grand here or there for shots that might embarrass somebody with the money to pay him off. More than the photos would be worth to the tabloids.'

'Maybe he was somehow connected to this story Gabe was working on and the killer is cleaning up loose ends.'

'What story?'

'He never told me.'

'Yeah, well, anything is possible,' he said, like it wasn't. 'You wanna go get a cup of coffee?'

'Something else I gotta do.'

'Sure. Guess I should write this up while it's fresh.'

We tapped fists goodbye, then I kicked away from the Cadillac to approach the patrolman sipping coffee by his cruiser. 'No press allowed,' he volunteered, in a tone no different from how he'd say screw off.

'I need you to call down one of the detectives,'

He didn't want to do it, thought I was trying to trick him into a photo-op, but ducked his head into the car to call it up. Somebody had to go get somebody to get the guy I wanted but when the response bleated from the radio the patrolman was surprised. 'Hang around,' he instructed. 'He'll be down when he can.'

I hadn't expected priority treatment and didn't get it. By the time Harker's partner strolled down the hill a couple reporters had arrived to mill in front of the patrol car. A bearded redhead with eyes like an angry dog's recognized him and shouted out a question. Detective James Douglas ignored it. 'You,' the patrolman commanded, pointing at me.

Douglas watched me lean under the police tape and walk up the hill to meet him. Another late night, a second murder in the same area with the same general *modus operandi* and I figured I might see tension or even simple fatigue crease his forehead but no readable expression marred the dull brown mask of his face.

'I got a witness,' I said.

Something sparked deep inside his eyes. This to him was a big reaction. I let him hang there for a moment, wondering what I meant.

'Somebody coming out of the photocopy shop down the street saw your partner push my face in the curb.' It was a lie but so what? It was their game, their rules. 'I could file a complaint.'

'These charges come up all the time. Believe me, they go nowhere,' he said, his voice slow with caution.

'That says a lot about the LAPD doesn't it?'

He didn't get defensive. He didn't get angry. He didn't get anything. 'You wouldn't be coming to see me if you were going to file a complaint,' he observed, again cautiously, a man walking the plank of deduction.

'Doesn't it scare you that he can lose control like that?'

He didn't answer. He just looked at me and waited. He knew I was going to offer a trade. His deliberate pace wasn't a prop of stupidity but its opposite.

'I need to find my husband's relatives. No matter what you think of me, they deserve to be told.'

His chin dipped to his chest and returned to level. He was still with me.

'Did you find an address book in the apartment? Any letters?'

'No letters from family, no. But we did get an address book.'

'Did you check it? His brother's name is Nigel.'

'We checked. Why, specifically, do you think he had family?'

'He told me about them.'

'We didn't find anybody named Burns. I don't remember a Nigel either. The name is odd enough to stick out.'

Not everybody writes down the names and numbers of their immediate family. His parents probably had lived in the same house with the same telephone number for decades. His brother might not have moved in years. Lots of people know the address and telephone number of their parents by heart. Right?

19

The receptionist at Crash Foto Agency flaunted nails and lipstick a shade of purple so dark as to be equal to black in all but the brightest sunlight and her scoop-neck blouse, mini-skirt, stockings and combat boots were blacker than fresh asphalt. Her hair glowed so blindingly blonde I suspected it came not out of a bottle but a barrel. A rhinestone stud sparkled in her right nostril and a gold ring glittered at the corner of her right eyebrow. When she answered the phone her tongue clicked out a response pierced by a silver stud. Most receptionists are babes and this one was no exception, though her hipster style was too extreme for all but the most extreme of companies. In a culture of suntans and fitness-club figures she was strobe-light pale and amphetamine slim. Crash represented the most aggressive paparazzi in the city, including Gabe. The outlaw image began at the front desk.

'Did it hurt?' I asked, and when her glance struck mine I pointed to my tongue. During my time in prison piercing and tattoos had become as common as mascara and nail polish to the fashion demi-monde.

'I was too tranked out to feel a thing. Who you looking for?'

'Information about someone who works here, or did, anyway. Gabriel Burns.'

'What kind of information?'

'Telephone numbers, mostly. People who knew him.'

'We're not allowed to give that out.' She checked my outfit, Keds to black leather jacket. 'You don't look like a cop. You some kinda reporter?'

'I'm his wife. Make that widow.' I slipped a photocopy out of the front pocket of my duffel. 'I didn't expect you'd just hand his employment records over, so I brought a copy of my marriage certificate. Here, you see the name on my driver licence matches.'

She put her nose to the documents then squinted to match the picture to my face. Something like sadness altered her expression. Not sadness itself, just something like it. 'Wow. I mean, wow. It was such a shock. Everybody here is really bummed about, you know, what happened.'

'I'm trying to locate his family, maybe somebody who knew him in England.'

When her platinum head bobbed I thought she'd help but that wasn't her intent at all. 'I'm sure someone will want to cooperate with you but nobody's in right now and I have very strict orders not to give out any personal information about our photographers.'

'You always follow orders?'

I knew a lot of people who looked like rebels but it was just that, a look. She knew I meant the question to provoke her but chose to let the insult stick. 'A job's a job.'

'Exactly,' I said. 'So what's so important about this one?'

She considered my question like she would a knife between her ribs. 'Wait here. If I get fired I'm sleeping on your couch.' When I thanked her she just said 'right' and pushed through a door to the side of the reception desk.

Crash wasn't a back door operation like Lester's; it occupied a suite of offices in a Westwood mid-rise fit for an advertising agency. The reception desk was smoked glass and burnished ash. A gallery of poster-sized photographs devoted to the Hollywood celebritocracy hung on walls lit by track lighting. The leather sofa and end chairs were in showroom condition and the carpet smelled like it was replaced monthly or whenever it lost that new carpet scent, whichever came first. Until then I hadn't realized how much money could be made in the business by its brokers.

'I can't actually let you keep this, OK?'

The receptionist laid a double-sided photocopy on the corner of the table. The form read Foreign Artist Employment Record and listed Gabe's residency permit and work visa numbers, his address, the name of the publication in England that sponsored his work visa, and in the space reserved for emergency notification, the name Charlotte Dixon. The telephone number appended to that name bore a 310 long-distance code, which would place her residence about seven thousand miles west of England. I turned the photocopy to face the receptionist and pinned the name with my forefinger. 'Do you have any idea who this Charlotte person is?'

She craned her neck to read the name in full and nodded like it meant something to her. 'Well, it's me,' she said.

'Why did he . . .' I didn't need to complete the sentence. Of course Gabe had a sex life before he'd met me; I just hadn't expected to discover it so posthumously.

'I was his first contact here at Crash. He was new in town, you know, didn't know anybody.'

'So. You were, ahhhh?'

She nodded emphatically, purple nails scrambling to underline the date on the marriage certificate. 'But don't worry, we were over months ago, certainly before you two did the Vegas thing.'

The door behind me squeezed open to a puffy-eyed

hipster with a flush of black stubble at his jaw and the tortured gait of an eighty-year-old arthritis victim. Despite the cosmopolitan elegance of his black slacks and grey herringbone sport coat, the man looked like he'd spent the night wrestling with pharmaceuticals and wild women and been brutally pinned by both. The only thing still erect about him was his pony tail, an absurd little organ of hair that stood above his head like an exclamation point.

'G'morn Char, I feel like death in a deep freeze. Do me a fave and get me a cup of something hot and black, 'kay?'

Charlotte did her best imitation of a bunny rabbit in headlights. I stepped forward to introduce myself. His puffed eyes dilated just enough to take me in. 'The new girl,' he guessed. His right hand cocked back like a cowboy six-shooter and shot an index finger at my chest. 'The Death Row pix. Nuclear work. How'd you know to be there, anyway?'

'Just got lucky.'

'If that's true, we'll never hear from you again. But something I see in the woman standing before me says it wasn't luck at all.'

Charlotte regained enough consciousness to announce that the man standing before me was Barry Scanlon, the owner of Crash Foto. He dipped his head and brought it back to level to confirm this information was essentially correct. 'You looking for representation?'

'Nina here is married to Gabe. Sorry. Was married.'

The brain vacated Scanlon's body for several mindless blinks of his eyes. I waited for some reaction but though his gaze remained fixed in the vicinity of my face the man behind the gaze just disappeared.

'Gabriel Burns,' Charlotte prompted. 'You know, the pho – '

'I know who he is,' he snapped. 'I just hadn't realized he'd gotten married.'

'Less than two weeks ago.' I didn't know if the news disturbed him or he'd just blanked. 'You mind if we talk?'

'Noooooo, 'course not.' He led me through the door into an open work area staffed by two young men who handled 35 mm negatives over a light table. Both men had tousled green hair and square black glasses. You could tell them apart by the different names stencilled on their white lab coats. The two glanced up from their work.

'Hi,' said Fred.

'Yeah. Hi,' said Barney.

'Our film techs,' Scanlon mumbled. 'Develop film for us, keep the archives in shape.'

'Gabe developed his film here?'

'Sure. We liked Gabe.'

'Yeah. He was funny.'

'Did he bring anything unusual to you in the past month or so?'

'The lack of production was the funny thing.'

'It was like he took a vacation.'

'Or something.'

'Yeah. Or something.'

'Do you mind if I look at the proof sheets?'

Fred and Barney fell into a state of suspended animation. I turned to Scanlon, who stared into the distance over my shoulder as though he hadn't a clue I'd just asked for something.

'I'd like to see what he was working on at the time of his murder,' I explained.

Charlotte poked her head and a steaming mug of coffee through the door. Scanlon held it beneath his nose for several deep breaths. 'Sure. No harm in looking.'

Barney slid open the top drawer of a horizontal file cabinet and Fred, moving like a second pair of hands controlled by the same brain, pulled out a half-dozen proof sheets wrapped in clear plastic sleeves. 'As you can see, he didn't bring us much.'

'This is like, a typical week for Gabe. Not a month.'

Each plastic sleeve was tabbed with Gabe's name and the date the negatives had been developed. The most recent date was from the previous week. The proof sheet inside that sleeve contained images from the film premiere, including a few of me he'd taken without my knowledge. The five other proof sheets from that same month were typical of the business: famous faces screened by the arm of a bodyguard or the doorframe of a waiting limo and candids of the half-famous coyly poised as though unaware of the camera lens. The photographs Gabe had taken on our Vegas trip were conspicuously absent. Either they had been removed from the files, or Gabe didn't bring all his film to be developed at Crash.

'Any idea why he shot so little?'

'Love,' guessed Barney.

'No, he was just burned out,' Fred said.

'No problems? No big project?' I pressed.

The two techs bounced glances off each other, and again, it was like somebody hit their pause button.

'Somebody reported him to the INS,' Scanlon admitted. 'I got a call from a government alien chaser a couple weeks ago. But his work papers were in perfect order. Personally, I thought he was being harassed. It happens in our business.'

'Any idea who reported him?'

'Any one of a dozen pissed-off movie stars. He had a talent for the unflattering shot.'

'Gabe was the best,' Fred pronounced.

'Yeah, he was,' agreed Barney.

Charlotte reclined with a copy of the *National Enquirer* spread on her lap, a felt-tip marker in her teeth, a stack of periodicals at her elbow and combat boots propped on the corner of the smoked glass. 'This is what I do most mornings, when it's slow,' she explained. 'Go through the media and mark agency photographs.'

'You knew Gabe pretty well – '

'Not that well, really. We were together only about a month.'

Three weeks more than I had. For a brief flush, I was jealous, not of their sex, but of their time. 'I'm trying to reach his family. Did he ever talk to you about them?'

'His royal father, you mean? Sure. All the time. His brother can't be hard to find.'

'Nigel? How?'

'Plays soccer for some English team. West Ham, isn't it? I remember it sounded like something you'd eat for breakfast.'

20

The London newspaper that sponsored Gabe's work visa was a men's rag more famous for its sports section and page three breasts than editorial integrity. The photo editor was helpful enough over the phone, but the problem, as he explained to me, was that he knew almost nothing about the journalists and photographers the paper sponsored overseas. Gabe only occasionally carried out an assignment for him, most often involving a British national of special interest to the local reading public. The paper sponsored his visa because it was handy having someone in town should a need arise, but Gabe wasn't on staff and they knew precious little about him. He suggested I try the regional British authorities.

At the British Consulate I grabbed a numbered slip from a red plastic dispenser attached to the wall and with a rainbow of ex-colonials from India, China and other remnants of the Empire waited for one of the five service counters to beep me. It could have been a harmless prank, Gabe's lie to Charlotte, his way of having fun. The idea that his brother sported the rayon shorts of a professional footballer struck me as absurd. You might tell a casual fling just about anything that strikes your fancy, but not someone you genuinely cared about. One by one the numbers clipped past until the electric counter matched the slip I held between thumb and forefinger. Before I reached the open window, a reedy brunette sized up my nationality and slipped a form on to the counter: 'Welcome to the United Kingdom: Facts for Visitors'.

When I told her my husband had been murdered she was unimpressed. The disposal or transport of the body was my responsibility, she said; I was the widow, not the British government. 'But I don't even know his parents,' I explained. 'Don't know where they live or how to contact them.'

She turned to an area behind the service window not directly in view. I heard a file cabinet rattle and a moment later, the flash and mechanical shuttle of a copy machine. She returned flourishing a document titled *Tracing Friends and Relatives*. It listed various private agencies that performed searches in the UK.

'Isn't there anything you – '

'The Consulate do not provide search services.'

The electronic beep sounded and an agitated man in a turban pressed against the counter, surrounded by four beautiful women in saris, whom I took to be his daughters. The reedy brunette met them with the same implacable efficiency with which she dismissed me.

The consulate form listed the Salvation Army Family Tracing Service among the institutions that traced relatives in the UK. I knew the Salvation Army. Sure, they dressed in funny uniforms and had a peculiar name but since childhood I'd been giving them my old clothes. The signal buzzed a half-dozen times before a voice creaked, 'Yes?' Then, 'Just a moment, let me find a pen.' The phone clattered to the table and a short time later, a plaintive bellow followed the sound of something crashing upon the floor. I imagined a little old man in a band uniform, the Cross of Calvary on his epaulettes. 'That was the spider plant,' the voice announced. 'And good riddance to the old thing, I say. Now, shall we begin?' To a backup chorus of ahems and ahas I related the few official facts I knew about Gabe.

'These things normally take time, but as this is an emer – ' He feebly hacked something from his throat, paused to recover, then continued, ' – gency I will give it my personal and immediate attention.'

I thanked him effusively and wrote off the call as a loss. My only break of the day was a parking spot in front of my apartment. I trusted this as a sign that my luck was improving. When I reached the top of the steps I discovered the front door ajar. The lock was forged from cheap metal and a kick to the side of the deadbolt was all it took to splinter the wood at the jamb. I nudged the door open with the back of my hand. My futon curled in a foetal position against the far wall, slit open from head to foot. The fruit crates that had served as my shelves lay splintered over scattered books and clothes. While I dialled the police department I pondered the significance of having my self-help books torn from their bindings. The dispatcher fielding calls said she'd send the next available patrol car to investigate. I picked my way through the ruins to the kitchenette. The bastard even slit the bottom of my box of cornflakes. Nothing had been taken except a crate containing my proof sheets, prints and negatives – the only items I valued and could not replace.

Two hours later a patrol car pulled into the red zone on the corner and two uniforms climbed the apartment steps to briefly nose around my apartment and then fill out a short form titled Victim Memo Slip. To the LAPD a beach area burglary didn't rate fingerprinting surfaces or interviewing neighbours who might have witnessed the break-in. It didn't even rate a report or full sheet of paper. The words memo and slip made it clear where I placed on the list of police priorities.

I locked up the apartment the best I could and slept out the afternoon on the back seat of the Cadillac with my face buried in Gabe's pillow. I tried to dream but remembered nothing when I awoke. I swam in the rough December sea just long enough to turn blue, then drove out to Beverly Hills, where I joined Hank Vulkovitch at the counter of Kate Mantilini. For a friendly guy Gabe didn't have many friends, at least the kind he didn't sleep with. Until I could locate his family and friends in England, I needed to talk to somebody who'd known him and Vulch was the only male friend he'd mentioned. He wore his trademark black leather jacket and Ray Bans despite the warmth and dim lighting. When I greeted him he stood and embraced me with stiff respect.

'I didn't know if it was appropriate to contact you through your agency and in the end I decided against it because after all I don't know you that well,' he admitted, partly to explain, partly to apologize. 'But I'm truly sorry about Gabe. Dave Schuman was a son-of-a-bitch and I can't say I'll miss him, but Gabe was the brightest new talent to come along since I began in this business. I'll miss him.'

Vulch had picked the restaurant. We sat beneath a mural of Marvelous Marvin Hagler connecting a left hook to the jaw of Thomas Hit Man Hearns. The thing was huge, took up half the wall. I remembered the fight, watching it with my dad. The painter had caught exactly right the rubber legs and slack torso of Hearns going down. My dad threw excited left jabs and right hooks in front of the television while the fight was going on. He liked to imitate the fighters, how this one would bob and weave and suddenly explode out of a crouch, how another would come straight on, all business to a bloody finish. After Hearns went down dad worked on perfecting my left hook. I was fifteen years old then, didn't have the heart to hit anybody.

Vulch asked, 'Is there anything I can help with? If you want to arrange a memorial service, a wake, whatever, I can call around to the other photographers, get a decent showing.'

I thanked him for the thought but couldn't commit until I heard what the family wanted. 'I knew him less than two weeks,' I said.

'You're kidding. The way he talked about you, it seemed like . . . well, certainly more than that.'

'It was a green card marriage.'

'OK.' He nodded like that made sense to him. 'I knew he was having some problems. But he was crazy about you, one look at his face when you walked into the room told me that.'

I let his opinion pass uncontested and unconfirmed. I couldn't judge what had been genuine and what false about Gabe's affections. 'Did he ever mention his family to you?'

'Something about his father, the royal pretender, and a brother involved in . . . in . . .'

'Law.'

'Broadcasting, wasn't it? On the BBC? I don't really remember. He didn't talk much about it.'

'What about coke? Did he ever do it?'

'I don't really know. Maybe at parties. Doesn't everybody? If you're asking whether or not he had a problem with it, not that I noticed. But why ask? Bury the sins with the man.'

'When a man is murdered his sins don't bury.'

The counter waitress, a gum-chewing throwback in ponytail and harlequin glasses, hustled over to ask what we wanted. To my surprise meat loaf was on the menu. I ordered it. From the blow-dried look of the diners around me it didn't seem a meat loaf crowd but when the dish came, tender, moist and lightly seasoned with thyme, I decided Beverly Hills wasn't such a wasteland after all.

'You've been in the business for some time,' I said.

'Since the first incarnation of Travolta. Twenty years.'

'Was it always so aggressive?'

'The guys I broke in with told me that back in the sixties, Liz Taylor and Richard Burton couldn't show their face in a window without the photo press hanging off the neighbouring balcony. The business has always been sharp-elbowed. It's the rules that changed. Used to be the studios ran things. A half-dozen creeps with cameras are hanging around Liz and Dick? Great publicity! When the agents took over the business it was the same thing. No such thing as too much publicity. But these days it's the actors who decide what gets made and what doesn't. Nobody has the power to tell them anything. They don't seem to understand that being a star isn't nine-to-noon, it's a full-time job. They take their ten million a picture and tell us to fuck off when we try to do our job, which is to make them even more famous so they can command fifteen million on the next.'

'You sound like Gabe did.'

'I sound like everybody. It used to be different. Sure, sometimes we went too far but when we did the studio threatened to blackball us and we pulled back. Now it's strictly adversarial. Stars don't like us so we try to get them. We no longer celebrate stardom, we tarnish it.'

'I sometimes think Gabe wanted to embarrass people.'

'That's the Fleet Street style. He hated the star system, distrusted the concept of celebrity. Maybe it had something to do with being English, you know, the class system they have over there. Me, I love celebrity. We argued about that quite a bit. Philosophically, we were opposed, but technically, we admired each other. Gabe could really get the shot.'

'Is that why he was killed? Because he got the shot? The wrong shot?'

He ran his finger along the ridge of his prodigious nose and stared at me in a way that made me think he wondered if I knew something he didn't. Like a lot of guys who have been around for ever, he prided himself on knowing. 'I was afraid some crazy actor had him killed before this second murder. There are people around town who know how to get something like that done and actors certainly have enough money to hire a hit. But then Schuman caught it the same way and those two had nothing to do with each other. So it's probably a lunatic.'

'You think somebody picked Gabe's name off a photo credit.'

'Think about it. We're princess killers. The stars complain we're ruining their lives. Sooner or later somebody was bound to go off his nut and pop a few paparazzi. That makes us all targets.'

'He was writing some kind of a story, an exposé maybe. Did he mention that to you?'

'He mentioned it, but didn't tell me specifically what. And he shouldn't have. No matter how much you trust a colleague, in our business you never divulge the details. He tells me, I tell somebody else and soon the whole damn town knows.'

'Did that happen? Did you tell somebody else?'

Vulch polished off his beer and stared at the glass. 'Shit, I'd like a cigarette. What an idiotic town, can't smoke in restaurants, can't smoke in bars. People are so afraid of dying here they forget how to live. We're surrounded by forty-watt light bulbs in a klieg light culture. Has everyone forgotten that candles that burn the hottest give off the most light? The stars once knew that. They set the tone for this town. Now everybody wants to live forever.' He swept his arm across the crowd. 'They'll all die, but they don't get it. Even forty-watt light bulbs pop. Nobody understands that until it's too late.'

I returned to Venice Beach to find half the neighbourhood on the sidewalk watching the law invade my apartment. Police cruisers double parked up and down the block, rooftop lights spraying beams of red and blue into the night. It gave the more stoned residents something other than television to watch. My first impulse was to gun the engine, afraid someone had spotted my plates the night I'd broken into Gabe's apartment, but a common break-in, even one that violated a crime scene, wouldn't rate so much law. I parked in the red zone and told the patrolman guarding the stairs I wanted to get into my apartment. A moment after he shouted my name up the steps Harker and Douglas hurried down. With a flanking manoeuvre they hustled me toward a cruiser. Douglas guided my head below the frame then slid next to me into the prisoner's compartment. I thought I was being arrested. Harker twisted around from behind the wheel. 'Who else has been in that apartment besides you?'

'I don't know, I don't have many friends.'

'Think,' he said with enough sarcasm to suggest I didn't do that so well.

'The landlord, my parole officer, that's about it.'

'Did you touch anything?'

'I kicked at a few things, then got out.'

'You left the apartment, when? Exact time.'

'You mean before the break-in or after?'

He looked at me like I was stupid. 'Before.'

They had whisked me into the back seat so fast I hadn't a moment to consider why. That was what they wanted. They didn't want me to compose. They wanted me to react. 'It's the scalp collector, isn't it?'

Harker glanced at his partner, not having a clue what I meant. 'Answer the question.'

'Dave Schuman. His apartment was broken into, wasn't it? Just like Gabe's. And torn to pieces, just like mine. You think I'm on the list for number three.'

Harker stared at me, angry, not giving away anything. I glanced over to Douglas. He blinked a very tired yes.

They advised me to visit relatives outside the city, and if that wasn't possible, to find a hotel room as far away as I could drive in a night without violating the terms of my parole. I stayed in my car instead. I didn't have anywhere else to go except around. After midnight, the population of Los Angeles County dwindles from nine million to a few thousand. Lone cars straggle through an immense grid of empty asphalt, lost or looking for trouble or just to get home. During daylight hours the sidewalks look merely empty. At night, they look neutron bombed. Humanity diminishes to dash-lit faces framed by automobile glass, and the ragged figures of the homeless racking up shopping cart miles. The city for six hours simulates a post-apocalyptic time when all but a few have fled or perished. This was the city I liked best, a city emptied of humanity, a city of traffic lights regulating an absence of cars, of brightly lit store interiors peopled by mannequins, a city where the few survivors gathered at gas stations like frightened animals to drink their fill and vanish back into the night.

At the rail of Griffith Park Observatory I watched sunrise wash out the carnival sprawl of lights from downtown Los Angeles to the sea. The call from England came when the sun had burned from red to blinding yellow and the first bus-load of tourists crowded the rail.

'We have some information for you,' the old voice announced. 'Regrettably incomplete, but on such short notice, it was the best we could do.'

I scrambled through my bag for a pen and pad, shocked to hear from him so soon. 'OK, shoot.'

'Shall we begin with the brother?'

'Nigel.'

'Yes. Nigel. We found a certificate of birth for Nigel Burns, son of Ethan and Sophie Burns, dated February 12, 1965, but curiously, we could find nothing extant in current records. We did, however, after some looking, discover a notice of his death, actually, dated November 22, 1974, the cause listed as accidental.'

I wrote down the dates as I would the symbols of an unknown alphabet: completely without understanding. 'Could there be some error? Two sets of Burns? A mix-up of records?'

'Two Gabriel Burns, both with a brother named Nigel? We did check, but with only one day to research, we might have missed something.'

I said, 'I see.'

'Shall we go on to the father?' The tone of apology in his voice frightened me. 'We did find record of a current address for Ethan Burns, though an unusual one: Brixton Prison.'

'Brixton Prison?' I grasped at an idea to make sense of the address. 'Is he a warden there?'

'I'm afraid madam – and I'm sorry if this is contrary to

what your dear late husband informed you – that he is currently incarcerated as an inmate of that institution.'

'I see.' For once that idiomatic phrase reflected something of the truth. I was beginning to see aspects of Gabe that formerly had been hidden beneath a shroud of lies. With his sense of irony, he might have considered an ex-con the perfect choice in a green card wife. 'And the mother?'

'Deceased,' he said, as flat and uninformative as the word itself.

'How?'

'Ah, well, I don't know what good it would do to go into that.'

'How!' I shouted. He was a nice man. He didn't deserve to be shouted at. But he knew, and was too nice to tell me, not understanding that I was not like him; I was not nice.

'I did check a bit of the background. But I warn you, the story clipping I found could be upsetting.'

'The truth,' I said, 'usually is.'

He read awkwardly, perhaps from embarrassment, or merely due to poor eyesight. ' "After hearing a complaint of noise from neighbours, police constables in Islington yesterday afternoon visited the terraced house registered to Mr Ethan Burns, actor, and Sophie Burns, his wife. When confronted by the neighbours' complaints and asked to explain the cause of the noise, Mr Burns led the constables to the body of his wife. He was taken to station, where, under direct questioning, he confessed to strangling her to death in a fit of jealous rage. Neighbours were shocked – " We can skip that part, I should think,' the old voice interjected. 'Ah, here's something – "Away at school at the time of the incident was a son, Gabriel, aged twelve. In the absence of other relatives, the child has been taken charge of by Social Services." That would be your husband, if I'm not mistaken? And here at the end, one more bit – "A matinee idol in his youth and at one time no stranger to the London stage, Mr Burns has not performed publicly for three years. Readers will remember him for his portrayal of King Richard the Third . . ." Well, we needn't go into that. A very sad affair, caused quite a sensation at the time. Mr Burns the elder quite lost his wits if I remember correctly, and most probably still misses them.' He cleared his throat with a great hacking sound. 'I'm terribly sorry to be the bearer of such news, Mrs Burns. Please accept my apologies and condolences.'

I don't remember driving down the hill. A merciful delirium settled over me in which I thought about nothing. The automobile can be a form of meditation for those with nowhere to go and no time to be there. The mind rests but the senses react to the flow of asphalt like a movie in which nothing happens except the illusion of something eternally about to happen. To drive a car nowhere is to chase freedom inside your head.

The pendant caught my eye while I waited at a traffic light on Melrose. I can't explain why I saw it just then, the seeming coincidence of timing. Other women might have passed me on the street wearing that same pendant but I had been blind to them, just as I had been blind to the truth about Gabe. The woman must have thought I was crazy when I jumped out of the Cadillac and called out to her. She looked not just startled but frightened. That I asked about fashion reassured her. Fashion was a safe subject. It was acceptable to show irrational interest in another woman's fashion accessory. She smiled, unaware that the twin to her pendant, which Gabe had told me he found while shooting on assignment in Papua New Guinea, dangled between my breasts. 'This? I found it at Maya. Do you know it?' At the shake of my head she whirled to point west. 'It's just a couple of blocks that way, on this side of the street.'

Maya had yet to open when I jogged up. I nosed the plate-glass window and spotted movement inside the shop. A retro-hippie in long braids, peasant skirt and fringe of leg hair opened the door a few minutes past the hour. I flashed the pendant on its string around my neck. 'Do you carry these?'

She jabbed her chin toward the back end of the shop. Past a bin of ten-dollar Javanese wood-puppets and next to a collection of hemp wallets I found twenty hanging on leather strings, each identical to the one around my neck. The hand-lettered ink sign above the row of pins that hung them read, 'Mayan Love Pendants, Hecho en Mexico'.

I fled the shop, stunned. The immediate neighbourhood looked familiar. Down the avenue I recognized the street that led to Gabe's apartment. The bastard hadn't the energy to shop more than a mile from his front door. I couldn't imagine what he'd been thinking, what kind of man he had really been beneath the lies and false histories. I couldn't from that moment trust any word, gesture or caress. I couldn't trust my own memories. The symbol of our relationship was a lie and a joke. What had I expected from a green card marriage? I hurled the pendant against the wall.

The case cracked with a certainty the relationship never had and the pieces – two halves and fragments – clattered to the cement. I swore at him then, called him a liar and a cheat and other things I have the decency not to repeat here. When I ran out of curses I thought of Gabe's body bled white and heaved upon the shore. I was sorry then that I'd cursed him. He'd been cursed enough.

It shouldn't have surprised me that Gabe had lied. People

lie in love affairs. It defines the form, a sort of *trompe l'oeil* of the heart. Falling in love is falling for the lies of your partner, and being in love is learning, once the lies are discovered, to live with them. I dropped to my knees to collect the pieces, not pretending I sought to glue them back together – it was too late for that in every sense – but thinking I might at least give them a decent burial, when I noticed that the pendant had contained something other than leather and cheap metal. Between the shattered halves of casing lay a thin magnetic disk wrapped in protective plastic, like a message in a bottle.

22

Frank answered the door looking like a hurricane had just made a pass through his hair. It took him some heavy lifting to blink enough light below his eyelids to see who had rung his bell before noon and stood at the doorway with a cup of Starbucks and a muffin in hand. 'Late deadline last night,' he mumbled. Unlike other men I'd known, Frank slept in pyjamas. The set he sported that morning was decorated with baseballs, bats, gloves and the insignia of the Chicago Cubs. He looked like a kid with a hyperactive thyroid. I pressed the coffee into his hand and nudged him out of the doorway. He stumbled into a living room cluttered with books, empty beer bottles and dirty socks, and collapsed on the sofa. 'I'd like it more if you came just before I went to sleep and not before I woke up. I look better that way and we might have more fun. Where are my cigarettes?'

He groped for a pack of Winstons on the end of the table, sipped at his coffee, took a bite of muffin and lit a cig. Frank was one of those organisms that could draw energy from tin cans, egg shells, old shoes – anything remotely organic. In his past life, he would have been a goat. He gazed at the plume of smoke with contentment. 'Every morning I wake with this serious doubt that life is worth living, but then, after my first cigarette, I usually conclude it is.'

'A filthy habit,' I said.

'Yes it is, isn't it?' Frank grinned, happy he'd offended me.

I slipped the magnetic disk on to the table out of immediate spill range. 'When you're ready.'

He jabbed the cigarette into the corner of his mouth and leaned over the table for a closer look. 'What is it?'

'You tell me.'

'I don't like intelligence tests. Am I allowed to ask where it came from?'

'It was Gabe's. Something I didn't know I had until this morning.'

Eyes squinted against the smoke, he moved the disk to the nearest corner, where he could keep a better watch on it. 'The guys at the paper are making a book that a serial killer is on the loose, murdering paparazzi. The problem is, nobody knows anything for sure because our sources have all gone to Death Valley.'

'What's in Death Valley?'

'A thousand square miles of desert. When a source doesn't want to talk to you, he's gone to Death Valley – dried up, evaporated. You hear anything?'

'The killer ransacks his victims' apartments before or after he kills them. I guess you'd call it his MO.'

'How do you know?'

'Because my apartment was torn up night before last and half the law in LA came to check it out.'

Frank dropped his cigarette into a beer bottle and swished it out. 'Jesus.' He set the bottle down on the table and said nothing for a minute, just looked at me like he didn't know what to do. 'You want to stay here? I can clear the beer bottles and socks off the couch. Hell, I'll even leave the toilet seat down.'

'I feel better on the move. But thanks.'

Frank picked up a couple of bottles and a corpse-ridden ashtray and legged awkwardly over the coffee table. I heard him clanking glass in the kitchen, saw a blur of Cubs pyjamas push through a door at the end of the hall. I thought about straightening the living-room while he was gone and just as quickly forgot about it. From what I saw cleaning up would be like trying to empty the ocean with a bucket.

'I kind of liked the pyjamas,' I said when he came back in jeans and a Bulls T-shirt.

'You wanna see the show lady, you gotta pay admission.' He blew a residue of ash and crumbs off the table, laid out a clean towel, flat-head screwdriver, needle-nose pliers and a 1.44 megabyte floppy disk. He worked the tip of the screwdriver under the floppy disk's metal slide, popped the catch and then pulled it free with the needle-nose pliers, revealing a rectangular opening in the plastic casing, and within that a dark magnetic material. The tip of the screwdriver wedged into the casing seam and cracked it apart at each of the four corners. The floppy split into two halves and a magnetic disk popped free. He laid it next to the disk I'd brought. The only difference between the two was the plastic wrapped around the one from Gabe. 'This what you were thinking?'

'That's what I was thinking.'

He slid Gabe's disk on to the towel and, careful not to touch the magnetic coating, positioned it on to the metal hub that held it to spin free within the casing, then snapped the halves together again. 'So far so good, eh? 'Course I can't promise anything. Floppy disks are not the most stable things. Whatever was on here could be wiped clean as chalk from a board.' He walked the disk into the kitchen and booted up a notebook computer on the kitchen table. A dictionary, thesaurus, note pad and coffee cup bristling with pens took up the rest of the dining space. In place of food, the kitchen counters were stacked with magazines, folders and reams of loose paper. The door to one of the cupboards leaned open to rows of books. 'Hey Frank, what do you eat, paper?'

'Look in the refrigerator.'

I swung open the refrigerator to three floors of bottled beer, a carton of milk, box of cornflakes and bag of Oreo cookies.

'When I want variety I order out for pizza.' His index finger traced the surface of the screen to a folder titled 'Party Animals', containing something he called JPEG files. I didn't know what he meant until he clicked on a file and the screen transformed into a night shot of an estate that, viewed from the side, looked like it had been designed by people who built Las Vegas casinos for a living. White marble pathways laced through a landscape of evergreens sculpted into the shapes of animals and wild women, leading to an immense fountain in which stood the statue of a bearded hunk gripping a trident. On the fountain's rim sat a bruiser in slacks, turtleneck and loose-fitting sport coat. Security. Behind the fountain loomed a mansion with a triangular marble pediment, stepped podium and Corinthian colonnade façade that could have been transported block by block from the Rome of Claudius.

The next photo abruptly changed scene and historical era. Four women wearing miniskirts up to their navels stepped out of a limousine. Each woman sported rock-video hair, photo-shoot make-up and a sculpted-for-sex body. 'This is starting to look like the Playboy Channel,' Frank said, not unhappily. I pointed to something hidden in the shadows near the hood of the limo that struck me as oddly incongruous, a German shepherd leashed by a plain strawberry blonde in a short house dress. 'Looks like the guard dog,' Frank guessed.

The next JPEG returned to a side view of the villa. Framed by a ground-floor window, two women nude from the waist up stripped each other for an audience of two women and two men. 'The obligatory lesbian scene,' Frank commented, like an expert too familiar with the routine. He positioned the arrow and clicked open the next file, titled 'Piña Noir', a close-up of one of the two strippers, a raven-tressed beauty with honey-coloured skin and a sultry stare. 'Yummy,' Frank opined and clicked again. That image focused on the heads of the two men, turned away from the camera to kiss their consorts. One of the men had long black hair pulled back into a ponytail and the other short brown hair parted to the side. 'Our mysterious hosts, I presume. The next shot should tell us who.'

But the JPEG he opened recorded an abrupt shift in action and character; the strawberry blonde in the house dress sat with her arms around the German shepherd, only she didn't seem to be wearing the house dress anymore. 'Oh my God,' Frank whispered, then he laughed like what he saw wasn't funny so much as too strange to believe.

'What is it?' I asked.

Frank answered by clicking the next JPEG. The focal length pulled back to show more of the room. An audience of four women and two men watched the strawberry blonde and German shepherd perform an act I never believed to be more than a vile myth. The faces of the men were too distant to identify in detail. The next shot brought them closer. The man on the left, still in his coat and tie if missing his pants, was a darkly handsome longhair with a granite jaw, known to millions as the action movie star, Damian Burke. The guy on the right with the plain-wrap haircut and glazed eyes was a politico I recognized from newspapers and billboards, Pete Danavitch.

'This is pure anthrax,' Frank exulted. 'We could wipe out half the political infrastructure of LA with these shots.'

I could hear a giant flushing sound for a couple of careers but didn't see how it could extend beyond that. 'How so?'

Frank ran a fingernail beneath the throat of the politico. 'As a county supervisor, Danavitch is the most powerful politician on the Westside. He talks like a liberal but acts like a conservative, which makes him popular with people who want to seem compassionate without having to pay for it. One of his pet political stands, appropriately enough, is animal rights.'

'Does that include bestiality?'

'No reporter has ever asked him. Until now.'

I didn't like the way he said that, like he planned to ambush Danavitch with the question the next chance he got. I said, 'This is not your story, not yet.'

He tossed up his hands in a palms out gesture of backing off. 'Just thinking aloud. The photographs are yours and no story without the photographs, right? Nothing the lawyers would let me publish, anyway.'

Even the tabloids had journalistic scruples, or at the very least legal departments worried about libel suits. 'Can you copy those photographs on to another disk, one I can give to the police?'

'Sure. I can also take rat poison but I'd rather not.'

'It's evidence in a murder investigation.'

'It's proof of a political scandal is what it is. If the cops see this the investigation will be dropped. Nobody cares about justice for a blackmailer.'

'You think he was trying to blackmail somebody?'

'Why else would he delay publishing the pics?'

'He claimed he was writing a story,' I blurted. I didn't know why the idea should shock me. I didn't know anything about the man, just what two people share in a few nights of passion, and that's nothing at all.

'Maybe he was but I don't see any proof of it on the disk. And if you give this to the cops they'll find a way to confiscate the original and nobody will ever write the story.'

'That's what you want to do, write the story?'

'Sure. When do we start?'

Sometimes people who seem interested in your welfare are mostly looking to help themselves. 'Just copy the disk like I asked you.'

I didn't know enough about computers to know how he did it but after some swapping files around he handed me two disks, one carefully marked as the original. If the photographs had led to Gabe's death, either through a story gone awry or a failed blackmail scheme, I knew where to begin looking. Most paparazzi plugged into an informer network. Gabe had a reputation for getting shots no one else had a clue existed and that meant original sources of information. An exclusive is almost always the result of good information and rarely luck. I'd seen for myself how easily he charmed women. The name given to one of the files, 'Piña Noir', wasn't a misspelled wine but a call girl.

The episode of *Meat Wagon* came on while I waited for Vulch in a 1940s joint on Fairfax named Tom Bergin's, an Irish bar with a dark wood interior that hadn't changed in fifty years. Neither had the bartender. I didn't notice the show was on – nobody watches television in bars except losers who can't keep a drink company – until the booth behind me rocked with barely legals hooting and retching at the screen. I moved my Jack Daniel's to the back end of the bar.

'Hey, that's her isn't it?' someone in the booth shouted. 'Sure it is! Look, she's even wearing the same jacket!' The heads in the booth went into a football huddle and one guy forearmed a tabletop beer in jumping free. When he walked over to check me out I could see he wasn't mean, just somebody who confused television with reality. Under different circumstances I might have thought him funny. But he was approaching me under a completely different set of different circumstances and was too drunk or too dim to sense how little I wanted him in my face. 'It is her!' he shouted back to his buddies and one of those buddies yelled back, 'It's all fake, isn't it? Ask her if it's all fake.'

He plonked his elbows on the bar to scrutinize me through wobbly eyes. 'It's you, isn't it? Up there on the box.'

'That's right, it's me.'

That coaxed a smile from him. 'It's totally fake, right? I

mean, like, you're really an actress, and the whole thing's a hoax, right?'

'No, it's real.'

He wouldn't let me fool him, like most people in the city he considered himself media wise. 'You gotta say that, because, like, it's in your contract.'

I stared straight ahead and sipped at my Jack Daniel's, giving him the chance to go away and knowing he wouldn't. He fumbled for a napkin along the inside edge of the bar and drew a pen from his pocket. 'What'd she say?' one of his buddies shouted. 'Ask her over for a drink!' suggested another and then somebody else joked, 'No, ask her for a date!' Everybody in the booth thought that was pretty funny. He pushed the pen and napkin next to my whiskey. 'Could you, like, give me your autograph?' He giggled like he was holding back a bigger laugh. 'And make it out to Dan?'

'You want my autograph?'

He nodded, legs crossed, elbows propped on the bar, face hanging over the wood. Easy.

'You sure you want my autograph?'

He nodded, grinned. He was sure.

I cut his elbows from under him with a swipe of my left arm and with my right backhanded his skull. His face took a very short flight and thwacked on to the bar top, making an impression as indelible as spilled beer. I flipped him over, took a last sip of Jack and signed my name on the vacant space of his forehead.

Zero, like his IQ.

Zero, like my tolerance for assholes.

Then I went out to wait for Vulch in the parking lot. Nobody said a word. The bartender had probably seen variations of the same thing a hundred times before. Once the adrenalin subsided I regretted what I'd done. He was just a dumb kid. He didn't deserve the knockout drop, and even if he did, I shouldn't have given it to him. If I felt that way after one autograph hound, how must a movie star feel after a thousand? I was lucky nobody had a camera, wanted to put my face in the tabloids.

The headlights to Vulkovitch's Mercedes caught me sleeping behind the wheel. Since Gabe's murder I hadn't slept more than a couple hours at a time. When I stopped moving, sleep swept over me like a sand dune. I stumbled out of the car, stretched, asked Vulch, 'What are the high-class hooker agencies in town, you know, the ones movie stars use.'

'Whatever do you want to know that for?' He lifted an aluminium case out of the trunk of the Mercedes and took a ticket from the attendant.

'I'm thinking of trading professions, getting into something with a little more dignity.'

Vulch thought that was funny enough to smile at. 'Madame Alex, now that Jody "Baby Doll" Gibson got busted. But if you're thinking of trying to recruit one of her girls as a source, good luck. When not practising their trade they have the tightest lips in town.'

He opened the aluminium case in the trunk of my Caddy, rested his palm on a black box big enough to fit a couple pair of shoes. 'You're lucky I have a spare – Barry Scanlon asked for it this morning and I had to tell him I promised you first.'

'The head of Crash Foto? Why would he want one?'

'Nothing works better than a tracking system if you want to follow somebody. The receiver runs on a high speed Intel processor. The signalling is digital, virtually untraceable, good up to three miles with a Mag Mount – the transmitter of choice if the person you want to follow isn't cooperative. Each transmitter has its own ID code so you can monitor up to ten targets.'

'Overkill,' I said. 'I just need one.'

'If it will do ten, it will do one.'

I got the message: shut up and listen.

He flicked the unit on and pointed to a backlit LCD display. 'This tells the distance to your target in feet, its position relative to the receiver and the direction it's travelling. If we were following somebody right now, this readout would tell you the target is, just for example, twenty thousand feet away and these directionals would show the target is due west and moving south.' He lifted a black metal cube from the case and let me heft it. 'That's a Mag Mount.' The thing was heavy enough to double as a paperweight. He knelt in front of the rear wheel and guided my hand beneath the car. 'It's magnetic, of course. If you put it on the frame here, away from the wheel and the rear axle, it can't be seen and if the target scrapes bottom coming out a driveway it won't be knocked off.'

'This all comes with an instruction book?'

'In the case. But the instruction book won't tell you one important point: If you're trying to conduct rolling surveillance, use an assistant either to – ' His glance jumped past my shoulder and his body followed a moment later. 'Hey! Hey!' he shouted, and sprinted toward a bearded truck of a guy opening the driver door to his Mercedes. I thought the guy had slipped the key from the parking attendant's box and was trying to steal himself an auto. The tyre iron was right there in the trunk. I grabbed it and took off, thinking I'd slip around to whack the guy on the back of his skull but he slid behind the wheel before I got to the bumper. The locks clicked first, then the engine caught.

'Call the cops!' I shouted. The parking attendant rolled his eyes and kept his arms folded across his chest. I thought maybe I'd crowbar the thief's skull through the driver window but Vulch braked me with a palm to my chest.

He hunched over eye-level with the guy behind the wheel and motioned him to roll down the window. It slid down a crack to a pair of eyes you'd find on a hyena. Vulch said, 'Be a sport and at least let me get my camera equipment out of the car.'

'You want your shit, *sport*, you can come get it at Cox Repossession Agency. We're in the book.'

The radial tread screamed and the Mercedes streaked out of the lot. A Ford Ranger pulled away from the curb and followed at high speed. The repo man's backup, I figured. I felt pretty stupid standing there with a tyre iron in my fist. But not as stupid as Vulch.

'Need a lift?' I asked.

Past ten o'clock at night there isn't a better city to drive in than Los Angeles. The freeways clear of traffic and will take you within ten minutes of anywhere in the city you want to go. The surface is smooth, the turns are easy and the signs well lit. You have to be drunk to get into any trouble. The occasional testosterone carboy will cut you up but most everybody just wants to get from point to point without making enemies. After I dropped Vulch at the repo agency I tuned to late-night college radio coming out of Long Beach and hit the Santa Monica Freeway. The dealership that leased out the Mercedes had really screwed him, Vulch had complained. You'd think a Mercedes would be trouble-free wheels but a half-dozen things had gone wrong with the car and the dealer wouldn't fix anything without trying to pin the costs on him. So he stopped paying the monthlies, right? Told the dealer when the car ran like it should he'd pay like he should. Never suspected the son-of-a-bitch would call a repo agency on him.

Debt is just another aspect of the Los Angeles lifestyle. Half the people on the Westside tried to look like they had more money than they really did. If you couldn't buy the clothes and drive the car, you were a nobody. You didn't belong. If you wanted to belong, you bought the big house, the car, the clothes – even if you could afford them only on credit. The culture valued appearance more than substance and it didn't matter how you got it as long as you had it. Vulch could have been telling me the truth or a tale but the distinction mattered little to me. I didn't judge him by his bank balance any more than I'd want him to judge me by mine.

I parked the Caddy downtown and crossed Figueroa to meet Detective Douglas at a twenty-four-hour eggs, sandwich and steak joint called the Pantry. Owned by the mayor, it was a popular place for cops to see and be seen, like a Polo Lounge for the law. Harker sat alone at a table by the bathrooms, his head tipped against the funky wooden partition that divided the regular tables from a row of stainless steel stools and counter service. A sign by the entrance said the place hadn't closed one minute since its founding in 1924 and by the look of the grease-stained ceiling the place should have shut its doors long ago for a good hosing out. Being the mayor means not having to worry about health inspectors. I strode down the walkway between tables, sure that half the eyes in the joint had me marked for a snitch. When I crossed into Harker's eye line I said, 'Where's Douglas?'

Harker wiped the hair on his upper lip with a paper napkin, smoothed the growth straight with a comb-like forefinger, pointed that same finger to the hard-backed chair across the table. 'Show me what you got.'

'Douglas said he'd be here,' I insisted.

Harker looked over his shoulder and inside the breast pocket of his checked blue sport coat. 'I don't see him. That must mean he's not here. If you don't have anything to show me you're just spoiling the view.'

I was a good citizen. The disk was evidence. For all my problems with the law I still believed in its essential integrity.

I sat down, slid the disk across the white formica tabletop, said, 'I found this hidden in something my husband gave me.'

Harker didn't pick it off the table, didn't look at it, didn't look at me, just watched a spot on the wall above the entrance. 'What's on it?'

'A couple of suspects and a motive for murder.'

Harker snorted and without moving his eyes from the spot behind my head slipped the disk into the side pocket of his sport coat. 'Sure, we'll look at it.'

By that he meant he'd glance at the plastic casing as he tossed the disk to the bottom of the case file. I took a chance I'd end up face-first again. I'd thought about that incident many times since it happened. Either he was crazy or something specific had set him off. I braced my hands against the table and set my feet at an angle clear of the chair. If I had to move quickly, I could. 'I've been widowed, betrayed and robbed, my PO officer is threatening to punch my ticket back to the Institute, you want to arrest me, and some freak out there aims to give me a dirt nap. But still, I'm a hell of a lot luckier than you.'

'Why's that?'

'Because I only knew my husband for a week and you knew whoever you're grieving a lot longer than that.'

The ripple started with a flutter of eyelids, cracked down his neck and through his torso like a shock wave. His hands shot from his cuffs to death lock the edge of the tabletop. I couldn't tell if he was about to leap the table and throttle me or just cry. The air burst from his lungs. He shifted his weight, relaxed his grip, stared again at empty space. 'You want your husband's body, it's yours. The coroner signed it over for release this afternoon. Any mortuary will take care of the details for you.'

I thanked him and after that we didn't have anything to say to each other. He didn't particularly trust me and I feared he'd still bust my butt back to jail at the first opportunity. Even if his attitude toward me softened to a grudging apathy he wasn't going to act on the information in the disk any time soon and he might not act at all. If he wouldn't, I would. I had no idea how I was going to get close enough to slip a Mag Mount under Damian Burke's Ferrari, Mercedes, or whatever six-figure chariot he drove but maybe the call girl Piña Noir could tell me that.

Once your apartment has been broken into it's hard to tell the difference between paranoia and honest fear. No one would be waiting in my darkened apartment while I climbed the steps but still I felt genuine dread as I keyed the door and swung it open. I flicked on the light switch, noticed white on my fingers. Fingerprint powder. It coated every surface that might reasonably be touched. I didn't think they'd caught any set of prints except mine. The person doing this might have the heart of a jackal but not the brain of one.

I picked through the clothes scattered on the carpet, searching for black jeans and a black long-sleeve cotton jersey to replace the gold bowling shirt and lime green plaid slacks I'd worn since the morning after Gabe's body had been found. I didn't mind the stink so much as the visibility, figured night work called for black. While I cleaned myself up I listened to messages. The only one that mattered went, 'Ah, Mary? Wait a minute, where is that – do I have the right number?' The mysteries of tape recording must have proved too complex because that was all my mom said before hanging up. She'd left countless messages just like that back when we still talked. The first nine digits of her phone number beeped beneath my fingertips. Mom was a devoted fan of trash television. The moment she got home from work she turned the television set to the talk shows and the set didn't go off until she fell asleep in front of it. She'd probably seen me on the box earlier that night, hadn't even known I'd been married let alone widowed. When I realized I didn't have anything to say to her I hung up.

Parked beneath a flickering streetlight, the Caddy was still warm enough to send shimmers of heat into the night air. I got behind the wheel, put on my seat belt and sent some spark to the engine. Many nights in prison I'd dreamed about the simple act of sitting with my mom over coffee. I had planned to tell her how beautiful I'd thought her when I was a child and how I'd lived for those moments when we might shut out the world and do something together, without my brothers, without my dad, just us two. Somehow those moments never happened. I dropped the transmission into drive and released the brake. When the tread grooved asphalt I flicked a glance at a shadow crossing my rear-view mirror. I thought it was a truck until a steel tube pressed against the skull bone at the base of my neck and a grim voice instructed me to take the 4th Street onramp to the Santa Monica Freeway. I had the wits to nod but little else until a mile down the road I worked up the courage to glance his way.

He sat hunched over the back of the passenger seat, left arm wedged under his chest for support, right arm crossed on top of his left, gun wrist resting on his left biceps. The more scared I seemed and the further we drove the more relaxed that gun hand got. I saw what could happen.

I was wearing a seat belt.

He wasn't.

25

The Caddy hit the rear end of the parked Beamer inside the right headlight. No dramatic jerk of the wheel, no warning, just a silent drift and a *kamikaze* stop of crunched metal from thirty miles an hour. He didn't have a chance to shoot. His body catapulted over the seat and drove his skull into the windshield before a scream reached his throat.

Even though braced and belted, the impact knocked the wits out of me. My brain believed we were still cruising along at thirty. Gradually, I became aware that the ringing in my ears was not from my own bell having been rung but from a car alarm. I threw the transmission into reverse and rocked the Caddy off the Beamer's trunk. The engine revved up fine and the wheel still turned in my hands. Once a felon, always a felon. I jammed the accelerator in a hit and run and didn't stop running until the scrape of metal on rubber forced me to the curb of a quiet residential street.

A moan from the floorboard told me the guy wasn't dead. His gun kicked at my feet – a Smith & Wesson .38 Chief's Special with a blue carbon steel finish and two-inch barrel, simple enough for any idiot to shoot. I jammed it under my belt and pulled my duffel bag out from under his deadweight arm. For a moment I considered doing something for him but decided instead to make sure he hadn't damaged my camera. I grabbed him by the hair, twisted his face toward me and tested out the Nikon with a flash exposure. The crack of light made him blink and moan. He wore blue jeans and a Golds' Gym sweatshirt layered under an unzipped Dodger windbreaker. By the hay-coloured hair and bushy moustache I recognized him as the jogger who had attacked us in Vegas. Blood puddled on the floor mat from a cut above his left eye, where his skull had spidered the windshield. In another minute it was going to ruin the carpet. I needed to do something about that.

The guy wasn't in any shape to walk so I had to drag him by his collar to the trunk of the Caddy. He didn't want to move and I wasn't strong enough to lift him solo but after a couple of whacks with the tyre iron he rolled on to his stomach and tried to get up. I grabbed him by the back of his belt, helped him into the trunk and slammed it shut. He didn't utter a word of complaint. I think he was happy to get away from me.

The Caddy's right front fender looked like a bicyclist signalling for a turn and the hood came up skewed on a bent hinge. The engine compartment had absorbed the impact without much visible damage. The radiator felt solidly mounted and none of the hoses had busted loose. The scraping noise I'd heard came from the front right tyre, where the wheel well had crumpled back and gouged the tread. Had I any decency I'd take the guy to the nearest emergency room, call Detective Douglas and tell him what had happened. I crowbarred the sheet metal away from the tyre and disconnected the headlight so I didn't spotlight cars on the right as I drove past. The Caddy was a tank. When I sped away from the curb it handled no worse than it ever did.

At the first stoplight I flipped open the jogger's wallet. The California driver licence listed his name as Richard Grimes.

The Culver City address probably wasn't any good but I took it down with the licence number. The next sleeve contained another licence, this one authorizing the bearer to conduct private investigations in the State of California. I'd worked with a couple private investigators once. The big time operators did legal legwork for law firms and worked the other side of the law as fixers for wealthy clients. Small-timers did whatever they had to short of murder to make a living. Maybe this one hadn't even stopped at that. No reason a private detective can't be a hired killer. If I took him to the emergency room, Douglas might pull another no-show. I couldn't afford decency.

You didn't have to be a killer to know the desert around Los Angeles was a fifty-thousand-square-mile body dump. Seemed like some hiker found a new set of bones every month or so. The desert sand is soft and you can get down a couple of feet without much trouble. After the first wind nobody can tell the ground has been disturbed except maybe the animals and if they find the body nothing will be left to identify. In the middle of the desert Grimes could scream all he wanted and the only answer would be the howl of a coyote that might soon gnaw his bones. I wasn't sure if I could kill Grimes in cold blood but I was ready to give my ethics the test. I drove east on the Antelope Valley Freeway, found a side road on the fringe of the Mojave Desert, then a dirt road after that.

He didn't move when I opened the trunk. I whacked him a good one on the shins with the tyre iron and that brought him out of his death sham quick enough. 'Get out,' I said.

'I can't move, lady,' he moaned. 'I think my neck might be broke.'

I swung the tyre iron like a hand axe, chopped his knee

hard enough to hear a crack. I hadn't intended to break anything but it wasn't a bad idea to hobble his wheels. He screamed out a few things about my character which he should have left unsaid but I didn't hold it against him. I said, 'Get out.'

'I can't get out, you broke my leg.' He rolled around in the trunk, his hands on his knee. His neck must have felt much better.

'If you don't get out now, I'll break your arms, then I'll drag you out by your neck.' I didn't sound angry. I said it like I was going to cross the street to buy a carton of milk.

He swung his legs over the rim of the trunk and steadied himself on the bumper. I had no doubt the windshield had messed up his equilibrium but not half as bad as he pretended. When he straightened and looked at where I'd brought him, he was more scared than when I'd hit him. I'd chosen the spot well, a ravine set up against the mountains, shielded by gully walls. No way anybody was going to see us. He had nowhere to run except into the sights of his own gun.

'Come around this side of the car.' I stepped back with the gun aimed at his chest, pointed the crowbar to the spot at the rear tyre where I wanted him.

He gimped around, tried to crouch on his heels, but the pain in his knee wouldn't let him. He settled his butt on to the dirt and straightened his legs. Blood had streamed from the cut above his right eye to stain his windbreaker. During the ride he'd stopped the bleeding with a white handkerchief that he'd half-tucked into the front pocket of his jeans. He didn't look too good and probably felt worse.

'I'm going to tell you a story. You want to hear a story?'

He looked at me like I was nuts and he didn't like it. Crazy people can do crazy things.

'Once upon a time, I had this boyfriend, and this boy-friend, he gave me something to deliver, and this something he gave me blew up. Killed the man I handed it to. My boyfriend was trying to rip off the people he was doing business with, you see?'

Grimes nodded, following me so far.

'You know what I did to this boyfriend?'

He shook his head. He didn't have a clue I was Pandora's Box and he'd just opened me.

'I shot him. Then the guys he ripped off came after me, because they thought I was part of the deal, see? And you know what I did to them?'

He stared wide-eyed, too afraid to guess.

'I shot them too. And last of all, the honcho who employed the guys I shot decided to try the job himself, and you know what I did to him?'

He was nodding now. He got it. 'You shot him?'

'That's right. And if you don't give me truthful answers here, you know what I'm going to do with you?'

'I got people who know where I am.'

I laughed at that one. 'I don't see anybody here but lizards. They your friends? I don't think so.' I pointed the tip of the crowbar down one end of the gully, then up the other end. 'Take a look around. Nobody's going to know what happens out here. Nobody's going to find your body. If you tell me the truth, you'll live. If you lie, you die.'

A struggle waged in his mind between his preconceptions of the gentler sex and the sight of the gun in my hand. Not many women are capable of shooting a man who hasn't beaten and abused her for years. But I hadn't been particu-larly gentle and that and the pain in his knee decided him. 'OK, I'll tell you what I know.'

'Good boy.' I smiled at him. I wasn't unfriendly. Even if

I had to kill him, I didn't want him to think badly of me. 'Let's start with Vegas. Why did you come after us?'

'I was supposed to collect enough dirt on the Englishman to force him out of the country, you know, get him in trouble with immigration, get his work visa pulled. After he married you I thought I'd try to scare him out. Might've done it too, except you bitchwhacked me. Didn't expect that.'

'This all your idea or you on payroll?' I didn't take offence at the bitchwhacked part, thought it amusing.

'You took my ID, you know what I do for a living. Personally, I got nothing against you except a broken leg.'

'Who's the client then?'

'I can't tell you that.'

I didn't mean to hit him. I meant the shot to go wide, but it had been a while since I'd shot a gun and I'd never been that good in the first place. A pistol isn't a surgical instrument; it's designed for blasting away up close in the hopes of doing general damage. I didn't think it would do my street cred any good to admit I'd just wanted to scare him, so I pretended his size twelve Nike was what I'd been aiming at all along. He screamed and clutched his foot like I'd just murdered his baby. I hadn't even hit it flush, just winged off a toe or two. I repeated, 'The client?'

He gasped, nodded, gave me a pleading look.

'If you don't talk a little faster, you'll bleed to death.'

'I deal with a guy named Mark Finster.' He clenched his teeth so hard the words came out with bite marks. 'But he's just a yuppie who tells me what to do and I don't even know if that's his real name. Uses a dead-letter drop to pay cash, always in blank envelopes. I call in on a direct line, leave a message on a machine, and he calls me back from a pay phone. I get the feeling there are legal issues to this that he's not comfortable with.'

'A murder charge would make anybody uncomfortable.'

'Nobody's killed anybody.' Grimes put enough scoff into his voice to sound half-convincing.

'Somebody's killed two people, one of them my husband, and I'm looking for a reason not to kill you. Want to help out here, give me one?'

'Because I didn't do it!'

'You can do better than that. Who does Finster work for?'

'Are you gonna shoot me again if I tell you I don't know?'

'I might.'

'He told me the Englishman had taken some photographs, was trying to extort some friends of his. That was why I was supposed to use all means of persuasion, because it was already a criminal situation. Except the negatives disappeared when the Englishman died and he got worried, thought you had them.'

'I don't.'

'Great, I'll tell him it's all a misunderstanding.'

'So who does Finster work for?'

'Lady, please don't shoot me again. He didn't tell me and I had no other way of knowing except the pictures and I never found those.'

'What kind of wheels does he drive?'

The question caught him off guard. 'A Toyota Land Cruiser – why?'

The smart thing would have been to shoot him through the head and bury him in the desert. I couldn't take him to the cops, not with a bullet punching his shoe and a four-hour gap between smacking the BMW and turning him in to explain. The way I looked at it, the cops would arrest us both and he'd be released on bail about the time they bussed me back to the Institute. Releasing him presented other problems. He knew where I lived. If I let him go he could terminate me simple as a drive-by shooting. But no matter what my reputation, I'm not a killer even if it's the smart thing to do.

We struck a deal. He'd tell his client I knew nothing about the photographs. I'd drive him back to his car. Neither of us would mention to the law what happened. If asked we'd maintain he hadn't tried to kidnap me and his injuries had resulted from an automobile accident. Grimes might have thought anything negotiated with a gun to his head was less a deal than a survival strategy so on the drive back he stayed in the trunk.

His set of wheels was a white Pontiac Grand Am parked in front of the RTD bus lot on Main Street, a couple of blocks from my apartment. Venice is not the cleanest city in America and you don't want to be crawling around the street an hour before sunrise but it took me a few tries before I positioned the Mag Mount where I thought it would hold. I drove to an all-nighter on Lincoln Boulevard to pick up doughnuts and two coffees to go and looped back to the Grand Am. The tyre iron stayed in my hand when I opened the trunk. Grimes squirmed out fast enough when he saw I'd stayed true to my word. In the limping scramble to his car I handed him a cup of coffee and a doughnut. He didn't bother to thank me.

The Caddy's big dash fit the tracking receiver behind the steering wheel like a natural part of the instrument panel. I chased the data north and then east until the footage to target compressed to zero at St John's Hospital. Behind the emergency entrance sign a red-vested parking valet leaned over the Grand Am's hood to wedge a claim ticket between windshield and wiper – first time I'd ever seen an emergency room you had to valet park to get to. I parked on a one-way street with clear sight lines and watched the valet nose the Grand Am on to Santa Monica Boulevard.

A Toyota Land Cruiser wheeled up to the emergency room an hour later. A young suit snatched a valet ticket and trotted toward the entrance. He moved too fast for a detailed look but the age and car matched. When the parking valet popped behind the wheel and swung on to Santa Monica, I followed. He turned right at the next block, then right again, circling to a parking lot on the opposite end of the hospital.

Spending that much money on a car must have scared Finster. By the just-out-of-the-box look of his Land Cruiser the nearest he'd come to off-road was his driveway. Like a lot of people in Los Angeles he wanted that off-road image but wasn't an off-road guy. Because he wasn't an off-road guy I didn't have to worry the Mag Mount I attached to his undercarriage would jar loose.

For the next hour I fed quarters into a meter across the street at fifteen minutes a pop. The city had more meter maids than cops. The moment the meter went red a helmeted enforcer was sure to bicycle past and slap a ticket on the windshield. When I was down to my last quarter Grimes crutched out of the emergency room entrance with a head wrap that made him look like a refugee from a budget mummy flick. His client kept pace next to him, his mouth jawing away and his arms flapping like an angry bird. He was a tall, pin-striped man with gelled black hair that curled so perfectly the distinct odour of a beautician's permanent wafted on the wind. Grimes slapped at him with his crutch like he would a pigeon. I couldn't tell what they were arguing about but both looked plenty mad and if Grimes actually connected with one of those swings he'd have one less client.

Finster took advantage of the delivery of his wheels to break off the argument, slam his $45,000 door and chirp the tyres on his way out of the drive. Grimes stood on the sidewalk giving him the finger until the Land Cruiser disappeared down the street and still he stood there middle finger raised like some statue of obscenity. When he turned his back to toss his crutches into the Grand Am I slid away from the curb.

I lost Finster beneath a Westwood high rise when he split off to monthly parking and I was routed to the visitor slots. At the ground floor I approached the security guard, a silver-haired black man with solemn almond eyes and asked, 'Excuse me sir, did you see a young suit come by here a minute ago, tall, black hair gelled back, glasses, drives a Toyota Land Cruiser?'

'About thirty people in this building fit that description,' he said. 'The latest one I saw went up to the 23rd floor.'

The elevator doors on the 23rd floor opened to a big-haired blonde receptionist sitting guard at a desk and switchboard. The gold-plated lettering on the oak veneer panelling behind her spray of hair read STONE, FELL AND HUGHES DEVELOPMENT CORPORATION. The office behind it took up the entire floor. I walked up and leaned palms down on her desk. 'Did a guy just come in here, tall, glasses, black hair gelled back?'

She smiled so pleasantly I figured pleasantness was part of her job description. 'That would be Mike Finley. Would you like me to ring him?'

Most people pick an alias close to the original and Mike Finley was a kissing cousin to Mark Finster. They had to be the same guy. 'No thanks, I mean, not yet. I just thought he was kinda cute, you know? Wondered what he was like.'

Her pleasant smile grew even more pleasant and her eyes sparkled. 'He's a real asshole,' she said. 'Believe me, you don't want to have anything to do with him.'

26

Ever since I went as a kid with my dad hunting for parts to fit his '62 Chevy pick-up I've loved junkyards. The smell of oil-soaked dirt and rusting engines, the unexpected beauty of scripted chrome, thrusting tail-fins, bug-eyed headlights and gap-toothed grilles, the very heat that sang from so many packed carcasses bleaching in rows of steel, glass and rubber thrilled me like an archaeologist exploring ancient ruins. I could roam for hours wondering who drove that rusting shell of a '48 Lincoln, sky blue '62 Ford Galaxy, or sun-faded yellow '64 Chevy Impala. What children or dreams were conceived on those now torn canvas seats, and which crumpled fender and spidered windshield turned the wheel to coffin? The pleasure I got out of a good junkyard was not much different than other people might find wandering through a cemetery, except most graveyard visitors don't get the side benefit of shopping for body parts.

Sandwiched between a Ford Thunderbird and a Chrysler Imperial I found what I was looking for, a 1976 Cadillac Eldorado with a showroom-condition right fender, even if the rest of the car looked like it had collided with a freight train. Armed with socket and crescent wrenches, a rubber mallet and a can of WD 40 lubricating solvent I popped the hood and went to work. Even properly equipped I just about tore a rotator cuff trying to torque loose the lug nuts bonding the fender to the wheel-well and frame. An hour of sweat pulled the fender unscratched, a baby blue I liked so much I thought I'd paint the whole car that colour. I prised loose the old fender and bolted on the new one right there at the junkyard, attached a new set of headlights and gave the grease monkey who ran the place the scrap. I drove out of the yard feeling about as proud of what I'd accomplished as I'd ever felt about anything.

The Little Chapel of the Dawn rested on a street corner in Santa Monica, a mock-Tudor-style mortuary fronted by trimmed hedges and a flower box appropriately pushing up daisies. The junkyard celebrated death; the mortuary buried or burned it. I preferred jet noise, clanging metal and the crunching of safety glass underfoot to piped church music and solemn whispers from men with the demeanour of professional grief. Despite my preferences, I didn't think the authorities would let me bury Gabe in a junkyard. I parked in front of a stone walkway that cut invitingly through the lawn to a welcome sign on the closed front door. The door had one of those old-fashioned brass front latches, friendlier than a doorknob, where you press on a thumb-sized flange inside a projecting brass 's' and the thing springs open. A rustic wood sitting group, padded by plaid cushions, welcomed me to a country cottage front parlour with warm wood-panelled walls and latticed windows. On the far wall hung a painting of big-eyed dogs frolicking on the grounds of an English estate. I wondered if I hadn't stumbled into a pet mortuary by mistake but the sixty-something receptionist didn't flinch when I informed her I'd come to make arrangements for my husband. Gabe would have howled with laughter. The Little Chapel of the Dawn perfectly complemented the Special Memory Wedding Chapel™ in Las Vegas; I married him in kitsch and I'd bury him in kitsch.

A dark-suited, sombre-lipped gentleman in his early sixties stepped into the parlour to ask, 'May I help you, madame?' like he didn't know what I was doing there. He didn't get many widows my age in Santa Monica. The morticians in South Central, Watts, the *barrios* of East Los Angeles, they handled young meat all the time, but Santa Monica was too white and too safe for brutally premature death. When I presented him with the coroner's release form he led me to the conference room, where he propped his elbows on a black-lacquer table, steepled his fingers beneath his chin and asked, 'Have you given any thought regarding how you wish to treat the remains of your loved one?'

'I want to burn him,' I said.

He blinked once, heavily. 'Cremation, you mean?'

'My husband was beaten, stabbed, strangled and drowned. I've seen road kill look better. Burning is the only way to give him back his dignity.'

He nodded once, solemn and dignified, to indicate he agreed that my decision made perfect sense. In a black leather notebook he jotted down the preference and said, 'To begin: we need some basic information about your husband, for example, his full name, the date and place of birth, that sort of thing.'

I dug our marriage certificate and Gabe's employment record from my duffel and did my best to answer the questions. I didn't know where he had been schooled, his educational degrees or professional associations, if any. Each field left blank testified how little I knew him.

'Maybe we had better move on to the arrangements themselves,' he suggested. 'How would you like to contain the cremains of your dear departed?'

'Cremains?'

'Forgive me, an industry term. The body is not reduced to

ash as some believe, but to skeletal fragments, which we grind into a fine powder and call the cremated remains, or cremains.' He laid a four-colour brochure on the edge of the table, folded open to the first page. 'We carry a wide selection of funerary urns, from this engraved sterling silver designer model to classic bronze – or for those on a budget, a cardboard box.'

The business of death chilled me. I left the Little Chapel of the Dawn needing to talk to somebody. In a city of fleeting affairs and transient friendships everybody needs one or two people they can depend on in a crisis. Though I counted Big Brenda as a friend I had not known her long or well. Frank might have done me a favour but not without expecting something in return; I didn't know him at all. If friendships were the measure of a woman I was pretty damn small. That left only family.

Though the people who worked the cash registers and stocked the shelves at K-Mart would be friendly enough I didn't think it right to walk into the store unannounced and ask for my mom. I didn't want to embarrass her. Every family has its dirty linen but nobody wants it walking into their place of work. I cruised the parking slots outside the store but didn't see her Ford Escort. She had probably car-pooled with a co-worker, maybe the younger woman I'd seen in her company on my last visit. I parked the Cadillac on the blacktop and waited for the change of shift. When she walked out I'd tell her that I was returning in person her call of the day before. Even if our talk lasted less than ten minutes the drive would have been worth it.

I recognized the co-worker when she came alone out of the employee entrance behind the store. With her home-permanent hairstyle and owlish glasses, she looked like my mother's true daughter. She jumped back and put her hand to her breast when I stepped out of my car and called to her. What tales she must have been told to appear so frightened.

'Sorry to bother you, but I'm looking for – '

She barricaded herself behind the wing of her car door. 'Haven't you heard?'

'Heard what?'

My mother had been admitted into Henry Mayo Memorial Hospital with a broken hip and a laceration above her left eye. My brother Ray had called the shift manager two days earlier to report it. Her co-workers had sent flowers and a get well card. An accident in the home, they all thought. I knew my father well enough to picture what happened. Some accident.

The Mayo was a modern community hospital built to serve the needs of an affluent commuter suburb that had paved over the oak and grass hills near my old home town. I jogged down a pink-tiled hall beyond the nursing station and poked my head into a bright and cheerful room with two beds and a window looking out to the central courtyard. My mom lay in the bed by the window, her eyes directed to the television set attached to the wall. I crept up to her bed and placed on her lap a golden yellow teddy bear that had caught my eye in the gift shop. A tag around the bear's neck read, I Love You.

'You shouldn't have,' my mom said when I bent to kiss her cheek. The bandage above her eye didn't conceal the bruising beneath it. She looked frail and broken in that room. I tried to smile. I failed.

She asked, 'You got my message?'

'Last night. But you didn't leave much of one.'

'I didn't want to be dramatic, dear.' She always knew how to understate things.

'He hit you, didn't he?'

She jerked her head aside to keep me from seeing the truth in her eyes. 'I fell,' she said.

I don't know why I was so angry. My dad hit everybody. When I was growing up I just accepted it. Everybody's dad lost their temper, mine more than most. Every week he hit somebody, every week somebody got their ears boxed or face slapped. Some weeks, it was my mom he hit. She never complained. She never left him. Maybe that was what angered me so much.

'Why do you lie about it? Just because you pretend he didn't hit you doesn't mean he won't do it again.'

'I told you, I fell.' Her voice was solemn, as though belief could convince her the world was flat. 'It happened coming down the front steps.'

'Don't you see that he's put you in the hospital?'

The woman in the bed by the door stirred beneath her covers.

'Please, Mary, don't raise your voice.'

'I'll lower my voice when you raise yours. Are you going to suffer in silence for the rest of your life?'

'We were preparing for bed and I forgot to, to get the mail. It was dark and the corner of the welcome mat was turned up. I was coming down the front steps – '

'No! He hit you and you fell. He started drinking after work and didn't stop. Maybe you said something that set him off and maybe he just felt mean, but he hit you, like he's always hit you, only you're getting older now, and you can't take it so well. This time when he knocked you down you broke. The next time he might kill you.'

'Quiet please!' The crisp white uniform of a nurse flashed through the door. The expression on her lined face was stern and her tone tolerated no nonsense. The hospital was no place for a family argument, she said. I did my mother no good and disturbed the other patients. I should go. I pulled my arm away when she reached for my elbow.

'I'll be quiet,' I promised.

'The nurse is right,' my mother said.

I felt small and bad. I said, 'I'm sorry, I just think you should defend yourself.'

'This is not the time or place,' the nurse insisted, her voice gentler but no less firm.

My mom turned her eyes back to the television set. 'You're just like him, Mary Alice, you're more like him than any of us. That's why you hate him, and why he hates you. It would be better for all of us if you didn't come back here for a while.'

With its sheer grey walls rising bluntly from Sunset Boulevard as though from a moat, its pitched black roof and central tower, the Chateau Marmont looked like the bastard child of aristocratic castles from the Loire Valley. The hotel had clung to the hillside above Hollywood since the 1920s, pines and eucalyptus shielding from public view the mock-sixteenth century edifice if not the excessive behaviour of its celebrity clientele. Early in its history, following the erotic adventures of Clark Gable and Jean Harlow, the Chateau Marmont developed a reputation as being a film-star fuck-pad extraordinaire. Successive generations of actors and recording stars found it a discreet environment for equally outrageous behaviour until a heroin-cocaine speedball blew John Belushi's brain out the roof of bungalow number three. It took the hotel a decade and a change of ownership to recover from the hangover but as she neared her seventieth birthday the Chateau Marmont had again become a film industry hangout and host to scandalous behaviour to rival that of its famous ghosts.

The woman who came to the door of my suite would have attracted any man or woman above the age of twelve and under the age of dead. It wasn't just the photogenic contrast of Polynesian black hair and beige skin with high cheekbones and sea-green eyes, or the sinuous obedience of her black mini and tube top, or even the tattoo panther that prowled the wild place between her hip and navel. A sexual energy vibrated from her entire being, halo to heels, an energy so polymorphous-perverse in appeal I half expected the carpet to pull up tacks and wrap her. When I stood back from the door she stepped into the room with an approving smile that warmed me in places I'd rather stay chilled. 'Love your show,' she said. 'Every Tuesday night my nose is glued to the tube, you gotta tell me, is everyone on the show true-to-life or are some of 'em actors?'

Like many high-class hookers Piña Noir wanted to be an actress and thought this was the way to meet the people who could make her one. I doubted she had watched more than one episode of *Meat Wagon* but as I'd borrowed Cass's identity when calling to ask for her services I didn't question her enthusiasm. Madame Alex wouldn't send one of her girls on a blind date. That wasn't the way the system worked. She had to know who I was. I'd flashed Cass's credit card to check into the hotel then insisted on paying cash for the room. I didn't want to leave a record, I said. They knew what I meant. Entertainment types used the hotel as a trysting place. Discretion was included in the room price. When Madame Alex returned my call, the front desk connected her to the woman registered as Cass Mitchel. She knew Cass's name from *LA 411*, the directory of everybody in the business. If the hotel accepted me as Cass, I was Cass. A cop couldn't use the name of a Hollywood player to sting a working girl. 'They're all real,' I said. 'The last thing anybody wants to be is on my show.'

Piña leaned against the counter between the living-room and mini-kitchen and snapped open her purselett. 'I always like getting the financial arrangements out of the way first – do you mind?'

'The envelope on the counter there belongs to you.' I spoke as light-heartedly as I could considering the envelope contained five one-hundred dollar bills.

Piña confirmed the amount and slipped the envelope into her purse. 'You know I don't do guys, don't you? I mean, I perform in front of 'em, but I don't do 'em. In case you're worried.' She slid her hands beneath her hair to cradle the back of her neck and stretched, bringing dramatic focus on to the thrust of her breasts and down to her dark radiance. She said, 'You're very attractive, you know that? I really go for that bad-girl look of yours.'

'It's not just a look, I really am a bad girl.'

'How bad?'

'Worse than you can imagine.'

'Yum. How do you like to be bad?'

I didn't think I should tell her that, at least, not yet. 'Please, make yourself comfortable.'

'How comfortable do you want me to get?'

I didn't believe she wanted to get comfortable at all. She wanted to get down to business and get out. 'No rush. Shall we have a drink first?' I brought out a bottle of Jack Daniel's, carried a couple of glasses and a bucket of ice to the coffee table. 'Sorry, guess I should have brought champagne, right? You look like a champagne kind of girl.'

She didn't know if that was a compliment or not but nodded like I had it right. 'It's OK, I'll drink whatever you're having.' She perched on the edge of the green-velveteen couch which, like the coffee table, the stuffed chair and everything else in the room, looked like it had been salvaged from a Beverly Hills flea market.

'I'm not bad like you,' I explained. 'I'm not bad because I use my sexuality to get things, or because I enjoy types of sex society disapproves. Sure, sometimes I do those things, but that's not why I'm bad. I'm bad because I hurt people.'

A woman like Piña, she'd experienced a lot in her twenty-two years, though of such a narrow range that she nodded like she understood exactly what I was saying even though she had no idea. 'As long as it's controlled an' nobody gets hurt a little pain is exciting. But I didn't know that was what you wanted, I didn't bring anything special.'

'I'm not talking about S & M. I'm talking about putting people in the hospital, I'm talking about putting people in the grave.'

Even though she still didn't understand what I was getting at, her black heels shifted on the carpet for secure footing and her red nails gripped the bourbon tight enough to crack a thinner glass. It was occurring to her that something about me wasn't right.

'Do you know why I asked for you? Who recommended you specifically?'

'Alex said one of your girlfriends knew me.'

'I lied.'

She cocked her head, all sensual burn reduced to cold ash. 'Then who?'

'Gabriel Burns.'

She set the drink down on the coffee table and snapped up from the couch. 'I have to go.'

I shoved her back down hard and kicked her heels out. With my hand at her throat I said, 'This is a wild hotel, people have a lot of parties here, screaming and yelling at all hours of the night. If you try to leave, I'll hurt you bad enough to make you stay. You scream everybody's just going to think we're having a really good time.'

Her crescent eyes stretched to oval with more than just

fear, as though the threat of violence fascinated as much as frightened her. Her head dropped slowly and came up again. Almost uncontrollably, I wanted to kiss her. Like a lot of my desires, that was someplace I didn't want to go. I backed off to sit on the edge of the chair between her and the front door.

'You're Nina, aren't 'cha?' Piña swung her heels back to the floor, reached for her glass and drained it in one smooth line of movement.

I took the bourbon from the table, poured her a refill, set the bottle on the floor by my side so she wouldn't feel tempted to use it on my head.

'Gabe talked 'bout you. He talked 'bout you so much I shoulda been offended, 'cept what he said made me just more interested.' She took down half the refill in one gulp and smiled at me with sexual bravado intact. 'He described you as a Tootsie Pop: hard on the outside, soft an' chewy on the inside. He was definitely right about the outside, makes me even more curious about the soft an' chewy part.'

'That soft part isn't soft anymore,' I said. 'And the hard part isn't sweet.'

She glanced slyly from beneath her lowered head like a child walking the edge of a fence. 'This act, pretending you like girls, it's not just an act, is it?'

I poured myself a shot, threw it down, chased it with half a glass of water. 'The way you talk about Gabe, seems to me you knew him pretty well. Were you sleeping with him?'

'You should give him credit for knowing the difference between his joystick an' his thumper.'

'So you slept with him.'

She had courage, I had to admit that. She stopped fidgeting with the glass and threw down a dead-on stare with as

much invitation in it as confession. 'It's one of the things
I do.'

'I thought you said you didn't do men.'

'Professionally, I don't.'

'Gabe was, what? Recreational?'

She stared at her hands and turned them palms up to
cup her face like a surgical mask. 'Gabe was a friend.' She
fought it briefly and lost badly, her eyes going bright red
and swelling furiously until the tears burst and streaked
mascara-black down her cheeks. Piña was a pretty girl but
she cried ugly.

The display moved me to pity but not any closer to my
own personal grief. I wasn't jealous of her relationship with
Gabe. In a strange way, I felt closer to her because she had
known him, had enjoyed his friendship and his body. Her
relationship didn't threaten mine, make it any less real or
unreal than it was or was not. That we had both known him
made me feel less alone. What brought up feelings of jealousy
and envy was the way she could cry about losing him. Some
have a facility for tears but for others to cry means complete
emotional destruction. I hadn't cried for five years. When I
said I had turned to stone I meant it. I worried that somewhere along the way, at Gabe's death or before, I had done
mortal injury to my soul. I wasn't even sure I still had a soul.

I stroked her hair and when I cupped the side of her face
in my palm she nestled into it like something lost. 'You were
his friend, so you'll help me, right? You'll help me do what
I gotta do so we can bury him, sleep eight hours in peace?'

She nuzzled into the palm of my hand, eyes clenched,
teeth nipping the inside of her lower lip. Sometimes simply
opening one's eyes can be an act of vulnerability. When Piña
opened hers I saw in the wide black iris a figure huddled as

though left naked on a rock in a vast sea, exposed and afraid. The way she looked at me, I was not unaware that she would then slip her face from my palm and seek my lips. I was not unaware that when she did so I would not turn my face away.

When I stopped wanting it to go further than that one kiss I pulled back and smiled to let her know it was OK but I was not ready for anything more than just that. She wiped beneath her eyes with the back of her forefinger, noticed the smudges of black mascara and showed them to me, laughing. 'I prob'ly look like the La Brea Tar Pits. You got any tissues?'

'In the bathroom,' I answered, and went to get them.

When I stepped back into the living-room the front door was open and she was gone.

28

Beyond the balcony of my suite a billboard of the Marlboro Man loomed like a giant cartoon ready to break his posts and rampage through the city, roping cars and six-gunning sky-scrapers. I wondered which of the cars streaming brake-light red below was Piña's running back to ground. Further down Sunset, Madonna strained against her plywood frame with breasts big enough to crush small cars, Nathan Lane mugged with a mouse the size of a killer whale and the thirty-foot-tall sunglassed face of Jack Nicholson howled at the moon. One Halloween or Oscar night they might come alive, leap free of the plywood, paint and paper that bound them, and with bodies to match the size of their stardom trample Hollywood to dust.

Piña was in the suite for close to an hour and all I discovered was that she'd slept with Gabe. I didn't learn what had happened the night the photographs were taken, how he had known about the party or where he'd waited with his camera. Cursing myself comes more naturally than cursing others. When I ran out of things to call myself I reached Frank on his cell phone, asked him what he knew about Stone, Fell and Hughes Development Corporation.

'One of the top ten land development companies in So Cal.' Tyres hummed beneath his voice. He was on the road, prowling for a story. 'Not as big as Irvine Ranch Company, which owns half of Orange County, but you see their signs on some of the top end housing projects on the Westside.'

'What do you mean, land development?'

'It's an oxymoron. They don't develop land, they bulldoze it and drop a couple hundred designer tract homes over rolling oak hills or pristine desert. You drive the ridge of the Santa Monica Mountains on Mulholland, you'll see one of their projects. Guard house out front, earth-coloured anti-tank wall and more electronic security gear than the Korean DMZ.'

'Do they have some Hollywood connection you think? Some side business in the movies?'

'The information highway is a two-way street. You want to invite me over for a drink, we'll talk about it?'

I hesitated long enough that he got offended. 'I'm not going to try to bone you, just have a drink.'

He whistled when I told him I was staying at the Chateau Marmont. At $300 a night business must be pretty good, he said. I didn't tell him about Piña. I was supposed to be a hardened con. The ease of her escape embarrassed me. I was guilty of naivete or stupidity and maybe both. What was it my parole officer said? Criminals are screw-ups.

During my five years in stir I'd lived in a society of criminals. Most were not bad people. We had a few killers but the cold-blooded ones were kept away from the rest. The majority served time on drug or prostitution charges. They never hurt anybody except themselves. A few had the inner strength and determination to change once they were released but most just went back to the same life that got them arrested, only older and more desperate. Prison might have taught them new ways to break old laws but it didn't make them any smarter. They were like dolls spinning atop a music box; when wound and released they danced to one tune only and every time in the same direction. The tune I danced to was no more complex nor the movement of my feet less predictable.

The confidence that I could discover who had killed Gabe struck me then as another example of how I'd screwed up my life. I'd already broken into an apartment, assaulted a kid in a bar and held a man at gunpoint, acts which could send me back to prison. When I did uncover something I couldn't trust the cops to do anything about it. I wasn't a professional investigator or even a talented amateur. My greatest asset was desperation. Frank was right to call me a fool, and not just for giving a copy of the disk to Harker. When I heard the knock on the door I decided to confess to just that. Only it wasn't Frank waiting for me at the door, black heels slung over her shoulder, tattoo puma on the prowl and a bottle of Moët & Chandon in hand.

'You were right. I am a champagne girl.' Piña stepped lightly inside and when I shut the door she backed me against the wall with a kiss that just about burned a hole through me. Life is full of surprises. I let the kiss flame out on its own, said, 'I appreciate the effort but this isn't what I want.'

'Sure it is. Sure you want it.'

She handed me the bottle and two glasses. I eased out the cork while she settled into a suggestively prone position on the couch and giggled like a bad little girl. 'I went down to the bar.'

All this time I'd been thinking of Piña as a grown woman. Few women had her sexual energy or experience but in other ways she wasn't more than a child. Maybe the child-woman duality was part of the appeal. I handed her a glass of champagne and sat across the coffee table. She was a little drunk and it took her a moment of pouting to determine I wasn't getting on to the couch with her. 'I had to prove to myself I could get away, y'know?' She put her feet to the floor and her knees together and rifled me a look equal parts anger and invitation. 'The way you were acting, talking 'bout putting people in the hospital, it was pretty scary. Sure, I'm sometimes attracted to danger an' I didn't get any vibe you were evil. But what if it was some *Aliens* scenario, y'know, when a monster busts out of someone's gut? People are walking 'round out there an' they look like you an' me, they look normal, but they're not. They're aliens. You get alone with one, in the wrong situation, an' you pray you pull a Ripley, you pray you find a way out.'

'Is Damian Burke that way? Does he have this thing in his gut?'

Piña had a youthful way of nodding, bobbing forward from the shoulders. 'Burke is totally evil but he's an actor, y'know? He controls it. You're sure he's got somethin' nasty deep in his gut but you can't prove it. It's like he plays with it, lets you see it for a second an' then pulls it back until you swear it wasn't ever there. You can't help yourself, you watch him because he's like, fascinating.'

'Tell me about the night Gabe took the photographs.'

'Which night?'

I couldn't tell if she was playing dumb or something else. 'I know you were there. Performing with another girl for Burke and a county supervisor, Pete Danavitch.'

'You mean the night with the dog.'

'Was there more than one night?'

A rhythmic tapping sounded from the front door as though someone attempted to knock out the tune to *Yellow Submarine*. A rod shot down Piña's back and she glanced to the bathroom door and then to the balcony.

I said, 'It's a friend.'

'Look, I don't want to be seen here, I don't want anybody to even know I'm talking to you, understand? It can be dangerous for me.'

'I called him after you left. He has nothing to do with you.'

Sure it was a small lie but it relaxed her. She slipped around the couch and into the bathroom. I got up, went to the door and opened it to Frank's smiling face.

'Evening, beautiful, if you got the booze, I got the news.'

I suspected one of Frank's problems in life was a case of bad timing. 'Sorry, I got a visitor.'

'But you just . . .' He leaned forward, out of the hall light, to get a clear look at my face. 'You have red lipstick all over your mouth.'

Piña's colour. I hadn't thought to check. 'Things have been interesting.'

Frank backed away like I'd just shot him in the gut. Maybe I had. He said, 'I'll bet.'

Before he turned to stride down the hall his lips tightened like he couldn't decide whether to scream or cry. That look told me what he'd wanted out of our relationship. I was less than a week a widow and the last thing I needed was mooning from the guy I was supposed to be working with. When he reached the head of the stairs I called out, 'Don't get too far ahead of the plot here, Frank.'

He gave me a little wave with the back of his hand, I couldn't figure if he was signalling he was OK or going down for the third time. Nothing worse than falling for a person and then seeing them with somebody else, all that rage and sadness but nowhere to put it except back inside. His fault; he never should have fallen for me.

'New boyfriend?' Piña smirked, I don't know what at, the

idea of boyfriends or my having one so soon after being widowed.

'Just a wanna be.' I hated myself for saying that.

'If it gets out I talked to you, I lose my job.'

'That may not be a bad thing.' I poured myself a shot of Jack to chase the champagne. Even good champagne was too sweet to drink by itself. I needed the bitter taste of fire.

'I'll keep my job, thanks. I'm not going to sling frappucinos in some coffee house.'

'It's an honourable job,' I pointed out. 'Half the actresses in Hollywood have waited tables. Can you name me a single hooker who went on to have a real career?'

It took her a moment, then she came up with, 'Sylvester Stallone.'

'He acted in one porno film. Not the same thing.'

'I thought you were cool,' she sulked. 'But I belong in this town more than you do, you're just a moralist.'

I laughed at that one. 'You're right, I'm not one to give out career advice. You can't screw up a life any better than I've screwed up mine.' She'd do what she wanted no matter where it led. People usually do. 'That night at Damian Burke's, was it set up through Madame Alex?'

'Everything is always set up through Madame Alex.'

'Who set it up, Burke or Danavitch?'

'Burke. He's a steady customer. He prob'ly knows every girl on the roster.'

'Did she know Danavitch was going to be there?'

Piña's shoulders lifted to her neck. 'I didn't even know who he was until you just said. But Alex, she knows stuff. She keeps a computer database, her lil' black book she calls it, contains the preferences of everybody she sends girls to. Sometimes I think she knows everything.'

If Piña didn't know Danavitch was going to be there, Gabe

didn't either. He had to be gunning for Burke. 'You told Gabe about the party that night, said Burke had ordered something extra special?'

Piña stared at the champagne glass, her ripe lower lip pinched between two sharp white teeth. Her green eyes turned inward with the calculation of what she desired subtracted by what she feared. 'If this gets out . . .'

'Why did you do it?'

'Money, why else? Gabe told me he might get as much as a hundred grand an' offered me twenty per cent. I trusted him.'

Sentiment and honour made me stupid. Always will. 'If the photographs ever get published, I'll do my best to honour Gabe's deal.'

'You have 'em? The photographs?' Beneath the casual tone glimmered an excitement I didn't think healthy.

'Just heard about them.' In a way, that wasn't even a lie. I didn't have the photographs themselves, just digital copies. 'Where did Gabe shoot from? Did you set that up?'

'The estate next to Burke's. The owner went back to Saudi Arabia or someplace an' the house is up for sale. Gabe knew the real estate agent.'

I hopped over the back of the chair to grab a pencil and pad and sat next to Piña on the couch. She snuggled closer, refilled champagne for both of us and yawned. 'Champagne makes me sleepy.'

'Burke played host and Danavitch the guest of honour.' Her warmth comforted and disturbed me. 'Who else was there?'

'Lezly, she's my partner. Sometimes I'll pair up with another girl, but most of the time, Lezly is the blonde in the show. Black hair an' blonde hair together, y'know, ebony an' ivory, it turns guys on.'

I wrote the name down. 'Who else besides Lezly?'

'The blow-job girls, Tiffany an' Darlene. An' then the other act. Kathy an' Rex.'

'Rex?'

'Yeah. The dog.'

'You think he'd talk?'

'Better'n Kathy. That girl's got the IQ of a chew-toy.'

'Nobody else?'

'Earl. He was 'round but I don't think he watched the show. Earl is 'round all the time, acts as Burke's bodyguard an' general houseboy.'

The bruiser sitting on the rim of the fountain in Gabe's photographs. 'This Earl, what's he like?'

'Angry.' Piña nudged my arm with her chin until I draped it around her, then nestled between my breast and shoulder. 'Hey, did you ever hear of the concept of degrees of separation?'

'What's that, some new kinda term people use before they get divorced?'

She giggled, slow and drowsy. 'No. It's like, how closely connected you are to somebody famous. Like, for example, I know somebody who knew somebody who knew somebody who knew somebody who knew somebody else who'd slept with George Washington. So me an' old George, we're five degrees of separation away from having sex together. Get it?'

'So one way or another we've both slept with everybody who ever existed in the world, is this what you're saying?'

'No.' She giggled and didn't stop, I could barely make out what she said between sleepy gusts of laughter. 'What I'm saying is, you're only one degree of separation away from sleeping with two Academy Award winners.'

'That's something to tell the grandchildren.'

The breath from her yawn spread warm and liquid-like across my breast. 'You're funny.'

'Why is Earl so angry?

When she didn't answer I thought she was preparing some in-depth critique of Earl's psyche, but when I broke out of my own reverie I heard rhythmic breathing and a soft snore. I guessed that meant we weren't going to have sex. The last of the champagne was in my glass. I downed it, lifted beneath Piña's knees and shoulders and carried her to bed. I wasn't used to sleeping in the same bed with somebody, had only done it twice in the past five years and both times with Gabe, but I was too tired to be strange about it and spun off to dreamland while taking off my shoes.

'Hey, you asleep? . . . I said, hey, Nina, are you asleep?'

The voice came at me like a light at the top of a deep, black well.

'I wanna tell you something. Can you hear me?'

I swam toward a diffuse glow of daylight. To surface from such depths of sleep hurt like a dreamer's case of the bends. Through an eyelash gauze I saw Piña's face over mine. My tongue struggled to find the right vowel. I thought I heard myself say, 'Yes.'

'Were you serious about giving me twenty per cent?'

I floated close enough to consciousness to nod.

'Then you should know it was two nights. Not one. That second night Burke was with somebody new. 'Bout thirty-five, went by the nickname Vinny. Lezly an' me, we didn't get five seconds into our show before Burke threw us out. Gabe was next door taking pictures, least he was s'posed to be, but I don't know for sure because I didn't talk to him again. That was the night before his body was found in the lake.'

Piña was out the door before I could struggle upright. I

bounced off a door frame, stumbled into the hall, heard heels clattering on stairs three floors down. Harsh desert sunlight blared through a window at the head of the stairway. I groped my way into the bathroom and ran cold water over my face, going over what she said again and again to make sure I knew what it meant. Gabe's body wasn't discovered the night he was killed; the gases of decomposition took twenty four hours to float him to the surface. Gabe had been murdered the night he had returned to photograph Burke.

The young actor slashed through the Marmont's pool like a blade, lithe chest and concave belly flashing at each turn, his legs lean and big kneed and his arms no more muscled than a young girl's. The morning sun sparkled at the tip of each ripple and wave and as he swam his slender feet kicked up a wake of diamonds. That high above Hollywood the traffic on Sunset faded to a distant rustle and the splash of his beautiful young body drifted into the trees like music. At the near end of the pool he swung his elbows on to the ledge to rest, water streaming from his troubled post-adolescent brow and over lips so pink and full the only proper thing to do was kiss them. I recognized his face from the magazines. That season he'd made his fame as one of the networks' premiere teen heart-throbs. In person I could see why; he was some boy, like a fruit at the peak of sweetness. In another year or two the image-makers would deem him not slim but skinny, a professional trainer would be hired and his beautiful boy's body would be gone forever.

'Hey, that coffee you got there?'

I had my sunglasses on – had to because of the hangover – and didn't think he'd noticed me staring at him. I said, 'It is.'

'Would you bring me a cup?'

That amused me enough to pour one from the room

189

service thermos and bring it to him. Up close, his eyes were the kind of hazel you keep staring at to see if they're green or brown. He took the coffee and watched me over the rim while he drank.

'Mornings, what a bitch, eh?'

The sunlight glinting from his grin just about blinded me.

'Bitch, bastard, depends on which sex gives you the most trouble.'

'That would definitely be a bitch in my case.'

It was hard to be offended. He was too charming. He could have said anything or nothing and charmed.

I said, 'Both sexes give me trouble.'

'Lucky you. You staying here at the hotel?'

'Did last night, maybe again tonight.'

He drained the coffee, asked, 'Want to go up to my room and fuck?'

The white deck shoes of a pool attendant clipped at the edge of my vision and in the eucalyptus branches overhead a mockingbird squawked.

'Well, no, but thanks for asking.'

'If you change your mind you know how to find me.' He handed me the cup and kicked back into the pool with a splash that shot a single bullet of chlorinated water into my sunglasses. I retreated to the shade beneath the sun umbrella and wondered why the physically perfect men even as boys are most always jerks.

Midway into my reading the calendar section of the *LA Times* my parole officer pushed through the gate beyond the diving board and stiffly glanced about the patio. Her hand rested on her purse like the butt of an Uzi. I held two fingers out in the sunlight to show her where I sat. By the time she strode over to the table I'd folded the *Times*, poured her a cup of coffee and kicked out a chair. Like me she wore dark sunglasses, although hers concealed vigilance rather than a hangover.

She took the chair and swung it around to face me but her concentration drifted to the young actor doing laps in the pool. 'A place like this must cost a small fortune.'

On the navy blue thigh of her pantsuit she tapped the hotel's promotional brochure, a cream-coloured price list inserted between the folds. It wasn't hard to read what she was thinking.

'You want to see my pay stubs, make sure I'm not dealing coke on the side?'

She snapped open her purse, shoved aside what I imagined to be hand-grenades, brass-knuckles and land mines to whip out a sheet of paper that looked like a form. 'The results of your A and T test.'

The form had numbers written on it that meant nothing to me.

'It's negative. You're clean. But you have other problems.'

'You mean problems other than a husband who got himself murdered? You mean different problems than that, like maybe, I can't go back to my apartment because it was broken into by the same guy who killed my husband and the cops think I'm next in line for a grass blanket? That problem? Or are you still hung up about the green card thing?'

'I checked the records. Mr Burns never visited or wrote you at California Institute for Women. Not once.'

When both players are wearing sunglasses a stare-down contest can go on for ever with no clear winner. 'You want to take me in now? Because if the past week is what so-called freedom is like I could do with a little more time in stir.'

'You think I'm a bitch.'

'I didn't say that.'

'In this job, I have to be a bitch.' Her lips were too thin and rigid to move much without snapping but a twitch along her cheek showed she was trying to smile or sneer, I couldn't figure which. 'I saw that television programme you were on, when you found ' – she rolled a different word around her tongue – 'your husband's body. If you were an actress you'd be making a million bucks a picture. I'm sorry. That was cynical, even for me. You weren't acting. You looked like somebody ripped your heart out of your chest. I could see he meant more to you than a few thousand bucks for a green card. I don't think there's a parole officer or judge in the world who would want to ticket you back to prison after seeing that.'

'You believe me?'

'I believe you.'

'Nobody in law enforcement has ever said something like that to me before.'

'Maybe you didn't deserve it.'

I raised eyebrows and shoulders to say I couldn't be the one to judge that. 'Then I'm clear?'

Her head wagged back and forth. Even when she was being soft the woman was hard. 'I'm in contact with the investigative officers in charge of your husband's case. Detective Harker tells me you have some ideas yourself about the way the investigation should be handled. He's afraid you might do something really stupid, like talk to potential suspects, look for evidence, in general screw up his investigation. You wouldn't do something that stupid would you?'

At the near end of the pool the young actor vaulted from the water and stretched his hairless chest toward the morning sun, drops glistening on his skin like rubies. His swimming suit wasn't large or baggy and didn't conceal that a certain part of him wasn't as thin as his arms and not at all boyish.

My parole officer's right forefinger arrowed between her eyebrows and slid the bridge of her sunglasses an inch toward the tip of her nose. Some things don't need shading, not a bit. She whispered, 'Wait a minute, isn't that – '

'Looks like him at a distance,' I said, 'but if you get up close, it isn't him at all.'

30

Once upon a time I'd been a straight citizen; I had a regular job, went to the hairdresser every month, never back-talked nobody except boyfriends no matter how much I was provoked. I knew how to look and act like a lower-middle-class good girl who said yes to everything except sex and even then didn't say no, just not now, who never wanted to be bad except in bed and then only with the right man, who never made trouble except when she drank a little too much at parties and who could always be counted on to do what was asked of her with pliant efficiency and without question. At JC Penny's and Target Drugs I purchased a big-hair wig, lavender miniskirt, white silk blouse, pantyhose and white heels high enough to give me vertigo. I laid the outfit on the bed heels to hair like a scary Halloween costume. Then I took a bubble bath. Nothing like a bubble bath to make a woman feel more like a girl.

Soaked and scented, I wedged tissue paper between my toes and painted my toenails a colour the bottle said was misty pomegranate, then did my fingernails to match. As the polish dried I replaced the multiple hoops in my right ear and the dagger stud in my left with a single pair of silver hearts my mom had given me on my sixteenth birthday. An eye-lash curler, eye-liner and mascara transformed my stark blue eyes into a pair of peacocks. It took a couple of tries to pin my hair back and settle the wig securely on my head. It felt so heavy I was half-afraid the thing would break my neck in a high wind. The wig was made from somebody else's hair blended with miracle synthetic and curled like a blonde waterfall down to my shoulders. In the product literature the manufacturer called this particular style the Dolly. In my skirt, blouse, earrings and wig I looked like one.

The only aspect of my appearance that seemed to throw the receptionist at Stone, Fell and Hughes was my hair, just about identical to hers in colour and cut, though I was pretty sure hers was not pre-owned. I asked, 'Could I speak with your Employment Opportunities Director please? Mr Finley asked me to come by.'

She pressed a series of digits with her palm flat against the board to avoid damaging her ultra-length crimson nails, spoke softly into her headset, then glanced up at me with a winning smile. 'If you'll have a seat, Mr Fielding will be out in just a minute.'

One minute stretched to twenty before a plump-faced forty-year-old with a cowlick and striped red tie popped through the door. His gaze travelled from my ankles to my eyes, taking several rest stops between, as he circled the reception desk to greet me. 'Miss?'

'Dahl, Miss Dahl.' I offered a limp-fingered grip and let my eyes go pleasantly blank when I smiled.

He wrapped my hand in a patronizing two-handed shake and sought to penetrate my character with a glance. 'Fielding here. Call me Jerry. Why don't we have a little talk in my office, hmmm?' He led me through an open-ceiling work area broken into a maze of cubicles. The walls were partitioned just low enough for some boss to nose over the top and see if you were playing computer games or really working. The bosses themselves had floor to ceiling walls and doors that closed. Mr Fielding was a boss.

'How do you know Mr Finley?' He made himself at home while perusing my résumé, kicking his oxfords up to the corner of his desk to recline near horizontal.

'Well, we met in the lobby and when I told him I was looking for employment he suggested I apply here.'

'Did he get your phone number?'

At first I didn't understand what he meant but then I did and knew just how to answer. I didn't say anything. I blushed.

Fielding grinned with *boys-will-be-boys* admiration. 'That's Finny.'

'That's what?'

'Finny. Mr Finley's nickname.' His eyes dropped back down to the résumé. He turned it over to confirm I'd written nothing on the back and tossed it on to his desk. 'I must hand it to him though, he chose well this time. The training and work experience all look good, and eighty-five words per minute is impressive.'

I certainly hoped it was. I'd invented the résumé that afternoon at a local copy shop that rented computers and printers by the hour, asked three different people what secretarial skills I should claim. A cat hopping across the keyboard could type more accurately than I.

'We don't have any immediate openings, but positions do pop up from time to time. If something does, I'll call and we'll arrange a formal interview to discuss responsibilities, salary, benefits – that sort of thing. And of course we'd administer a test to verify your word-processing and typing skills.'

I folded my hands on my lap and puckered my mouth to angles of prim righteousness. 'I expect to be tested. After all, if you don't verify the information I could claim just about anything, couldn't I?'

He made a sudden movement to place both feet on the floor and said, 'I'm happy you understand,' a signal the interview was over. He took my hand, prattled on about how grateful he was that I had chosen this company to apply to, and just as he released his grip said, as though forgetting something of small but still critical importance, 'Oh – I didn't see anything here about marital status?'

'Single,' I smiled. 'But still hopeful.'

He plucked a pen from the inside pocket of his suit as though ready to note that on my résumé and joked, 'Then so am I.'

Some joke.

As I stepped into the hall I asked with polite urgency, 'The little girl's room?'

He pointed to his right, no hesitation at all. 'Just around that corner, second door to your left.'

A woman about my age stood at the sink washing her hands when I pushed through the door. She bent her hips away from the sink to keep dry her knee-length grey skirt and matching jacket. Her mouse-brown hair had been trimmed in no-nonsense style just above her shoulders. She couldn't hide her smirk when I asked which office belonged to Mr Finley, but then, she didn't try. I was getting a feel for his taste in women. I fitted right in. Her directions were as precise as a blueprint. I thanked her, backed into a stall, lowered the toilet lid and dialled Frank. The answering service picked up – he'd turned off his cell phone. For two hours I entertained myself by reading the graffiti and flushing the toilet. 'The brighter the tie, the bigger the dick,' one line went. I wasn't sure what it meant but I agreed with at least one interpretation.

Out in the hall I heard the white noise of ventilation ducts, fluorescent tubes and electronic equipment but no voices and no footsteps other than my own. I passed the entrance, counted off the doors and stepped into an office twice the size of Fielding's. The pictures on the desk were all of Finley doing manly things with his buddies. Fielding said people called him Finny. With his dark hair and Euro-style, he could pass for Italian. When he was introduced people probably heard Vinny. Somebody like Piña would naturally slide the F to a V, to something she'd heard before. I picked the cell phone from my purse and tried Frank again.

He answered with a brusque 'Whaddyawant?' In the background, I heard clattering plates and conversation.

'Hey, you eating dinner? You alone?'

The line went dead. I touched redial, listened to the phone ring five or six times, hung up, touched redial again. This far into the evening, he needed to stay wired to any calls coming in. If he shut off his cell phone, he shut off his sources. When he finally picked up I said, 'I don't have a lot of time for phone games.'

'What was that you were playing last night?'

'Interviewing a witness.'

'You always interview witnesses on your back?'

He didn't mean it. He was angry. I let it go. 'I wasn't playing games. When I called you I didn't expect her to show up.'

'Her? I never figured you for a lesbian.'

'Sure, Frank. That's why I won't sleep with you. Get it now?'

He hung up on me again. I hit redial one more time. After fifteen rings I gave it up. In a city of nine million strangers I had one less friend. I sat in Finley's chair and looked around. It was a nice chair. With the controls to slide the seat, backrest and arms this way or that it had more moves than an amusement park ride. The bottom half of his computer screen looked like the best place to catch his eye. The envelope would be the first thing he saw when he entered the office. If he still worried about the photographs Gabe had taken, I'd leave him a colour photocopy of one and see what that stick did to his beehive.

His desk drawers looked like some manufacturer's display model, organized into neat sections for writing tools in one drawer and company letterhead in the next. A beige four-drawer filing cabinet took up the space between desk and wall. The top drawer sprang open to a tab labelled Tinseltown Estates. The file behind it ran to the back and didn't end until the middle of the third drawer down. I pulled out the first item behind the tab, a thick blue home-bound report titled *Tinseltown Estates – Where the Stars Shine Night and Day.*

A faint scratching of nails sounded at the door. I eased shut the drawer and sat, trying to look invited. The door slivered open to the startled face and doppelganger hair of the receptionist. Her first reaction was to back out of the office, forget she'd even seen me. She expected Finley and it didn't bode well that she came face to face instead with a blonde who could have been split from her same egg. But before she closed the door suspicion subverted jealousy and she said, 'You know you shouldn't be in here.'

'You're absolutely right, I mean, Finny's an hour late already and a girl's gotta have some self-respect, ya know?'

'I meant it's after hours, against the rules.'

'I didn't mean to break any rules. He just told me to wait in his office.'

'This isn't the way to get a job here. Not through Finny. A lot of girls come up here but none of them ever gets hired.'

Women are always tougher on each other than on anyone else. I knew what she was getting at. She was calling me a slut. 'I should be like you – get hired before I drop into his office late at night?'

'I think you should leave. If Mr Finley returns, I'll tell him you're waiting in the downstairs lobby.' She reached inside the office and shut off the lights.

31

Little Chapel of the Dawn packaged all six foot of Gabe into a cardboard box that wouldn't fit a pair of shoes. Not much remains after the water boils out; a hundred and seventy pounds reduced to ounces and a few mixed memories. The cardboard box rested on an oak table in the Little Chapel itself, amid twin vases spilling over with yellow roses. The house organist played 'God Save the Queen' while I walked down the aisle to retrieve the ashes. The funeral director stood at the back, hands folded and head lowered. In a place like Little Chapel of the Dawn even camp took on a solemn note. It was like Gabe and I were getting married again, only this time the vow wasn't unto death but into it. When I lifted the box it was still warm from the oven, like bread.

I was determined that death would not separate us, not yet. When I got the box into the Caddy I set him on the seat next to me and opened the plastic pouch, stamped Personal Effects, that the coroner had delivered with the body. The contents were barely plural: one leather wallet, water damaged; one set of glasses, black; and one Swatch, not waterproof. The wallet contained twenty-three US dollars and five English pounds, Visa and Blockbuster Video cards and a California driver licence. The absence of house or car keys meant whoever killed him used the keys to gain entrance into his apartment. I pulled the driver licence, set it aside with his glasses, his watch and a tube of super glue. The rest I tossed into the glove box.

Midway between the glove box and steering wheel, about the spot a hula doll would go, I super-glued Gabe's ashes to the dash. His glasses fitted the cardboard box like a face. Below the glasses, I fixed a playing card illustration of a daggered heart, and beneath that, his driver licence. Amid fragments of the amulet he'd given me I stuck his watch. I liked the way that expressed how time went bang. The shrine would be a work in progress, a place to pin my griefs and hopes. I said a little prayer for Gabe's soul to the plastic Jesus I attached to the top and asked forgiveness for all the bad things I'd done and even worse things I was certain to do in the future.

When Finley pulled within range the transmitter let out a little beep and a few minutes later I spotted his Land Cruiser racing down Wilshire. Finley was in the hurry, not me. He didn't have much time to beat the clock if he wanted to park and get up to his office before nine. The report on Tinseltown Estates lay folded open on my lap. The first page of the report began with a poetic pitch, layered over an architect's rendering of a hilltop housing development:

Tinseltown Estates

Where the stars shine night and day,
And the gentle smogless breezes play,
Your estate above the city rests,
Secure you've bought the very best.
With only the finest materials in use,
Each estate has magnificent views
And neighbours from the silver screen;
Life here is the best it's ever been!

Except for the dodgy rhyme of 'use' and 'views' it sounded pretty good to me; whoever wrote it could make a good living in the greeting-card business. Maybe Finley was a sensitive soul behind the executive façade, not that poetry made him any less likely a killer. Lots of women I knew at the Institute wrote poems and the prison poet laureate was a woman doing life times five for salting the potato salad with arsenic at her in-laws' Fourth of July picnic.

Page two looked pretty impressive, an artist's four-colour rendition of a tropical mountain rising from the arid basin of the city. On the opposite page, the project was described in prose:

Tinseltown Estates
'Where the stars shine night and day'

A visionary real-estate project destined in future years to be mentioned in the same breathless whisper with Beverly Hills and Bel Air, Tinseltown Estates is an exclusive residential community to be nestled amid 350 lush hillside acres on Mount Lee, with sweeping views over Lake Hollywood to Downtown, Universal City and the Pacific Ocean. Each custom home will be hand-crafted with only the finest materials and set amid winding country roads on two-acre tropically landscaped lots. Being driven up the halcyon slopes of Tinseltown Estates, high above the stress and noise of the city below, will be like coming home to heaven. And just as the stars shine in heaven, Tinseltown Estates will boast its own galaxy of luminaries, thanks to the exclusive partnership between its developers, Stone, Fell and Hughes Development Corporation, and its investor partners – all legends of the silver screen – the Tinseltown Players Corporation. And because security is of equal concern to executive, investor and celebrity alike, Tinseltown

Estates will be a gated community with its own highly trained internal security force and perimeter protection based on the most modern technology available.

Prices start at just $2.5 million.

A few pages into the report, the text listed the members of the Tinseltown Players Corporation. As corporations go it was a small one, just four men and one woman, but all five belonged to that exclusive club of actors whom the studios trust can open a picture from Kalamazoo to Katmandu on the strength of their name alone. Damian Burke was not the most famous name on the list but as an action-picture star who in his most recent role as the President's bodyguard single-handedly eviscerated forty-two neo-Nazis, thirteen Arab terrorists and a Stinger missile in full flight, his name was prominently displayed under the title, Special Security Consultant.

Finley bolted from his hole a few minutes before noon, blasting from underground parking in a wild screech of tyres that turned the head of the single pedestrian on the block. He wove wildly from lane to lane and cut up other drivers indiscriminately – acting like a typical LA driver in an upscale car – then swerved into a four-wheel skidding U-turn. The manoeuvre slowed a speeding pack of onrushing Mercedes and BMWs, which sounded their horns in appreciation of the opportunity to use their ABS braking systems and rack-and-pinion steering if not yet the air-bags. But Finley wasn't finished yet; he rocketed forward and darted to a squealing left turn across traffic, heading north toward Sunset Boulevard. I needed only to pull on to Wilshire and turn left to track him. He pushed the speedometer up to sixty, sixty-five between traffic lights like he thought the devil was on his tail. Maybe she was.

The roads branching east and west from Beechwood Canyon simultaneously climb elevation and income levels – the higher the elevation the higher the cost of the home – up to the ridge tops of the Hollywood Hills, where the city below glistens in miniature from skyscraper to sea like a model ready for camera. What the real-estate hucksters called 'million-dollar views' up here they meant literally; vacant lots listed at that price. The tracking system led me up one of these ridge tops to Finley's Land Cruiser, caged behind spiked gates painted Versace gold. A granite-paved drive curved through a neatly trimmed paradise of bougain-villea, hibiscus hedges and flawless lawn to rest at the feet of two huge topiary lions. The beasts had been grown to guard the steps leading to the Corinthian colonnade of Burke's California-Neo-Romanesque mansion, the kind of hyphenated architectural rubbish people with more money than taste have favoured in Los Angeles since its inception as loose-marble capital of the world.

Just beyond Burke's estate the road dead-ended against the eastern boundary of Griffith Park. I turned around at the cul-de-sac, noted the servo-cameras at the top of the golden gates and coasted down the hill to a classic split-level California bungalow, all straight lines and clean angles. A real estate company's For Sale sign speared the ground beside a stepped brick path. Ask for Peter St John! the sign urged.

I dialled the telephone number and did just that.

32

Peter St John sported a cheerfully tragic look about him, as though he had once entertained more glamorous ambitions than selling real estate but was determined to make the best of his disillusion. Something of the college thespian had lasted to his mid-thirties in the elaborate gentility of his gestures and the careful flair of his dress. From his jaunty step to the gold handkerchief that jutted just so from the breast pocket of his blue blazer it seemed he wished the character he played to convey better breeding than his own. He was certainly handsome enough to be an actor – a wispy Rogaine blond with square jaw and spacious blue eyes – but deviation from the script, such as me, gave him trouble.

Improvisation is the unteachable art of acting and St John in this regard was artless. I didn't look like the Miss Dahl he'd spoken to on the phone, personal assistant to a furniture magnate from Sweden. I didn't look like anybody's personal assistant except maybe Joan Jett's or Courtney Love's but the odds I had appeared randomly were considerably longer. He couldn't decide whether to retain his salesman mask, all cheery and welcoming, or his get-rid-of-a-lost-stranger face. Maybe his inability to improvise was why he was still selling real estate and not movie tickets. He leaned his shoulders forward, cocked his head courteously to the side, said, 'Miss . . .?.'

'Nina Zero.'

He tried to be just helpful enough to brush me off gently. 'If you're here to see the house I have an appointment with another client at the moment, but – '

'Miss Dahl won't be keeping the appointment.'

'She – ?'

'Gabriel Burns was my husband.'

He stepped back as though I was something communicable. 'I – I – I don't believe I know Mr Bu-bu-rns.'

His hands shook so bad I had to take the keys and open the door myself. Inside, the house was empty of all but floors and walls and the walls at the back were glass framing a view across the canyon and down to Hollywood. That view was all the furniture I'd ever need. St John locked and bolted the door and then fell back against it.

'You can't tell them about this.'

'Which *them* you talking about?'

'Anybody. Particularly my agency.'

I pointed him down a hall that led in the direction of Burke's property. The walls were neatly laid brick and the light fixtures on the ceiling were asymmetrical triangles blown from frosted glass. It was a really fine house. 'What, you got kids, afraid you'll get fired, they'll go hungry?'

'No, I don't live with, no, no kids. But I have house payments, car payments, my God, I just bought a new living-room arrangement direct from Milan.'

The hall extended past room after room with window walls facing the canyon and ended at a room so big I wanted to strap on a pair of roller blades. St John couldn't help himself. He reverted to his role and announced, 'The master suite.'

I guessed bedroom wasn't a grand enough word. Through the half-opened door into the bathroom I glimpsed something like a jacuzzi or sunken hot tub, my familiarity with the plumbing of the rich insufficient to tell me which. I walked across the floor to the brick wall at the far end, where I'd hoped to find a window looking on to Burke's estate.

'Tell me what happened the night my husband was here, the night before his body was found.'

'He, he was here that night?'

'That makes you very close to being an accessory to murder, doesn't it?'

The wall facing the canyon was glass brick at the ceiling and sliding glass doors at the parquet floor. I flicked up a latch and stepped on to a wooden terrace constructed on stilts over the descending hillside. To the north the land sloped down to Burke's estate, nestled against the back ridge of the canyon, then rose sharply to hilltops in Griffith Park. From the porch corner off the master suite I looked across thirty yards of landscaping directly into Burke's living-room windows.

'What was Gabe's deal with you? Straight cash or percentage?'

St John blurted, 'Excuse me just a moment,' and hurried into the bathroom. I crouched on my heels and examined the flooring for blood, scrape marks, a torn corner of yellow Kodak or green Fuji packaging, any sign at all that Gabe had been here and what had happened to him. The angle matched and the windows looked identical to the ones from the computer disk. With sticks, a telephoto lens and fast film he could have shot straight through the wall of glass that gave Burke his view down the canyon. Funny how people with windows rarely consider it's as easy to see in as out. The floor was clean, any evidence swept up or kicked over the edge or not left at all.

I rapped on the bathroom door to hurry St John along.

He called out, 'Busy!' I gave him another two minutes before I hammered again. His fair skin when he stepped out had bleached transparent and the blood beneath it blotched red and blue. Water dripped from his face and hands and soaked the collar of his shirt where he'd splashed himself at the sink and then remembered the house was empty – no towels. I didn't enjoy watching him suffer. The Westside of Los Angeles can be an expensive place if you want to live high because the people with money here have a lot of money and they live very high. The ones who pretend to have money but don't can fall with nothing between them and concrete poverty except a few terrifying seconds. When you lose your job the fall begins.

I took his elbow, led him on to the porch for some air, confided, 'I'd say I've got you by the balls but I'm not sure you have any.'

In a sudden, frustrated gesture he ripped the tails of his white shirt from his pants and used them to wipe his face. 'It was a percentage. He promised me ten per cent. Five to ten thousand dollars, he said, maybe more, just to let him have the keys for a night.'

'But then it turned into two nights.'

'Why didn't he just publish the damn pictures!' He jammed the shirt-tails into his pants but didn't get the button line straight and ripped them out again. 'Whose idea was it to blackmail them? Was it yours?'

'Who said it was blackmail?'

He dropped his hands to his sides, looked down at the wrinkled shirt-tails and pressed them flat against his trousers. 'Nobody. I just guessed that was it. When he didn't, you know, when I didn't see anything in the papers.'

'Gabe didn't tell you that was why he needed the keys? You just guessed he was blackmailing Burke?'

His head went sideways and then up and then down and sideways again in a confused figure eight. 'He didn't, no, he didn't tell me anything, but, hey, why else wouldn't, you know, the pictures be published? Had to be blackmail.'

Most people aren't good liars. White lies or even tinted ones are voiced without a stutter but when they lie about their own bad behaviour a direct question gives them gridlock. They sweat, their voice clamps like brakes on a wheel, they pretend to do something else when they lie so you can't see how bad they are at it. Sometimes it's only one thing that gives them away. With St John, it was everything, starting with his shirt-tails. When his hand dipped into his trousers again I slipped the back of my hip under his and yanked him down to the wood. Before he could kick I pulled his tie and swung my elbow into his face. The crack told me I'd hit my mark. I let go of his tie, stepped back. He rolled on to his knees, blood spurting from his nostrils.

'Oh God, lady, you broke my nose!'

'Well, now you can go to a plastic surgeon, get it fixed the way you've always wanted.'

He stayed on his knees and tried to stop the bleeding with a hand to his nostrils. The guy had no clue that sooner or later he'd bleed to death that way. I knelt next to him and put my arm on his shoulder. He tried to push me away. I gently eased him back toward the railing. 'Come on,' I encouraged him, 'sit on your butt, put your head back on the rail here, that's the only way to get the blood to stop.'

He was pliant as a child, leaned his head back and pressed his fingers against the sides of his nose like I showed him. I was sorry I hit him, it was like hitting a kid, I felt really bad about it. 'Peter,' I said, my voice sad, 'don't lie to me. I'm under a lot of pressure here. Do you know what I did this morning?'

He moaned that no, he didn't.

'I picked up my husband's ashes. Compared to that, your nose, your job, they just don't mean much. So please, who told you Gabe was blackmailing somebody?'

'If you tell them I talked, they'll kill me, OK? Well, maybe not kill, but, oh God, a broken leg for sure. And my job, well that's gone anyway, isn't it?'

'Shhhhh. I'm not going to tell them anything, OK? And if you say what happened, no lies, no omissions, I won't contact your work either.'

'It's all going to come out anyway. I mean, it's murder, right?'

'That's what the law says.'

'The guy next door, not Burke, the bodyguard. Earl. He said it was blackmail.' The truth was working its way loose, I could feel it, like an abscessed tooth. 'He knew someone had been here, he'd seen one of the photographs, and the angle, this was the only place it could have been taken from. Earl, he made me, my job, nothing I could do, he said he'd get me fired.'

'What did Earl make you do?'

'Give him a set of keys to the house.'

'What else?'

'Call him. You know, when, it, I mean I, when it – '

I stroked his brow, calmed him like a hurt child, whispered it was OK.

'When Burns asked to borrow keys again. I called Earl, told him he would be here that night.'

I left St John on the terrace, fingers pressed against his nostrils while he waited for the bleeding to stop. I couldn't hate him even though his phone call likely led to Gabe's murder. He didn't betray Gabe for any reason more venal than self-preservation. I don't think either of us had hard feelings about the other. I got what I needed to know and he got a broken nose to soothe the guilt of his betrayal. A fair trade, in my estimation.

Just beyond the bungalow's foundation the ice plant sloped sharply to leave such a wedge of air between the terrace and the ground that the fan-shaped plane of wood seemed about to sail into the canyon on a gust of wind. The ice plant provided good foothold at the roots but the leaves were thick and slippery and as I crept down the slope along the terrace pilings I had to kick and dig with each step. Beneath the edge of the terrace my eye caught scraps of cellophane, sun-faded strips of coloured cardboard, a Miller beer can, a clear plastic glass, and further than I thought it could have fallen, tucked into the ice plant so just the bottom rim poked out, an empty film box, Kodak-yellow and marked ASA 1000.

'Can I ask what you're doing down there?'

I glanced up to a little bull pawing the ground at the rear corner of the bungalow, just before the hill began its slope into ice plant. What he lacked in height he compensated in bulk, probably packed two hundred pounds into a five-foot-nine frame. Most of the body builders I've met are short of six feet, work out their Napoleon complexes with weights. He'd come out the same way I had, through an unlocked gate just to the side of the parking overhang.

I said, 'Sure, you can ask,' and slipped the film box into my pocket. I ran my hand over the top of the ice plant, found a cigarette butt and threw it further down to where the ice plant stopped and the hill steepened to hard-packed dirt over stone.

'Answer me!'

'I said you could ask. I didn't say I'd answer.'

He pointed his finger at me, even took a threatening step down the hillside. 'Get up here, now!'

It didn't take much to bait him, just a middle finger waved like a red cape and he charged down the slope. I let myself scream and hopped from one foot to the next like I was more afraid of falling than getting caught. The scream had some viscera in it; the guy was big and built and projected enough murderous testosterone to scare the teeth out of a rabid dog.

He wasn't bad on his feet for a wide one – I had to admire his sense of balance as he pounded through the ice plant – but after a dozen steps he was moving too fast to control his speed or lateral movement and when I planted my feet and sprung up slope I caught him at the ankle hard enough to give my shoulder a plum-sized bruise. He flailed out to grab any part of me he could reach but he was already flying; gravity gave him just enough time and space to tuck before he hit back first onto the hardpan dirt and loose rock at the ice plant's fringe. At that speed and angle the canyon slope provided just enough resistance to sandpaper him raw as he bounced and kicked but did not significantly slow him until he tore into a clump of sagebrush another dozen yards down. The combined drag of that and his fingernails clawing into sandstone finally stopped his momentum. I regretted that he'd halted short of a considerable drop off to the canyon bottom but without climbing down and pushing him the last couple of feet there was nothing I could do about it. He lay there for about twenty seconds, clinging to the rock and I hope thanking God he'd survived, before he slowly pushed himself up to hands and knees.

The best thing to do was get myself up the hill and gone before he came back to his belligerent senses. But I couldn't help myself, I had to say something. I called out, 'Hey Earl!'

His head wagged from side to side and slowly came up to fix me with a baleful stare.

'Next time, bring your sister!'

33

Madame Alex lived appropriately enough in 90069, a zip code that straddles the hills above Sunset Boulevard from Laurel Canyon to the border of Beverly Hills. By the look of her house – an old-Hollywood-style hacienda built into the hillside, shaded by the graceful fans of fifty-foot eucalyptus trees – the business of procuring for celebrities was a profitable one. The property didn't look anything like a bordello; even the neighbours might not know they lived next door to Hollywood's most notorious madam. I parked the Caddy on the opposite side of the street, slid over to the passenger seat and waited while the sky lit smog red and burned to cinder black. The only sign of activity inside the house occurred when an immense shadow blotted the single back-lit curtain draping the first floor window. Foot traffic in the age of out call and cell phones had been a naïve expectation. I looked up the number from my notebook and gave Madame Alex a call.

'Cass! How wonderful to hear from you again! I'm so very, very sorry about what happened the other night.'

I wondered what she meant by that. 'But I had a fabulous time! I was hoping to see Piña again tonight.'

'Forgive me, she's engaged. I have a very special girl I'd like to introduce to you.'

'I prefer Piña, thanks. What about tomorrow night?'

'She's not free, no. Now this girl, her name is Sindee and she's a beautiful blonde California girl.'

'I'd really like to see Piña.'

'I'm very, very sorry but Piña is very strict on this. She thinks you're wonderful but she just doesn't do water sports.'

'Water sports? Is that what she told you?'

'Please, Cass, we're women of the world. It's nothing to be ashamed of. It's just that some girls go for it and others don't.'

I said, 'Oh?'

'Now Sindee,' she confided, 'is a beach-bunny type, she surfs, she swims, she's very into water sports of *all* kinds.'

I cruised down the hill thinking Piña's message to back off couldn't be clearer. I wasn't likely to see her again, at least not professionally. Then the phone rang with Lester's voice at the end of the ether. He frequently called after sunset with a tip about some actor or another. His call didn't surprise me but his tone did. He called me Nina and with a slow, careful diction I hadn't heard from him asked me to stop by his office that evening. He'd not once called me Nina since our relationship began. He always called me Shooter.

'What, Lester, did the doctor change your medication? I mean, you always sound like you're on drugs, but this sounds like a whole different spectrum of narcotic.'

'No, Nina, I'm fine, I'm – I'm just a little tired. I have a cheque for you from *People* magazine. They made it out to you personally.'

'So?'

'You need to sign it over to the agency so we can run it through our accounts.'

I said I'd swing by in half an hour. The moment the connection closed my thumb punched out a number and two rings later a voice announced that I'd reached 911, emergency services.

'It's my boss. I think he's just had a heart attack. I was talking to him on the phone and after he said he had chest pains I heard him groan and there was this big thump like he'd fallen to the floor and now I can't reach him at all. Can you send – '

'What's the address where your boss is now?'

I gave it, with his name and mine. I wasn't absolutely certain something was wrong but why else would Lester invent a story about picking up a cheque? He was very strict about money. Every time somebody bought one of my photographs they paid the agency, which took its percentage and then passed the rest to me. Any cheque made out to me directly would be returned to sender.

Lester's suite was accessible through a rear door that opened directly on to the parking lot. Running a paparazzi agency is a night business, with photographers dropping off film well into the blue hours just before dawn. Lester needed that back door to take deliveries. By the looks of the broken glass in the lobby and the still-ringing burglar alarm the paramedics hadn't known about it and had crashed through the front.

The back door swung open to a short hallway. Through the wedge of space between the door to his office and the jamb I watched two hunks in medical whites kneel over five-foot-two Lester, stretched prone on the carpet. A cervical collar wrapped his neck and a beige strip of foam curved around his skull from jaw to forehead. One paramedic prodded his chest while the other prepared a bandage to apply to a cut above his eye. Lester yelped when the paramedic pressed his rib-cage.

I poked my head around the door. Two of the three fax machines had been knocked to the carpet and the light table upended with enough force to break the glass. Over by the desk paper and film swamped the floor ankle deep. Each of the four file cabinets had been emptied of prints and negatives and then toppled.

The paramedic pulled his hands back to rest flat on his thighs and glanced up at me with patient brown eyes. 'Are you a relative?'

'I made the call to 911.'

'I gotta admit ma'am, this is the strangest-looking heart attack I've ever seen.' He tried to be serious about it but when he got a good look at me the lower half of his face split into a smile. He kept his hair clipped short and a stubble of strawberry blond on his very square jaw. He had a gravity to him that came from saving lives every day and I liked that.

'If you knew he'd been assaulted why didn't you just report that?'

'I didn't know he'd been assaulted.'

'Then why call?'

'He sounded like he had a gun to his head. If I'd called the cops and said I think my agent might be in trouble they would have sent someone around in what, four or five hours?'

He admitted I had a point.

I knelt next to Lester, afraid to touch him. That he'd been attacked was my fault. Had he never met me he'd still be pacing the room with his usual manic fervour. I owed him for his pain and I'd pay that debt when I paid Gabe's. 'Did you recognize them? Just yes or no.'

'The bastards wore ski masks. Jesus, they really trashed the place, didn't they? Something about a set of negatives.

When they didn't find those they wanted you. I had to make that call.'

I put my finger to his lips. 'You held out the best you could.'

The paramedics rolled him gently to one side and slipped the stretcher beneath his hips and shoulders. His eyes glimmered not with physical pain but shame. 'I didn't hold out two minutes,' he said. 'I didn't have the courage to last even that long.'

While the emergency room personnel at St John's Hospital patched Lester together again I walked down the street to an all-night drugstore. The masks concealed the faces of his assailants but not their identities. I'd taunted Earl that afternoon. The real-estate agent had told him who I was, what questions I'd asked. Lester was payback. My imagination hummed with fantasies of ringing the bell at the gate to Burke's estate and shooting whoever came out to answer. It made me feel better but didn't solve any problems except the immediate craving for revenge. I bought a case of weight watchers' liquid diet and a box of straws for Lester's broken jaw and a canister of pepper spray for me. I couldn't risk carrying a gun in my duffel bag but against a guy the size of Earl I'd need something more than my fists.

Two fractured ribs hurt Lester to walk no less than his compression-braced and wired jaw hurt him to talk. Still, he managed better than twenty words a step up the stairs of his West Hollywood apartment, mostly about how happy he was to secure a legal prescription for Percodan. He wanted to know why two goons should beat the hell out of him looking for negs shot by an English paparazzo. Didn't they know Gabe was represented by Crash Foto? I took his keys and half-carried him through a spare and tidy living-room on to a four-poster bed.

'Not the boots, clean sheets.' He tried to bend and unlace the big-heeled Doc Martens that boosted him up to five-foot-four. I held him back with a hand on his shoulder, slipped off first one boot, then the other. He allowed me to unbutton and remove his shirt but tried to paw me away from stripping off his jeans.

'I've seen plenty of naked men so don't think you've got anything special to hide.' Underneath his jeans he was all fur, like a little bear. I guided his feet beneath the down comforter.

'You're the first woman to see me naked since my mother.'

I was about to tell him nobody's sex life is that bad when I noticed the Robert Mapplethorpe and Bruce Webber prints. His sex life had nothing to do with women. 'Our loss,' I said.

'Right.' He giggled until the pain stopped him. 'If short, skinny and hairy guys ever come into style I'm going to be a ten.'

Like many Santa Monica apartment buildings from the early 1960s, the one in which Frank lived enclosed a central courtyard landscaped with browned evergreen hedges and an amoeba-shaped swimming pool. The Southern California fascination with space and stardom was captured by gold glitter rolled into the structure's stucco façade and in the name, originally the Stardust Apartments until some wag reversed the central d to spell out Starbust. Frank lived on the second floor, up a set of concrete steps flanked by wrought-iron railing. It took five minutes of applying my knuckles to the wood to rouse him and when the door did snap open his body blocked the wedge at the jamb. I felt about as welcome as a Jehovah's Witness peddling copies of *Watchtower* door to door.

'You going to let me in?' I hoisted the tray of coffee and breakfast pastry I'd brought to improve my reception.

'Let's go down to the pool.'

I followed him to a splash of morning sun at the base of the stairs, where he unbuttoned his Chicago Blackhawks windbreaker and collapsed into a plastic chair. For a man who couldn't run more than fifty yards without stopping for a cigarette he showed a lively interest in sports apparel. 'This weather is sick,' he complained. 'Middle of December and you can sunbathe.'

'Next you're going to tell me you miss the seasons.'

'No, I'm gonna tell you we'll all die of skin cancer.' Frank took a muffin and cup of coffee from the tray and lit a cigarette. 'The cops, they say anything since you gave them the disk?'

'Not a word. You still think I made a big mistake in handing it over?'

He blew a stream of blue smoke toward the pool, home-sick for the kind of breath you can see in cold weather. 'Yeah, I do. Any chance you can see me as a really mascu-line-looking woman so we can sleep together?'

The blankness of his expression betrayed the joke. If he could joke about it, our friendship would survive. I said, 'Depends on how cute you look in a dress.'

'I'm bow-legged and hate to shave my legs so I guess that means we gotta change the rules of engagement here.'

'How so?'

'I don't need you to play me for a sucker. Don't get me wrong, I like you, but it's not like I'm in love with you. Not saying I couldn't be if something like that was to happen. If, say, one night we were to find each other humping like bunnies, I'd probably be the happiest guy in town. But I still have a life. You gotta give me tit for tat here.'

'What exactly you looking for?'

'The story. I wanna write about Danavitch and Burke.'

'You want to steal Gabe's story.'

'You don't know he was writing a story. Not really. Just as likely he was blackmailing both of them. I'll even wait until you decide to publish the photographs. In return, I'll answer your questions, tell you what I learn from my inves-tigation. And if I can keep your husband's name out of the story, I will.'

I stared at the thin layer of scum forming along the surface of the pool, wondering how I could tell him no and not lose his help.

'I don't need your permission for this,' he said. 'I saw the images on the disk. I can write the story without you.'

'You'd do that?'

'You know the definition of a Hollywood friend? Someone who stabs you in the front. Yeah, I'd do that. But not without warning you.'

Reluctantly, I offered my hand across the gap between our chairs. I couldn't stop him from writing the story by refusing to cooperate but by agreeing I could influence what came out when. Frank stuffed a chunk of muffin into his mouth, wiped his hand on the breast of his windbreaker and we shook on the deal. No reason I had to tell him everything I knew. If he found out what I knew on his own, fine.

'I want to know about Danavitch,' I said. 'I know what the mayor is supposed to do, but not the board of supervisors.'

'The mayor rules the city of Los Angeles and about three million people. LA County has, what, nine, ten million people? The supervisors' jurisdiction includes Los Angeles the city, plus another eighty incorporated cities. That's a lot of power for just five people.'

'Exactly what do they supervise?'

'Just about every government service you can think of. The sheriff department, fire department, animal control – '

'What about building permits?'

'Even better than building permits, they control zoning. In most areas the supervisors dictate what the land is used for – residential, commercial or open space. As you can imagine, real estate development companies are major contributors to the supes' election campaigns.'

'So if some company wanted to build a hundred homes

somewhere in the city the first step would be to get the land zoned for new residential construction, and the supervisors could do that, is that it?'

'All it takes is a majority of three. Each supervisor runs his district like a fiefdom. In most zoning matters, the supervisors yield to the one whose district is directly impacted.'

'Sort of like, you don't pee in my backyard, I won't pee in yours?'

'Exactly. You think Danavitch was in the pocket of this real estate company you mentioned a couple nights ago?'

A cell phone rang. Frank and I reached simultaneously into our jacket pockets, a moment repeated throughout the city a thousand times a day. Frank made a face at me when the next ring sounded in my hand and not his.

'Hey girlfriend, I hear you were looking for me.' The voice was young but already scratched at the edges. Piña's voice.

'Still am.'

'You called to tell me you found the negatives, right?'

I moved to the far end of the pool and spoke softly. 'Not yet. I want to see you again.'

'Jus' business or you wanna get cosy?'

'I want to talk about the night Gabe was killed.'

'That's a pop'lar topic. You got competition, girlfriend.'

'What do you mean, competition?'

'A journalist wants to talk 'bout the same thing.'

I turned and burned a look into my colleague across the pool. 'Is his name Frank Adams?' Frank glanced up at the mention of his name, a 'Who me?' expression above the half-muffin wedged in his mouth.

'Somebody else. I shouldn't even tell you but I want to be honest 'bout it. Ten grand just to talk.'

'And you're thinking about accepting?'

'Yeah. Maybe a little more than thinking.'

'You've already accepted.' Her no answer was all the answer I needed. 'Why are you acting like such a . . . such a . . .'

'Whore?' She didn't say the word without bitterness.

'I thought you were Gabe's friend, maybe we might be friends too.'

'I got expenses, y'know?'

'Meet me before you meet him. At least do me that favour.'

'You're too persuasive in person, girlfriend. If you don't seduce me, you'll beat me up.'

'Then name the place you feel safe from both.'

The sound of her laugh came across the line like rustling leaves. 'No place on earth. But y'know the Tower Records on Westwood Boulevard? I might see you there 'bout four. Maybe I'll tell you then why I think Gabe had a partner nobody knows about.'

'What partner?'

She hung up without answering. I slipped the phone back into my side pocket and walked back to Frank's side of the pool to collect my duffel. 'The area around Lake Hollywood, is that, whose district is that?'

'Danavitch's. His district begins in the Hollywood Hills and stretches west to Santa Monica. But where you goin'?'

'Something just came up.'

'You gonna tell me about Stone, Fell and Hughes?'

I walked backwards a few steps, imitated a phone with my thumb and little finger and said, 'Later.' Out in the car I turned off my cell phone. Like I said, if he wanted to write a story that was fine but I didn't have to help him.

I took surface streets to Westwood and caught up on my sleep in a shady corner of the UCLA Medical Centre parking lot. At two dollars for all-day parking, it was the cheapest hotel in town if you brought your own sheets. The Caddy's big bench seat was so comfortable I didn't drag myself up when my wrist watch alarm sounded and didn't get to Tower Records until a quarter past the hour. I browsed the CD stacks while I waited for Piña to show, glancing at every fresh face to swing through the door. I was disappointed but not really surprised when none of those faces were Piña's. The easiest way to blow somebody off is to agree to meet and then fail to show. She didn't owe me anything, at least nothing worth ten grand. She'd told me someone else was willing to pay for the story. That was favour enough. On my way past the cash register I picked up a copy of 'Lady In Satin', Billie Holiday's final recording, in which gin and cigarettes have damaged her voice as much as pain and longing had long scarred her heart. When I needed her pain to feel my own, I'd buy a bottle of bourbon and listen to it.

But just at that moment I had someone else's pain in mind.

35

I don't believe you can judge a man by what he drinks but you can tell a lot about someone's character and aspirations by where they choose to drink, no matter whether it's milk or vodka filling the glass. The zinc and blue resin bar where Finley stopped after work buzzed with those perfect people you find in LA who by the age of thirty have yet to acquire a wrinkle or lose one strand of hair, as though they regularly send not just their clothes but their entire bodies out to be dry cleaned. In the crush of the bar scene they tried to pick each other up, waved about nouvelle nothings from the adjacent restaurant, or, in a few desperate, isolated instances, actually drank. Finley had entered alone and after he spoke a few words to a brunette who quickly fled I guessed that he had not come to eat and, by the pale green bottle of Pelegrino on the bar before him, certainly not to drink.

I hooked the Caddy into the back alley and found a parking slot behind a beauty salon closed for the night. A caged security light illuminated the back door and in fading arcs diminished to darkness at the far slot. It was a good spot for bad business. I touched up my face by the light on the vanity mirror, circled to the trunk and dolled myself up in the blonde wig, a Wonder Bra and tight-fitting black cocktail dress guaranteed to flick the tongue of Finley's reptilian brain. Before locking the car I stashed the pistol under the seat and the tyre iron under the lip of the trunk, just to the side of an artist's portfolio stocked with photos of naked blondes.

I didn't blame the men for looking when I walked into the bar; I couldn't have advertised myself better with neon and half-price stickers. I slipped through the crowd, deflected the offer of a drink, nudged up to the bar next to Finley and ordered a Jack Daniel's neat, water back. I focused on the movement of the bartender's hands as he poured the bourbon and set it down before me. Then I allowed myself to glance to the mirror behind the bottled bar and, just as I figured, Finley was staring. When he caught my eyes he smiled.

'That's a strong drink for a little lady.'

'This little lady has just worked a *long, hard* day under *hot* lights and she needs a *stiff* drink.'

That turned his attention full frontal. Finny was designer slick from Bruno Magli foot to Armani cuffs. I could see how some women would think him attractive. He was tall enough to look up to and his eyes were nice in a lost-little-boy way and he certainly dressed like he had some money in his creased trousers. Finley was like a lot of LA guys in their mid-twenties to late thirties regarding the importance he placed in surface values, from the clothes he wore to the car he drove and the bar he patronized after work; some people do not mature into themselves so much as construct an image of who they want to become and then imitate it. Trying to hold a conversation with one of these is like talking to a twelve-year-old boy behind a Tom Cruise mask. He looks good and he sure can smile but behind that it's all zits and caca jokes. The lenses of Finny's Armani glasses looked so thin I wondered if they corrected not a defect of vision but image; like the Pelegrino water at his side they served no useful purpose except to suggest he was a serious person, perhaps even intellectual.

The notion that he was intellectual was promptly dispelled by his next conversational gambit, which was to ask the quintessential LA question, the one strangers inevitably ask of each another within a minute of meeting in this town. 'What kind of job do you, I mean, what do you do?'

I told him I was a model. Men like models in the same way they like marlins and other beautiful creatures: as something to catch and stuff.

'A beautiful girl like you, I'm not surprised. What sort of model are you, I mean, what do you model?'

'Nothing particular,' I said. 'I just, you know, model.'

'No, no, let me guess then. You're a product model, one of those women whose hands we see holding the dish detergent or the shapely legs inside a pair of nylons. Am I right?'

I giggled like I thought he was awfully charming. 'No, you're wrong.'

He stepped back, took our little game as an excuse to eyeball me toes to hair. I was a little short of five foot ten and my style less than *haute couture* but he wasn't interested in accuracy at that point; he wanted to get laid. 'You're a fashion model.'

I swung my blonde curls back and forth like a veil. 'Wrong again. I definitely don't model with clothes, I mean, sometimes I'll wear heels and a garter belt but it's not exactly like Victoria's Secret if you understand what I'm saying, the underwear is not the thing.'

'You model in the nu – I mean you, magazines, that sort of modelling?' The question came out in spurts, like he had a sudden problem controlling his breath.

'Magazines, yeah, I've done a lot of magazine work, but

most of the money now is in video.' Then I remembered that little move Piña made, where she put her hands behind her neck and stretched. So I did that too and said, 'I guess you could say what I model is myself.'

'Well, that's – ' his glasses slipped down his nose in the sudden flush of hormones and with a deft movement of his forefinger he poked them back into place ' – that's just, yes, really interesting, just fascinating, really.'

'The way I look at it, God gave me this body, and it's like I'm an athlete, he didn't give me a beautiful body to hide it away, he gave it to me to share with others.'

'I think, yes, that's very generous.' The way he looked at me it was like I was an open net with no goalie, no way he could miss this one. 'Maybe I've seen you?' He closed his eyes and shook his head, afraid I'd get the wrong idea. 'I mean, I don't subscribe to a lot of magazines, or watch a lot of, well, videos, but maybe? I've seen you? In one of your spreads, I mean layouts, I mean, what would you call it?'

'Pictorials.'

'Pectorals! Of course! Maybe I've seen one of your, uhh, *pic*torials, though again, I don't really look at those things, I mean I look at them but not all the time?'

I put my hand on his arm to calm him. 'Let me, no, you wouldn't have seen *that* one, but how about *Playboy*? October '98? The girl-girl pictorial? I wanted the centrefold, you know, it's good exposure when you get to be the *peeoh'em* – sorry, that's show-biz speak for Playmate of the Month – but I guess just being featured is honour enough.'

'*Playboy*, I mean, wow, that's the top end of the business isn't it? No, no, I think it's just, fabulous, really, that you were in any part of the magazine, I mean, if you want my opinion, they really made the wrong decision there, you should have been the centrefold, but, yes, I mean, just getting in at all.'

I didn't make it sound like a come on, like once we got to the car I'd ask him for money. I knew enough about women who took off their clothes for a living from my time in stir. Sure, some hate themselves, but some are professionals, proud of their skills and how good they look, even if they're usually doing so many drugs they don't look that way for long. 'Hey, you know I have my portfolio out in the car, maybe I could – no, I can't bring it in here – but maybe I could show it to you, out in my car?'

Finley answered by signalling the barman and tossing a twenty on to the zinc. 'I'd really like that, I mean, I think what you do is really interesting and I have an idea, I'm really hungry, maybe we could go, get something to eat?'

I gave him my arm, let him lead me out of the bar. I'm sure he thought he was a real wolf and I was some lamb, yum yum juicy, he was going to have himself a nice meal. On the way to the alley we had not one single awkward moment until we reached the trunk and I picked the keys from my clutch-purse.

'It's kind of dark,' he observed.

I smiled up at him and popped the latch. 'Don't worry, I have a good trunk light.'

I reached across him with my left hand to flip open the portfolio to the first page, the movement screening my right hand as it gripped the tyre iron under the lip of the trunk. The portfolio featured an anonymous blonde who, considering the contortions of her body and the angle of the shots, could have passed for me or any other blonde. Naturally, Finley bent over the trunk to get a closer view and when he did that I didn't have to hit him very hard, just a tap above the join between neck and skull and he toppled into the trunk so neatly all I had to worry about was the legs sticking out. I patted down his coat, removed his keys, wallet and cell phone and folded him up like a suitcase. At the top of the dumpster across the alley the green of a cat's eyes glowed curious but wary.

'That's the way you catch a mouse,' I said.

She skittered off the dumpster when I started the engine. I marvelled that my hands didn't shake much at all, said to Gabe in his cardboard box, 'You know, I really have a talent for this, one small twist of motive and I could be a real criminal.' Then I laughed, because by almost any reading of the legal code I was a real criminal. I'd committed and been convicted of crimes, done time and after my release committed more crimes. Hell, I wasn't just a criminal, I was a recidivist. I shouted my laughter like a victory cry, heard an echo coming from the back of the car, a muffled scream. I turned on the radio to a college radio station playing trip hop, turned it up full blast and cruised.

The only sign of the planned development on the mountain above Lake Hollywood was the newly graded dirt curving away from the main fire road. Anybody driving up the dead-end street and stopping at the locked access gate would think the cut just another fire block. In the swirling dust of the Cadillac's high beams I flipped through Finley's key chain until I found the one that sprung the gate's padlock. Overhead the scissors-bright wings of an airliner sliced through the moonlit sky, trailed by the fabric-ripping sound of its engines. In the mountain beyond the gate the brush rustled and chirruped with a hundred species of animals and reptiles. To the unpractised eye the terrain might have seemed barren but even that small patch of remaining desert teemed with prickly pear, mariola, cholla and sand verbena among the rough and choking scrub brush. A mountain range rippled through Los Angeles like a spine and despite the steady encroachment of civilization the hills remained wild with coyotes and owls, which feasted on neighbouring cats and small dogs as often as jackrabbits.

At the hard lateral edge of the Caddy's headlights the gashed hillside spilled off the road in fresh clumps of dirt and uprooted brush. No rain had fallen since the road was cut and no living thing yet had taken root or tramped the churned soil. As the road corkscrewed around the mountain

it ascended to ever more spectacular views of the surrounding land and city, passing the four points of the compass from
Universal City to the west through Burbank and Griffith Park
to Hollywood in the south. At the peak the road terminated
in a circle of graded earth and the intended future home of
Tinseltown Estates.

I got out of the car and climbed over the rocks to where
the land sheered away to a radiant scape of lights. From that
height Los Angeles was among the most beautiful cities in
the world, a luminescent grid of neon displays and street
lights cut by rivers of bright white and flashing red. Traffic
flowed from one far horizon to the other, branching through
diminishing streams to a single pair of headlights cruising
a residential street. To the east and west the city lights had
no visible end, as though glass, filament, trace vapours
and electricity had vanquished the earth's landscape. To the
opposing sides of north and south the lights scattered to
darkness up the imposing wall of the San Gabriel Mountains
or into the immense black sheet of the Pacific Ocean.

The mountain top above Lake Hollywood was the
geographic core of this megalopolis of light. The valleys at
the base of the mountain cradled the Southern California
film industry, from Warner Brothers, NBC and Disney in
Burbank to Paramount Pictures and the thousand small
production companies of Hollywood itself. In the parlance of
real estate agents the mountain had the defining element
of the Southern California good life: location, location, location. And when the end came, as it must even for the richest
and most famous, the mountain sloped conveniently into the
manicured green of Forest Lawn Memorial Park, the final
venue of choice for those who could afford it.

I made a pile of Dolly on the passenger seat, adding blonde

curls to the heels and black cocktail dress. I dressed for a violent bit of business: dark jeans and a lightweight polyester pullover anonymous enough to toss aside if bloodstained. I felt beneath the seat for the revolver and checked the cylinder. One spent bullet in five. I left the spent casing in its chamber, flipped the cylinder shut, leaned back against the seat and closed my eyes to focus on what I needed to do. The thumps and shouts from the trunk had quieted to an occasional anguished cry for help. From the back seat I lifted a brand new gardening spade, carried it to the front of the Caddy and chopped it into the ground. The spade was short with a rectangular blade. It would make a good weapon if he tried to use it that way. But I didn't think he'd try. If he did, I'd shoot him. I held the revolver against my thigh, popped open the trunk and stepped back.

When his eyes peeped above the rim of the trunk he whispered, 'You're *her*, aren't you?'

'Which her you talking about?'

'The one who – who – who – who – ' he closed his eyes and a little shudder rattled his gelled black curls ' – put Grimes in the hospital.'

'This is Grimes' gun, so if I shoot you, he'll take the fall for it. You on good terms with him?'

'N-n-n-n-no.' The word shook from his mouth.

'Then you should do what I say so you don't get shot, don't you think? Take off your shoes, socks too, and climb out of the trunk.'

He was very obedient. I got no bad vibes from him at all, just fear. His shoes were the slip on and off kind that had little tassels above the toes. When his bare feet came down on to the desert soil he grimaced and shifted his weight to find a foothold without rocks or burrs. 'I – I want to apologize.' His glasses had twisted off one ear and first looking at me to see if it was OK he took both hands and set them straight again.

'What are you apologizing for?'

'Grimes. If he said or did anything to make you upset.'

'Apologies are lousy compensation. I don't accept apologies.'

'Fair enough. But still, this gun, there's no reason for that. I've raised most of the money. We've been waiting to hear from you.'

'What money are you talking about?'

A smile wrenched the corner of his mouth, like I was testing him with a question so easy it had to be a trick. 'The two hundred and fifty grand. I mean, for the pictures, right?'

'You think I'm blackmailing you.'

'Yes, well, blackmail is a harsh word, but, ummmm, aren't you?'

'Let's take a little walk.'

Finny peered around the darkness. 'Where?'

'Follow the headlights.'

Take almost any city boy and walk him barefoot through the desert and you'll understand how the word tenderfoot came about. Finny didn't so much walk over the barbed earth as try to hop above it on the tips of his toes. I didn't take any pleasure in his torment. His torment was just beginning. The sight of the spade arrowed into the ground stunned him into a terrified stillness.

I circled to stand in the glare of the headlights. 'Pick it up.'

He forgot how rough the ground was, took one step and another with no herky-jerk in his legs at all. He squinted at me, slack-jawed, then turned back to stare at the shovel. He couldn't bring himself to reach out and touch it.

'The night before they fished my husband from the lake you attended a sex party at Damian Burke's estate.'

'I can't, I wasn't, you can't really mean this, can you?'

I didn't point the gun at him, I just tapped it against my thigh to remind him it was there. 'Pick up the shovel.'

He looked at the gun, then the shovel, then the gun again before reaching with heart-sick reluctance to grasp the handle. 'This is ridiculous! I mean, what, I'm supposed to be digging my own grave here? I wasn't even there the whole time, just the start, I didn't have anything to do with, I wasn't there at the end.'

'Are you nervous because you're an accessory to murder? Or because you were an active participant?'

'I didn't, I didn't, I mean, it wasn't supposed to end like that, look, I never imagined anything like that would, what happened, it just, boggles.'

'Dig,' I commanded.

Though the steel is hot rolled into a curl the back rim of a shovel is not designed for the bare foot. It's not easy to dig a hole in hard dirt without boots or shoes. Each of the organs is connected to a particular spot on the sole of the foot, and when you put the arch of your foot to the back rim of a shovel and kick down you can feel it up through your hip and into your kidneys. I didn't expect Finny to dig all that fast. I just wanted him to dig.

'I'm a fair-minded person. Maybe you could tell me why I shouldn't believe you hired Grimes to get my husband deported, and when that didn't work, had him killed?'

'No, really, I'm not a violent guy, the whole idea of blood makes me just, incredibly nervous, I mean' – he leaned the shovel against his hip and held his trembling hands out straight – 'are these the hands of a killer?'

'Don't give me acting. Everybody in this town can cry on cue. Give me reasons. Start with the night Gabe took pictures of Danavitch.'

'I'm, I'm, I'm, I have to throw up, OK?' He barely had time to bend at the waist. His face swelled to a terrible, bloated red and when his stomach wrenched again and again he gasped with the strangled panic of a drowning man.

I'm not a sadist. I didn't enjoy watching him suffer. Part of me wanted to put my hand on his shoulder, tell him he was going to be OK. Some people are capable of killing but most aren't and if I read Finny right he was part of the most. But he knew what happened and his silence made him complicit. So I didn't say anything, didn't do anything except wait while he wretched and fumbled at the last for a handkerchief to wipe his mouth. Sometimes you have to spill a little fluid if you want to get the sickness out.

'Dig,' I said.

He scrambled to retrieve the shovel and scratched the blade against dirt. The faltering edge of the headlight beams cast his face in shadow. He was crying, I think.

'Tell me about the night with Danavitch.'

'I can't, I mean, I wasn't there, I, I only learned what happened the next morning, when Earl called. He said he'd seen something next door, noted the licence plate, wanted it traced and I had a guy who could do that. Earl is Burke's – '

'I know who Earl is. So you called Grimes.'

'I did, yes. Information like that, it's his, his business. He asked somebody at the DMV to run the plates and when Burke heard they belonged to a photographer it was like somebody had, I don't know, driven a stake through his heart. Earl wanted to go kill the guy right away, but that's just Earl, I mean, he always wants to kill something.'

I barely heard his voice over the scraping of the shovel as he dug. He wasn't making much progress. About three inches under the topsoil the mountain turned to hardpan so solid he'd need a pick-axe to break it up. 'Drop the shovel and kneel down in the dirt.'

'Lady, no, I mean, I'm telling you everything, don't, please, I'll, no, it's not fair, I'll do anything you want just don't, don't . . .' He dropped the shovel and kneeled.

I figured I had his full cooperation then. No need to torture him any further. It wasn't mercy that moved me. I would have kept him digging all night if it served my purpose. I stood out of the glare of the headlights and let him see me as a human being. I even smiled at him. 'I don't want to hurt you, not if I can help it, but I really need your help on this, because some things I just don't understand.'

'Can I, can I help?'

'First thing I don't understand is the dog. Put ten men in a room with ten hookers, make it a freebie and seven would do something illegal. But bestiality is a whole different category, isn't it? No question in most people's minds, it's not simply perverse, it's a violation of humanity, not to mention the poor dumb animal. So when I first saw the pictures of that girl and her dog, I thought these had to be the dumbest, sickest people alive.'

Finny nodded aggressively, he wanted to leave me in no doubt he agreed, he said, 'Yes, yes, yes.'

'But then another thought kept going around in my head, What if it wasn't stupid? What if Finley had set it up to blackmail Burke and Danavitch?'

'No no no, not me, I didn't set up anything, I don't have those kinds of thoughts. Burke told me he was going to party with Danavitch and the girls and I did guess by that he meant prostitutes but no, blackmailing him wasn't my idea and I didn't learn about the dog until later. I mean, stupid, stupid, stupid.'

'Why would Burke need to blackmail Danavitch?'

'Not blackmail, no, wrong word. Insurance. That's the way Burke put it. Danavitch was just mesmerized by the Hollywood thing, that was how we got him to commit to Tinseltown Estates in the first place. But he was starting to flip-flop on the zoning issue, promising us it was a done deal one day and then complaining that it would kill him politically if he pushed it through the board. Burke wanted to make sure he didn't back out of the project.'

'Why would it hurt him politically?'

'Half the no-growth nuts in the state live in his district. I mean, you've heard of the People's Republic of Santa Monica? To the real estate community, the entire Westside is the Union of Soviet Socialist Communities. No matter how much we donate to his campaigns, Danavitch has to pretend to be a low-growth politician, and, well, just look at where we are. This is the biggest privately held plot of undeveloped mountain land between the city centre and the Pacific Ocean.'

'What would happen if you lost Danavitch?'

'We'd lose the project.'

'I still don't get what Burke was thinking. Danavitch could just deny it, you know, a dog, nobody would believe it. Did he expect to use the girls as a witness?'

He bit his lower lip and shook his head like he really didn't want to say this but he did anyway. 'Well, no, there were the video tapes.'

'What video tapes?'

'Burke has the whole house wired for video. You can't even use the facilities without some camera peeping you.'

I laughed at that. Burke didn't have a moral problem with blackmail, he just didn't like being on the receiving end. The way I was laughing, Finny didn't look too comfortable; he kept inching away from me a kneecap at a time.

'You start with the idea of blackmailing Danavitch and get blackmailed by somebody else. I'm sorry, I just think that's funny. How did the blackmailer contact you?'

He gulped at the air, swallowed, gulped again. 'Something came in the mail first, not the photographs themselves but, what do you call it, when all the pictures are really small and on one page?'

'A proof sheet.'

'Right, that's it. Then a few days later, Earl fielded a call from someone who claimed to have access to the negatives.'

'And you assumed it was the same guy who took the photos?'

'We thought it might be his partner but we really didn't know. This voice on the phone, he didn't make it sound like blackmail, he just said he knew how damaging they could be if published and he wanted to help us. He thought he could broker a deal, get the photographer to give them up for a price. According to Earl, he made it sound like he was doing us a favour.'

'How much?'

'A million bucks.'

At least Gabe hadn't died for a pittance. That much money could turn almost anyone into a blackmailer – or a murderer. 'And you were going to contribute, what, the two-hundred and fifty thousand?'

'No, that came later.'

'A separate blackmail demand?'

Finny looked hopeful, expecting now to live. He nodded

like a beaten dog wags its tail. 'Three days after the, you know, the body was found.'

'The same voice?'

'No voice at all. A written note this time, like the kind you see in the movies, with the letters all cut up out of newsprint? That was why I sent Grimes after you. I thought you had inherited the negatives and were trying to make a new deal. I mean, aren't you?'

'Why would I need a new deal?'

'Your husband, maybe you thought my company would be safer to blackmail because, because . . .'

'The first deal got my husband killed.'

'Exactly. Seems logical, right? I mean, right?'

'Tell me about the night you murdered my husband.'

'No, not me. I didn't, I didn't set it up. I was just, like, there.'

'Who set it up?'

'Burke. The party was a trap. But nobody ever said anything about, oh God, I mean, murder? I didn't agree to that. Sure, I knew they were going to beat him up, they even said they wanted to plant some coke on him and call the police, get him deported.'

'Where did they murder him? Tell me how it happened.'

'They told me they didn't kill him, he must have crawled into the lake on his own, I didn't see it, I didn't see anything, I don't know anything, I just, I just, I just – '

I pointed the gun at his face. He threw his arms over his head and curled into a ball, as though that was going to do him any good against a bullet.

'I didn't see it! I didn't want any part of it but Burke bragged he wasn't just a movie star, he did his own stunts, and it was just insane, the photographer was already bleeding when we got next door because of what Earl had done to him but that wasn't enough. He tied him up and he, it was just sickening, I mean, the guy already told them what they wanted to know, what was the point? But still he didn't stop, he just kept hitting him, wanted me to help drag him back to the house but I just, ran, I got in my car and took off.'

'Back to what house?'

'Burke's! Back to Burke's house.'

I left him barefoot on the top of the mountain, didn't have enough decency to leave him his shoes for the walk down. Maybe he'd hedged about his role in things but he'd told me the basic truth. His confession should have gratified me. I'd learned most of what I needed to know to take revenge in clear conscience. But I didn't feel clear, I didn't feel clean and I didn't feel like I had much conscience.

37

The security cameras at the top corners of Burke's gilded gates may not have been manned twenty-four hours a day but if the house was as wired for video as Finley claimed I didn't mistake them for decoys. Signs warning of electronic security measures and private armed response decorate half the houses in LA. Many are a bluff, nothing more than a stake in the ground or a decal glued to a window. I didn't think Burke's system was a bluff. An obsidian buzzer rested in a brass plate on the gate post. I pressed it, stepped back and took a flash picture of the camera lens. I wanted Earl to know I watched them as closely as they watched me.

He made his appearance about ten minutes after I'd rung the bell, strut-waddling down the granite drive in the heavy-footed style typical of over-pumped body builders. I noted with some pride the bandages at his elbows, gained from his slide down the hill the day before. He grinned and puffed out his chest as he neared the end of the drive. Through the bars of the gate gleamed the white block letters printed on his T-shirt, SHUT UP BITCH.

'I know it's late,' I said. 'Did I catch you in the middle of a wank?'

'What's a wank?'

'It's what you used to do before you took so many steroids your pecker fell off.'

His grin flattened. 'If you're trying to trick me into beating the shit out of you, you're very close to succeeding.'

'You're good at beating the shit out of people, aren't you?'

'I've had some practice.'

'You know the King's Road Café on Beverly?'

'Not my kind of place,' he sniffed.

'I'll meet you there in thirty minutes. We'll talk about the photographs.'

The King's Road Café and neighbouring newsstand were prime sources of show-biz information. The pre-war neighbourhood apartment buildings and duplexes bordered the talent agencies of Beverly Hills, attracting a core of young actors and actresses who aspired to but couldn't yet afford the 90210 zip code. Both newsstand and café were good spots to catch candids of young celebutants thumbing the film and gossip magazines. Tables lined the sidewalk to allow customers to soak up automobile exhaust with the fresh California sunshine. The tables stayed out at night to accommodate tourists and the half-dozen or so tobacco smokers left on the Westside. The vast majority of non-smokers sat inside, watching the puffers out the plate glass windows like animals in a zoo.

Earl looked like he belonged inside less than the smokers. The clientele of the Kings Road Café favoured the flat biceps, distressed blue jeans and can't-remember-my-last-haircut look of the professional arts set. Earl carried far too obvious a load of testosterone in his razor-cut head and baby-bull shoulders to blend anywhere except a gym. He had the sense to drape a black leather jacket over his SHUT UP BITCH T-shirt.

I'd chosen a table with clear sight lines to the front and back doors and sat with my back to the wall. In my right jacket pocket I fingered the canister of pepper spray. I kicked out the chair opposite mine when he came up to the table. He turned it around and sat with pneumatic forearms curled around the tines of the backrest. I'd grown up with that style of sitting. My dad sat that way all the time.

'Sorry about your husband,' he said, not sorry at all.

'It was a green card marriage, strictly business.' I focused on a spot six inches behind his head when I spoke, my eyes flat of anger and mercy. He didn't mean anything to me, the look said, he was just there. It was the kind of look I gave any predator to convince it I'm not just meat, I have teeth and claws of my own. 'I needed the money. Still do.'

'The real-estate agent told me what you wanted.' The barbed way he said that gave me the idea Peter St John had a rough time after I'd left. 'He seemed to think you didn't know your husband was blackmailing us.'

'Like I said, we weren't particularly close. You mind telling me the asking price?'

The lie creased his eyes before it passed his lips. 'A hundred grand.'

'That's a lot of money.'

'Woulda been if he'd lived.'

'If I were to find a set of prints, offer them to you instead of the tabloids, would the price still stand?'

'You don't know shit, do you? A hundred for the negatives. Prints would be worth far less, maybe twenty.'

'I thought *you* had the negatives.'

The waitress popped into the conversation with a friendly, 'How we doing tonight?' She poised the tip of her pen on the order pad and smiled like we were all good friends. I said everything was fine, thanks, and ordered a plain coffee. Earl asked for herbal tea. When she took the order to the kitchen I said, 'Of course you have the negs. You set the guy up, waited for him to show, then took the keys and tossed the apartment, right?'

'We didn't set the trap. The voice on the phone did.'

'What voice?'

Earl amused himself by bending his spoon into a circle. 'The Brit didn't call. Some other guy did. Said he could broker a deal for the negatives. Some days later he called again. Turned out he couldn't talk him out of publication, at least, that's what he told us. Said he felt real bad about it. If we wanted to throw another party, he'd make sure some-body showed up with a camera. We set it up and he was right, the Brit didn't have a clue he'd been back-stabbed.'

'So you beat him up and tossed his apartment.'

'You have a genuine talent for being half-right. The apartment was already trashed when I got there.'

'And the voice?'

'Never heard from him again.'

If I believed what Earl said then somebody else searched Gabe's apartment first. The voice on the phone knew the apartment would be empty. But if the voice had searched the apartment and found the negatives he would have followed through with the sale. Either the negatives weren't in the apartment or they were later taken from him. The problem with that logic was that I didn't particularly trust what Earl told me. 'According to you, the negatives are still out there somewhere.'

He gripped his fork and without taking his eyes off me twisted the metal into a neat spiral. 'I wouldn't be talking to you if they weren't.'

'That why you attacked my agent – you thought I had them?'

'You mean that little queer in Santa Monica? Never touched him.'

'Like you didn't kill the Brit, right? He crawled into the lake all by himself. You thought he'd lied to you, is that what happened? Or did Burke lose control, kill him while you went to get the negatives?'

'Some people make the mistake of thinking because I'm big and like to work out I'm stupid. You going to be one of those?'

There are times to talk and times to keep your mouth shut and this was a time for silence but the crack about Lester provoked me. 'I don't think you're stupid at all. If anything, you're too clever. You beat the location of the negatives out of my husband and tossed his apartment. When you got back to the estate you found Burke confused reality with the movies and committed murder. You dumped the body in the lake with enough cocaine on him to make it look drug related. You told Burke that somebody else got to the apartment first and stole the negatives. When the voice called again – I'm guessing it was another paparazzo named Dave Schuman – you killed him. You knew you couldn't get away with blackmailing Burke so you struck a set of prints and sent them to Mike Finley with a demand for a quarter million. You've let me snoop around this far because as long as I'm still alive Finley will think I'm the one blackmailing him. I wish I was as smart as you. But if I come up with another set of prints you'll have to deal with me and the price will be much dearer than twenty grand.'

I saw the move before he made it but had forgotten the speed and strength a violent man is capable of. Glasses and silverware flew across the laps of the people sitting next to us and crashed to the floor. I drew the canister of pepper spray from my jacket pocket as I sprang to my feet but Earl came up with the entire table in his paws. Before I could get my hand up he charged forward. The edge caught me at the waist and he rolled forward to flatten me against the wall, the table at my throat. Then he flexed his deltoids and squished me against the brick like a bug.

'Somebody want to call the police?' The request came out with my last wheeze of breath.

There must have been a dozen cell phones in the room but nobody moved. I love LA.

'Nobody's gonna help you, bitch.' His jaw moved an inch from my ear, the breath a mix of poison and mint. 'Not anybody in here and certainly not the police.' He tossed the table aside like a film prop and walked out, his splay-footed waddle no more hurried than when he came in.

The couple next to me picked stray silverware from their platters of skinless roast chicken. Nobody looked at me directly, as though offended by the bad taste of getting assaulted in public. Restaurants had long been favoured by the city's lovers as the ideal location in which to break up an affair. Scenes like the one I'd survived happened all the time. They probably thought I'd just told Earl I was sleeping with his personal trainer.

38

When driving Los Angeles at night there seems no end to the lights and asphalt but then the grid of streets crashes against the San Gabriel Mountains rising from the desert like a black tidal wave. Along a sixty mile edge the city goes dark, lights smashing street by street at the massive base of mountains rearing 10,000 feet above sea level. Big Brenda lived where the sprawl broke against the mountains' flanks. Hers was a nice middle-class neighbourhood of post-war homes on tree-lined streets that curled up and quit at the first serious incline. At two o'clock in the morning the houses were dark shells. The peculiarities of her occupation required Brenda to be a night person. The only lit windows on the block belonged to her.

The man next to Brenda when she opened the door stood a full head shorter than her and half an arm length wider. At first sight he looked fat but when we shook hands – Brenda introduced him as her old man, Raul – I understood he was hard as a bowling ball. He had the heavy kind of eyelids that made him look like he was sleepy all the time and lips that didn't seem to move at all when he talked. When he took my hand he held it firmly enough that I'd have to gnaw it off at the wrist if he didn't want to let go. 'This is Nina? The tough *chica* you been bragging about? No way! She don' look so tough, she look like *la niña gringa*.'

I didn't know if I was supposed to laugh. I said, 'Yeah, *mucho gusto* to you too.'

Brenda took his head in the crook of her arm, gave him a smack on the forehead. 'Don't listen to him, he's got nothing between his ears but *el viento*. Funny man, make yourself useful and go get us a beer.'

Brenda led me into the living-room and sat me down on a showroom-white colonial-style couch while she took the matching end-chair. The television set – a big Sony mounted into a mahogany veneer wall unit decorated with framed photographs and crystal baubles – played the Home Shopping Network with the sound off. Above the fireplace was an art warehouse reproduction of the face of Christ lit by divine light and on the opposite wall was a blow-up of a wedding picture too old to be anybody present. Nothing anywhere seemed out of its appointed spot nor had it gone more than a day without dusting. I first thought she had constructed the room as a front for her parole officer but that was a condescending notion and I discounted it. Brenda may have been a career criminal but still she didn't aspire to anything different than to be middle class.

'So what's on your mind *cariño*, you lock your keys in your trunk again?'

She laughed like that was funny and I guess it was but I wasn't in a laughing mood. 'I want us to partner up to hit a house.'

Her eyes held me in a grave visual embrace that warned me I had better be serious. 'I thought you'd be smart enough to stay out of the life. What's in this house you want to hit?'

'A video tape, maybe several video tapes.'

She didn't immediately understand the value of the prize and that annoyed her. After all, you never know which of your friends will turn out to be cranks. The irritation edged her voice when she shouted at Raul to hurry up with the beer. A bottle of Dos XX sailed out of the kitchen. Brenda snared it one handed. Raul was polite enough to deliver mine surface mail. He sat down on the other end of the couch, twisted the cap from his bottle and put it in his front shirt pocket with what looked like five or six others.

'They have *Snow White and the Seven Dwarfs*?' He asked, no smile. 'That's a good tape. I'd steal that. *The Lion King* too. Anything by Disney.'

'The tapes are locked up in a Hollywood Hills estate owned by a movie star. The estate has gates, video surveillance, a bodyguard and an alarm system hooked up to an armed response service. He won't be expecting a visit so it doesn't get any harder than just that. The tapes show the murder of my husband.' I didn't waste time with the beer; I took half of it down at one go. 'I can't promise you any money from this job because there won't be any. The tapes will go to the cops. But before he died my husband took some photographs of this same actor I should be able to sell to the tabloids. I'll cut you a piece of that, say fifty per cent. Should be worth fifty grand to you, maybe more, maybe less.'

'If the job pays no money, the job pays no money,' Brenda said. 'You want revenge, we can't take your money to help.'

'Sure we can,' Raul objected. 'She's your friend, she's got no money, I say fine, put her up on the couch, drive her to the welfare office, but no way risk going to jail. No money, no job.'

'Maybe we don't even need you.'

Raul got a little excited, shifted to the edge of the couch, pointed the sipping end of his beer at Brenda. 'You need me. The alarm, remember? What you know about alarms? *El electricista soy yo*. I do the alarm.'

The conversation shifted into a Spanish too fast and complex for my jailhouse vocabulary but I understood enough to know Raul was talking respect and risk against Brenda's obligation to friendship. I took advantage long enough to slap down the last of my beer. 'I want to pay,' I said. They didn't shut up. People rarely do when they get into a good argument. I walked into the kitchen to get myself another beer. When I came back out they stopped arguing to stare at me. Maybe they thought it a rude thing to do, just walk into the kitchen and help myself. 'The offer is not negotiable. The photographs got my husband killed. Any money, well, it's blood money. I don't want it.'

Raul's sleepy eyes opened a notch. 'So where's my *cerveza*?'

I gave him mine. He opened it and put the bottle cap in his shirt pocket. That was the way he kept track of how much he drank, but I couldn't tell if it was to limit himself or because he was trying to set some kind of record. He had about a dozen bottle caps in his shirt pocket when Brenda took him off to bed.

Associating with a known felon or felons is technically a parole violation. In a car town like Los Angeles Brenda and I didn't have to worry about being seen together at our homes or in cafés or even walking the sidewalk. The cops had no presence in those places but they owned the freeways and surface streets. Police in Los Angeles memorized not faces but cars and licence plate numbers. A licence plate is like a name tag strung around your neck for every cop to read as you drive by. Late the next morning Brenda and Raul split from me at the front drive and followed in the Jeep Cherokee.

Forty separate highways and freeways split Los Angeles County like a jigsaw puzzle. From the Sierra Madre foothills we negotiated four of them in traffic ranging from slow to stagnant. The traffic gave me time to work things out. Half of the rant I'd thrown at Earl the night before I believed I could prove but the rest was speculation. He'd beaten Gabe and searched his apartment, that much was certain. The voice on the phone had to be Dave Schuman. Gabe had accused him of trying to scavenge his exclusives. He'd followed us to Vegas and could have tailed Gabe the night he'd photographed the sex party at Burke's estate. When he realized what Gabe had shot he'd tried to broker a deal. I didn't know if Gabe had played along and then backed out or been a willing participant up to the moment of his death, but the proof sheet mailed to Burke proved his involvement. The blackmailer didn't find the proof sheet in a trash bin. Gabe must have given it to him. If a willing participant in the scheme, his greed had killed him as much as the murderer's knife. The more I learned about why he had been murdered the more my feelings for him changed. In the first few days after his death, I'd ached with loss and the terrible injustice of his murder. The killers had taken my chance at love with his life. Though we had not known each other long or well, I'd felt passion and hope. As I discovered the circumstances of his death, I realized my love for him would have led nowhere.

From the Beechwood Canyon off ramp it should have been less than fifteen minutes up the canyon to Burke's estate but a black and white swung onto my tail and popped its siren as I crossed Franklin. I was naïve enough to hope it was a routine traffic stop until the reflection of the LAPD officer in my rear-view mirror pointed a big gun at my head. It's hard not to scream and curl into a ball when somebody points a gun at your head. Those who do are inevitably shot.

His partner wiped across the windshield, the trajectory of his sights inscribing an arc into my skull, and planted his boots just up-fender from the side mirror. He knew where to position himself for maximum field-of-fire. If I tried to drop prone on to the seat I'd be dead before I touched canvas. The uniform in the mirror swung open the door and ordered me to kneel to the pavement. I kneeled and when ordered went down face first. I remembered how to take orders, how to disappear in the minutia of obedience. He pulled first one hand behind my back, then the other, cuffed them in place and left me face down on the street.

They stood over me to talk. I heard numbers recited and slang for the local police stations. They called me in and when they heard what they needed to know a pair of black boots nudged my shoulder. I rolled over on to my back, sat up, kicked my legs sideways to kneel and stand. My shirt had soaked through with sweat. The Jeep Cherokee rolled past as I waited for them to load me into the cage. Brenda didn't swing her head to rubberneck the scene and I didn't make a big deal of watching her go. Before turning on to Franklin she flashed her brake lights three times. I think she meant to wish me luck.

I've been few places lonelier than the back of a squad car. Not even a cell compares. In a cell, you've arrived at a place you expect to stay awhile. As cold and bare and hard as it is, it's home. You can look forward to getting out some day. In the back cage of a squad car you're baggage on the first leg of a long, bad trip. You have nothing to look forward to, not to staying cramped and cuffed inside nor to getting out, because oh the places you'll go, county jail to courthouse to prison and all its attendant facilities; none of them will be any improvement on the awful place you're in at the moment. When I saw one of the officers pull from under the front seat of the Caddy the .38 pistol I'd taken from Grimes I was sure I'd just bought a ticket for the full, bad ride.

39

Once in the system you have no choice but to go where the ticket books you. I was Mirandized and driven to the Hollywood station, pulled from the back seat like a suitcase and carried by the handle of my upper arm to the far end of a wooden bench. A metal rail ran parallel beneath the seat. I was chained to it and abandoned. On the opposite end of the bench a junkie nodded out, his chin buried in his chest and an imaginary cigarette smoking between his middle and forefingers. While I waited two officers brought in a woman with long black hair and a lip stud. Dense tattoo vines crawled up her arms from wrist to shoulder. She slipped me a conspirator's grin as they pulled her past the bench and into a tempered-glass observation room. The observation room was reserved for minors; she looked seventeen going on thirty-seven.

The circulation in my hands had diminished to a stinging numbness by the time Douglas walked through the door. To some people pain might be a distraction but physical suffering stilled my emotions and sharpened my mind to clearer focus. He didn't offer any formalities of greeting and neither did I. He clipped the cuffs and led me through the detectives' bullpen, a clattering, paper-strewn space with about twenty rickety desks and a half-dozen movie posters on the wall. The Hollywood station takes its show-biz legacy seriously;

seven Hollywood Walk of Fame-style stars lay embedded in the concrete walk leading to the front entrance, each star emblazoned with the name of a legendary policeman and the LAPD badge.

'You've been advised of your right to counsel?' Douglas closed the door to a room that smelled like fear and boredom. It was one of three interview rooms used for suspects. I'd been there before; after my husband's body had been found Harker had interviewed me in that room or one just like it.

'I'll waive it until I hear the charges.'

He drew a pen and notebook from the side pocket of his beige windbreaker and glanced over the arresting officer's report. 'Possession of a firearm, that's the charge we're holding you on. That alone should be enough to revoke your parole.'

'I have a story for the gun. First, it isn't mine.'

'Doesn't matter. It was under the seat of your car. That's possession.'

'I didn't know it was there.'

'Technically, that also doesn't matter.'

'Technically we'd all be in jail if they caught us at the wrong moment.'

A wry smile chipped at his blank façade. Douglas wasn't a bad guy as far as cops went. He dipped his chin once, as much a sign that he was willing to listen as I'd ever get.

'The gun belongs to a private detective named Richard Grimes.' His eyes drifted off course when he heard the name. I hadn't been talking long enough to bore him; he knew Grimes. 'We were driving in my car about four days ago when a pick-up truck ran a red light – this was about three, three-thirty in the morning. Grimes, he was in the back seat, and when we hit he went flying over the front and whacked into the dash. The pick-up truck, it was a straight hit-and-run, I never got his plates. Grimes was banged up pretty bad, first thing I noticed was a gash on his head. Then I saw the gun on the floor and I knew it was his but I didn't know what to do with it. I picked it up, wanted to give it back to him but he wasn't moving. I couldn't just put it in one of his pockets and I sure as hell didn't want to hold it either so I figured the best thing to do was throw it under the seat. Then in the rush of getting him to the hospital I just forgot about it.'

He didn't bother to take notes. 'Good story. Hit-and-run driver, explains your fingerprints on the weapon, Grimes has a head injury so if he doesn't tell the same story you can say he just doesn't remember.'

'Check the admissions sheet at St John's. He'll be there.'

'I'll check more than the admissions sheet. I'll check with Grimes and I'll check your car. But the fact remains, the gun was in your possession. You're going back to prison.'

The way he said that sounded less threat than fact. They had intended from the start to revoke my parole and with the gun I had given them the weapon to do it. 'Why was I pulled over?'

'For questioning. '

'What do you mean, for questioning? About what?'

'Where you were between four and ten p.m. yesterday?'

Given the time frame, it had to be Finny. He decided he feared me more than the law and filed a complaint. Douglas sat rigidly erect, pushing the arresting officer's report with his forefinger and pulling it back with his ring finger. He wasn't the one going to jail here. To him, I was just a job. He couldn't care less what happened to me.

'I'll talk to that lawyer now.'

'A murder investigation.'

That surprised me. I didn't expect to be innocent. 'Whose murder?'

'Liliana Tutuila.'

The name meant nothing to me. 'Never heard of the woman. Every time you get an unsolved, you going to call me in for questioning?'

He coughed once and eyed me over the ridge of his fist. 'You might know her by an alias: Piña Noir.'

I rocked back in my chair as though the first and last name were blows. First Gabe, now Piña. Mine was the kiss of death. Had she never met me she might still be alive. I made the mistake of thinking out loud. 'What am I supposed to do now? Can you tell me that? Feel guilty for the rest of my life?'

He started to take notes then. 'You were angry at her because – why – she and your husband were lovers? Or because you two were lovers?'

I flung my head down, cracked it against the wood table hard enough to make the legs jump. I had no choice. The pain and anger flashed through me like a fireball and the only way to stop it was to put myself out before I burned to cinders. Douglas leapt across the table and cuffed my wrists to the chair. His fingers reached to my forehead and came down with blood. When the pain began to vibrate above my eye I knew the fireball had blown through me. The door popped open and he called out he needed a med-kit.

'You plan to report police brutality? Is that what this is about? You should know the room is wired for sound and your little display is on tape.'

'You disgust me,' I said.

He stepped away as though I'd just bit him. He had no idea where I was coming from. 'She went to meet you yesterday afternoon and wasn't seen alive after that. You don't have a clean alibi for the night of your husband's murder and you were seen arguing with Dave Schuman a few days before he was killed. Care to explain?'

'Coincidence.'

A dogsbody shouldered the door wide enough to toss a med-kit on to the table. Douglas broke it open and doused his hands with rubbing alcohol, directing the pinkish spill onto a wad of cotton. 'Coincidence ranks up there with mistaken identity in the top ten of stupid defences. The court doesn't like to hear the word – ever. I suggest you come up with something else.' When he finished wiping the excess from his hands he returned the alcohol to the med-kit and snapped it shut again. No kindness there, just AIDS awareness. Blood trickled into the corner of my eye. I squeezed it out, took a breath, went on.

'She gave me a call yesterday. I wanted to talk to her. She agreed to meet at Tower Records at four but never showed up.'

'Why did you want to talk to her?'

'She said she was going to tell a journalist what she knew about the night my husband was murdered. I wanted to stop her.'

'How did you plan to stop her?'

'Begging, pleading, whatever.'

'Not say, with a knife?' When he didn't get an answer to that question he tried another. 'What was your relationship, exactly?'

'Friends.'

'Did you pay to have sex with her?'

'I paid to talk to her. For her time. Not for sex.'

'The sex was a freebie?'

'The sex is none of your business.'

'That must mean it was good. Too good to share?'

'You've seen the photographs from the disk – what are you hassling me for? Go talk to Damian Burke or Supervisor Danavitch.'

I didn't appreciate the way his eyes flickered across my face, like he measured me for a strait-jacket.

'You did look at the disk, didn't you? Don't tell me you haven't even seen it.'

'I looked at it.'

'Then you know.'

'The disk was blank.'

'How?'

He didn't bother to answer and his expression betrayed nothing except the suspicion that I was a murderous lunatic. Maybe he never saw the copy Frank had made. I'd delivered the disk not to him but to Harker, who could have glanced at the images and wiped it clean. Protecting a major politician would be a smart career move but maybe it went deeper than that. Harker could have known about the photographs all along and attempted to blackmail no that was a crazy idea but maybe he wanted to cover it up because the scandal would ruin Danavitch's career and why not blackmail he knew how to make the deaths seem like a serial killing and all these ideas gyred around in my head until I could no longer separate fact from paranoia. 'There were photographs on that disk, digital copies. That's why the killer ransacks the apartments. He's looking for the negatives.'

'You've got this all figured out, don't you?'

'No, not all.'

'Don't think much of the job we're doing?'

'I'm sure you're doing – '

'Think you can do the job better?'

'I can help – '

'Sure you can help. Know how?'

'Yeah, I can – '

'You can tell me now what else might be in your car.'

Gabe's original disk was in the car. I hadn't taken the precaution to properly hide it. Anybody feeling under the dash would find it taped to the inside rim. If the disk disappeared I didn't have another copy. Without the photographs I couldn't prove anything and I'd have several years in a hard, cold place to dwell on my incompetence. I said, 'Nothing.'

Douglas saw a nervous catch in my eyes or maybe like any predator he sensed when another creature feared him. 'Detective Harker is searching your car this afternoon. As an ex-con you don't have to be told that evidence connecting you to any of the three murders will put you on the fast track to the gas chamber.'

'Then go ahead and order the cyanide capsule.'

He took that as an admission of guilt, made a little note in his book. 'What will he find in the car?'

'The question is, what is he going to plant?'

'What are you trying to insinuate?'

'I'm not insinuating anything. I'm saying Harker will find in the car whatever evidence he needs to put me away – '

'Stop right there – '

' – and when I protest that it's planted nobody will believe me because I'm an ex-con and my word isn't good enough to spit on.'

'You're right there. It isn't.'

'Are you forgetting the night you pulled me over outside Hancock Park? You were ready to plant evidence then.'

Anger ripened his skin to the colour of black cherries. 'You give me a blank disk, slam your head on the table hard enough to draw blood and then accuse me and my partner of some conspiracy to tamper with evidence. Yes, I think you're a liar and yes, you are a suspect. If I can't connect you to Tutuila I'll find something else because I think you're too dangerous to walk the streets.'

I said, 'I'll take that lawyer now.'

40

A private security guard employed by one of the armed response services noticed the car first. He had been on routine patrol above Lake Hollywood and stopped because the parking lights had been left on. Kids and young lovers often parked on the street to slip through the fence and drink and screw around in the hills above. He didn't think it anything more serious than that until he noticed the corner of a leather jacket sticking out of the trunk. He was well enough trained not to force the trunk himself. If he read the papers and suspected what was inside he wouldn't want to look. He called the LAPD.

Like the scalp collector, Piña had been stabbed and dumped into the trunk of her own car. She had either been murdered on the street where the car was found or driven into the hills after being killed elsewhere. If the police had found conclusive forensic evidence to prove either scenario they weren't talking about it. She had been stabbed in the back and chest and slashed above the ankle of one leg. The inside of the trunk bore scratch marks. Paint chips were imbedded in the soft flesh under her shredded fingernails. Death had not been instantaneous. She might have tried to inscribe something in the paint before she died. Nobody had yet been able to decipher what she had written, if she had written anything at all. She might have scratched the paint inadvertently as she flailed out at the end of her life.

A lawyer told me this after I had been processed through the Inmate Reception Center of the Twin Towers, a complex of four high-rise, high-security octagons set across the freeway from downtown Los Angeles. With its eight stories of hardened concrete, archer-slit-style windows, tempered glass cells and inmate monitoring system the Twin Towers complex was Los Angeles County's 21st century version of the medieval prison tower. Accused felons awaiting trial were held there, along with prisoners convicted on misdemeanor charges. It opened while I was doing hard time at California Institute for Women. The facility might have been new but the receiving deputy was no different from the woman who had processed me at the old jail five years before. I stood barefoot on the cold floor with my legs spread and arms lifted. She ran gloved hands through my hair, looked into my ears, nose and mouth, felt around the wiring of my bra and patted down my legs. Her hands were quick and sure. She removed my cuffs and when the electronic lock sprang back I walked unescorted into holding tank number two.

Four women in similar circumstances sullenly eyed my entrance. Three walls of the tank were concrete and the fourth, glass, looked out on to the corridor, or rather, looked in at us. An aluminium bench lined the two far walls. One woman tried to sleep but the bench was too narrow and every five minutes or so she slipped off. After the third fall she gave up and slept on the floor. Messages, names and telephone numbers had been scratched into the concrete with the only sharp object remaining to the prisoners: their fingernails. One message went, 'Help, I've been abducted by aliens.'

An hour later my number was called and the same deputy

or one who looked just like her led me into a room with a bathtub. I removed my black jeans, pullover, bra and panties. Once again she examined my hair, ears, nose and mouth, this time gripping a club-like flashlight. I spread my fingers, lifted my arms and feet, bent over and pulled apart my buttocks. She directed the beam of the flashlight down my throat and up my vagina and rectum. These manoeuvres she performed with quiet professionalism. She would process a dozen prisoners that day. I was no more a human being to her than meat is an animal to a butcher. While I bathed and then cleaned the tub, she turned the pockets of my jeans inside out, felt carefully at the seams and at the stitching of my pullover and placed each article into a blue plastic sack with a string tie. She unhooked the nozzle to a tank of parasiticide attached to the wall and directed me to lift my arms, turn from front to back and bend over while she sprayed the now public recesses of my body with Kwell. The acrid odour was as familiar as it was vile. Prison perfume. Every new inmate reeked of it. At the door she gave me a jail dress and pair of thongs. I was allowed to keep my underwear.

After I'd been processed they let me see a lawyer. I didn't know and hadn't called the one who appeared on the other side of the tempered-glass partition to talk to me. He said a mutual friend had suggested I needed legal help. Brenda must have called him though he didn't name the friend and I didn't ask. He had the dishevelled hair and eccentric threads of a rich old lefty and the folksy manner of a friend to the downtrodden, a guy who once he starts pulling on your ear won't stop until you agree with everything he says. First thing he did was kick his chair back on to the rear tines and put his feet up so I could admire his snake-skin cowboy boots and blue jeans. The business card he pulled from the side pocket of his leather jacket read, Charles H. Belinsky,

People's Advocate. The jacket looked hand-made in a style inspired by those once worn by Native Americans, with leather fringe that hung six inches from the sleeves and breast. His bola tie had a chunk of turquoise big enough to bring down Goliath. He was in his sixties and had been married and divorced at least once a decade since his twenties. His newest ex-wife was twenty-eight. I started to call him mister but he rumbled with the insult and insisted I call him Chuck.

Belinsky was a man of strong opinions regarding the inadequacies of the criminal *in*justice system, as he called it. The police were holding me on illegal possession of a firearm – fair enough – but the hostile manner of my arrest was outrageous. I had not been wanted for anything except questioning in a case where no reasonable person would consider me a suspect. The way he saw it, they were fishing for bass without a licence and accidentally caught a trout. If the judge was a good game warden he'd rule they couldn't go fishing for one and catch the other. Were I anything but a convicted felon they'd have to toss me back in the lake. Felons were fish of a different stripe. Every season was open season on felons and that was my predicament. I could holler that the gun was under the seat buried beneath a month of newspapers but the police officer would testify that the gun was in plain sight when he visually inventoried the car interior. No judge in the world would suppress the seizure. Once the court rules the gun was constitutionally seized, the fire is stoked, the frying pan is smoking, and I'm on it, about to be cooked. So the best thing for me to do, he advised, was give them bigger fish to fry. Did I know anybody a little higher up the food chain? If the police thought they could catch a bigger fish based on something I told them, they might be willing to let me off the hook.

'They don't want to go higher up the food chain, trust me.'

'Why not?'

'Because it involves a major movie star and a county supervisor watching a girl have sex with a dog.'

That slapped all four of his chair legs down to earth and a notebook on to the table. I gave an account of my time since the night of Gabe's death, omitting the events that could get me into further trouble – the green card arrangement, hit-and-run on a parked car, three instances of assault and one kidnapping – but otherwise didn't veer from the truth any more than was necessary. He took meticulous notes in a sloping script. The pen, I noticed, was Cartier. We agreed that he should first interview Frank Adams, who had seen the digital photographs of Burke and Danavitch and could establish the beginning of my alibi for Piña's murder. If Frank couldn't or wouldn't corroborate the contents of the disk, Belinsky suggested we might want to consider refining our story to something we might be able to prove. I think this was his gentle way of telling me that he didn't believe a word of what I said. About Gabe's last night alive and who I thought had killed him I said nothing. He already suspected I might be crazy – no need to prove it to him.

At the Twin Towers, violent offenders are secured in tempered-glass cells, watched around the clock from a central control room. Everybody else on the women's side is held in dorm-style housing. I got a glass cell. The cells were originally designed to hold one inmate. I shared mine with two others. Yvonne had two black eyes and a balloon lip. She'd shot her husband. I didn't need to ask why. Louisa was a working girl on the needle. Normally she wasn't a violent offender but she was booked in with two prior convictions and withdrawal pains. She wasn't particularly pleasant company but then I don't guess any of us were. After a maximum security dinner – no knives, forks, pepper or talking – I was pulled out of the cell for an interview with my parole officer.

'You didn't last long, did you?' Her tone was part taunt, part regret and all contempt. I sat in the chair provided for me, folded my hands on the desk and stared straight ahead. She didn't bother wrinkling the crisp blue sheet of her skirt on the chair opposite mine; while I sat she paced between my back and the door. 'When were you released? Two weeks ago?'

'Something like that.'

'That's not a record by the way but it does put you in the upper ten per cent.'

'The gun isn't mine.' I knew from experience that consistency is one of the few weapons a convict can wield.

'How could you be so stupid?' Her face appeared over my neck sharp-angled as an axe. 'Possession of a handgun, it's automatic. Parole is revoked. You finish out your sentence plus the extra weight of the handgun.'

'It was in my car by mistake.'

'You were sentenced to seven years and you served four. That's a three-year mistake.'

I came as close to begging as I ever would. She didn't owe me any favours. 'It was a stupid mistake, I'll agree with that, but it wasn't a criminal one. I hope when you make your decision whether to support me or not you'll take that into consideration. I hope you understand I'm trying to do the right thing.'

'While you're at it, you'd better hope your story about the gun checks out one hundred per cent because if it doesn't this conversation will be our last.'

She flashed out of the room like a zipper sealing up my body bag.

By habit I fell back into the rules and rhythms of the system. Everything required to control the inmates was located on the floor that housed us. Our movements were tightly supervised and regulated. They moved us from our cells and back like products on a disassembly line, stripping away our freedom, our independence and dignity. It was no different in this way than any other penal institution, just more efficient. I knew how to do easy time. The mingled essence of parasiticides, industrial cleaning solutions and too many bodies in too little space smelled so familiar that after a few hours I no longer noticed it. I did what they told me to do when they told me and above all I did it silently.

The aspect of jail I appreciated most was the time it allowed for concentrated thought, even if the impending length of my incarceration rendered that thinking purely theoretical. Though I suspected Earl of complicity in my husband's murder he might have told the truth about the negatives. If the scalp collector had been the one to betray Gabe, then he would have tossed the apartment first, while Earl was occupied with the beating. Perhaps Gabe had implied he stored the negatives in his flat. Schuman's rage at not finding those million-dollar strips of celluloid had resulted in the destruction I'd seen the night of my break-in. If the negatives were in the apartment and Gabe had confessed their location, Earl would have found them straight away. And if Earl had the negatives, why did he try to beat their location out of Lester? Just to fool everybody into thinking he was still looking for them? It seemed more likely, knowing what I did of his character, that Gabe lied to the scalp collector and lied to Earl and hid the negatives with someone else.

I slept hard and deep that night and when I awoke the face of one of my cell mates had changed age and colour.

I stepped back on to the conveyor belt of the system, happy for the moment that I had been removed from the temptation to do myself more harm in the free world. At the end of a concrete corridor lit by a twitching fluorescent tube a steel door opened to a small room and the seated figure of Detective Keith Harker, dressed like a corporate executive in a blue suit and red striped tie. With the controlled aggressiveness of his every gesture, from the stone in his glance to the coiled hunch of his shoulders when he rolled his neck to crack the tension, he would always look like what he did for a living, no matter how he dressed. He was a hunter. The smell of spilled blood clung to him. When he looked at me I broke into a sweat.

'You do have a talent for trouble,' he said, just enough playfulness in his voice to sound condescending. 'Married to one murder victim. Seen arguing with a second. Supposed to be meeting a third at the time of her death.'

'I told Douglas what happened.'

'You sure convinced him. He's ready to book you a one-way ticket back to CIW.'

I didn't get it. I asked, 'Then why are you here?'

'Because I interviewed Grimes.'

Then I got it. Even if Grimes stuck to the story we'd agreed to tell, Harker wouldn't need to falsify, just twist the testimony and I'd twist with it. 'How does he look? Last time I saw him was at the hospital.'

Harker stroked the left wing of his moustache with his right forefinger, like he was trying to tamp down a smile. 'He doesn't look so good. I've never seen so many unusual injuries from a car accident. His leg for instance, how do you suppose he broke his – whatchacallit – his patella?'

I thought about it, offered, 'Probably got his boot hung up

in the rear seat while the rest of his body was flying to the front.'

'Probably right. The simplest explanation is usually the best. And the gunshot wound? How did he get shot in the foot, you think?'

'Happened when we hit the pick-up. Had the thing in his shoulder holster and at impact it went off.'

'That's what he said. But I still don't get it.' Harker backed away from the table and hung his coat on the chair. Beneath the shoulder of his coat he wore a hand-tooled Mexican leather holster. He'd checked the gun at reception. He cupped his hand around the butt of the holster and did what looked like an awkward dance; he bent his left knee to bring the foot up behind him and, hopping to keep his balance, sighted down the leather barrel. 'See, he's right handed, and he packs under his left shoulder, so to shoot himself in his foot, the leg would have to – hell, I can't do it, he'd have to be double jointed.'

I saw what he was getting at and the trap behind it: how was I supposed to know the angle of the entry wound? 'Doesn't look so hard to me.' I stood with both feet flat on the floor, put my hand under my shoulder like it was a gun with the barrel pointing down. 'Straight shot down to the foot, no mystery to it at all.'

He watched me not like a cop eyeballing a suspect or a guy across the bar who thinks if he stares hard enough your blouse will fall off but like a surfer looks at a curling wave or a climber the sheer face of a cliff; his look conveyed respect and more than a little aggression. He gently pressed my hand against my breast and sighted down my finger. 'He wasn't shot in the top of the foot. The bullet entered the sole of his foot and exited the top. Of course you couldn't know that unless you pulled the trigger yourself.' With gentle insistence he pressed against my hand until the finger rotated to point at the ceiling. Then he blew once on the tip, like a gunfighter. 'You understand the problem I have with this. How could someone shoot himself in the bottom of his foot?'

'You ever been in an automobile accident? A serious one? You go from forty miles an hour to zero in a hundredth of a second. That puts the body through some serious contortions. On impact his feet could have twisted up to his ears.' I don't know why I tried to convince him. Even if I was innocent – and I wasn't – he'd report what he needed to put me away. I sat back down, folded my hands in front of me and waited.

'You'd think if the gun went off in the car, I'd find the spent bullet somewhere. Unless the bullet deflected off his foot out the open side window. Was the side window open?'

I hadn't thought of the bullet. It's what you don't see that trips you up. 'I don't remember.'

Harker tucked the file he'd brought into the room under his arm, stood over me, watched the top of my head for a solid minute. 'That thing on your dashboard, that box, is it what I think it is?'

'If you think it's my husband it is, at least what's left of him.'

'Why is his murder so important to you? It was a green card marriage. We don't care about that any more. You don't have to prove anything. Why don't you do yourself a favour and let it go?'

That luxury wasn't available when somebody might be trying to kill me, I could have said. Or that their accusations had forced me into it as an act of self-preservation. Or that I wanted justice and revenge, even if I didn't precisely know what those two words meant or how I'd feel if I received some approximation of both. I could have said any or all of that, but I didn't. I just said, 'I have ghosts.'

'I can warn you about ghosts. They make you crazy.' Harker opened the door, called the guard, looked at me over his shoulder. 'But I think I've warned you too late.'

41

On the morning of my court appearance the guards loaded me with a half-dozen other women into a panel-van and cuffed my wrists to the seat. The ride was brief and silent. Our thoughts were private and our fears unspeakable. The next few hours would determine the course of years for each of us. Some would be released outright, others on bail, some returned to jail to curse the crime of being caught and too poor to pay, and the others, the damned, sentenced to spend a portion of their lives in a place even devils fear to tread. We did not know the face or spirit of our judge, who would speak for us or against us, or what we would say ourselves if called upon to speak. We were angry, confused, afraid and largely ignorant of our fates, and this made us silent.

The rear doors of the van swung open to a subterranean garage marked 'inmate transfer area'. From all we could see during the blacked-out journey we had been delivered into hell. The guards pulled us one by one out of the van and herded us in a group down an angled corridor to a room with a concrete floor and caged fluorescent lights. This served as the holding area. We waited, some standing, most sitting on low benches. When one by one our case was called gloved hands led us by the arm up an elevator and down a secure hallway. At the end of the hall a door swung open to the courtroom where our fates would be decided. The faces in the courtroom largely ignored us as we entered, each absorbed in routine documents, consultation, coffee.

Belinsky stood when I entered the courtroom and made an elaborate show of offering me a chair beside his. In this small way he wished to remind the court that I was human. The judge swirled the tip of her pen over a document as I crossed beneath the bench, oblivious to his gesture. She read carefully through glasses suspended from a neck-chain that picked up the silver highlights in her crow-black hair. The fluorescent lights drained the colour of blood from her skin. I knew enough not to believe that because she was a woman she'd be merciful; one just like her had put me away the first time. In the front row of reserved seats Detective Douglas read a copy of *Scandal Times* propped on his knee. LAX BOMBER BABE BAGGED FOR SNAPPER SNUFFS, the headline ran. In the gallery behind him, I spotted Frank amid the spectators. He observed me without recognition, professional enough to cut my throat with his pen.

'Are they going to arraign me for murder here?' I asked Belinsky, shocked by the headline.

'No, friend, the issue to be decided today is the gun found in your car, and only the gun.' Measured against the sheriff uniforms, magisterial robes and slick suits, he cut an iconoclastic figure with his fringed leather jacket, blue jeans and bolo tie. No doubt he meant to. 'Now, I had me a little talk with the prosecutor, and – no surprise here – he insisted that the judge would find the gun was legally seized. If they were of the mind to prosecute they could. Even if they don't prosecute, the court can still rule that the gun warrants revocation of your parole. You follow me?'

'The frying pan or the fire, I'm cooked either way,' I said.

He tapped my hand once, lightly. 'Exactly. I can tell you're the type of person I don't have to say things twice to. So

I paid a social call to your friend, Mr Frank Adams, who admitted to having a copy of this disk you mentioned and – '

'Wait a minute, he wasn't supposed to . . .' It didn't take long to work out what happened. 'He gave me the wrong disk!' Frank kept the copy I asked him to make for the police and gave me a blank. No wonder Douglas thought I was a lunatic.

'Regardless of how the disk came into his possession he's sitting at the poker table now so we have to deal him into the game. He was generous enough to confirm for me in very graphic detail the pictorial content of this disk. Unfortunately, he refused to allow me to use it as a chit to bargain your legal exoneration.'

'Bastard!' I said it loud enough to turn the disapproving eye of the judge my way.

'Like all members of his chosen profession, I'm sure he's lower than the tits of a pregnant wiener dog. He did confide to me that the moment your parole was revoked the contents of the disk would be submitted for publication.'

My parole officer strode into the court just as the bailiff read out a case number with my legal name – Mary Alice Baker – attached. She clipped past the defence table without a glance in my direction and pulled out a chair next to the prosecutor. I lost all credibility with Douglas and Harker when I gave them a blank disk as evidence and now the State was poised to put me away for another four years because Frank wouldn't turn over the copy he'd switched with the blank. He'd betrayed me not once but twice. My parole officer spoke rapidly and heatedly into the prosecutor's ear.

'But I have been up to some mischief on your behalf,' Belinsky announced. 'We'll soon see to what result.'

The prosecutor scooted out his chair and stood. His hair

was carefully combed back in a style popular in the year of his father's birth and his face framed a pair of square black glasses of the type favoured by the plastic-pocket protector set. I had the uncomfortable feeling that he scrubbed his nails every night after work but never got them clean enough to satisfy him. Everything about him – from the way he dressed to how he stood and read his notes – screamed out a second-rate law school and the determination to make up for it by aggressive effort. He set aside his notes when the judge called upon him and announced in the curt tones of a man whose foot is being stepped on, 'After careful review of the charges, the State declines to prosecute.'

Belinsky wrapped his arm around my shoulder and squeezed. I was too shocked to respond. 'Mr Prosecutor here doesn't have much of a bark this morning. When a big dog barks, the little dog listens. And Mr Prosecutor is a little dog.'

The judge announced that she had recorded the State's decision but clearly a gun had been found in my car and even though the State decided not to prosecute it was a violation of the terms of my parole. The gun had been in my car and extenuating circumstances or not I had been driving that car. The issue then, was one of parole violation. What, she asked, did the parole officer assigned to my case recommend?

'Your parole officer,' Belinsky confided, 'looks like the kind of little dog that just might bite a big dog on his hind parts.'

My parole officer stood and while she consulted her notes on the table smoothed a crease from her navy blue skirt and straightened the red, white and blue scarf around her neck. She made these adjustments not in a nervous flutter but with the hard, precise control of a very angry person. She didn't look at me at all. 'Your honour, though the parolee's explanation of how the gun came to be in her car was largely corroborated by the registered owner of that gun, their stories are not completely consistent.'

'That the gun was mistakenly jarred loose in an automobile accident, is that correct?' The judge moved her finger along a line in the documents before her.

'Yes your honour. For example, the owner of the gun, Mr Richard Grimes, reported – '

'Stop right there, please.' The judge held up a single forefinger and turned a page. 'A private detective, it reads here. Licensed to carry a firearm. Is that correct?'

'It is correct.' Even from my distance I could see her grit teeth. It galled her to be interrupted.

After too long a silence the judge peered over the top of her glasses. 'Please continue.'

My parole officer downed a half-glass of water and cleared her throat. 'Happy to continue, your honour. Mr Grimes stated that the vehicle that Ms Baker was driving struck, and I quote his testimony, "something on the right, a parked car, I think". Ms Baker contends that her vehicle struck a hit-and-run pick-up truck in an intersection.'

'Yes, but he doesn't remember exactly, does he? Due to a concussion and other injuries?'

'I'm merely documenting the discrepancies for the court, I'm not drawing conclusions.'

'We have a very full load today, so perhaps you should draw some. Do you have any reason to suspect either the licensed owner of the gun or Ms – ' the judge dipped into her notes and came up ' – Baker have not told the truth?'

'One or both have not accurately recalled events, your honour. I'll leave the question of truth up to the court.'

The judge turned a look of utmost patience on my parole officer. 'This is your case, officer. I respect your determination to set the facts straight before the court. It seems like a tempest in a teapot to me but you are best positioned to determine whether the parolee is making a sincere effort to rehabilitate herself and abide by the terms of her parole. What dispensation do you recommend?'

Belinsky reached out to grab my hand and squeezed it. His eyes were closed and his lips moved silently in what could have been prayer. That worried me some. I wanted my parole officer to look at me just once before she pronounced sentence but I didn't warrant even that.

'Tempest in a teapot or not, I don't believe any possession of a handgun by a parolee, however accidental, is ever fully justified. After careful and serious consideration, I reluctantly recommend continuing her on parole.'

'Parole is continued,' the judge announced, no consideration to it at all, just bang decided. Like many citizens hauled before the court, I was so mystified by the Byzantine workings of the law I had little idea what happened even after events were concluded.

'Why are they letting me go?'

'Because the big dog barked,' Belinsky said. 'Oh, I put a little bug in big dog's ear that made him itch and bark like mad.'

'Supervisor Danavitch?'

'You are a quick study, friend. I did give him a call to confide what Mr Adams possessed and what would happen if you were reincarcerated. He expressed a sincere desire to work with you in keeping the material on that disk private.'

'I can't promise that.'

He took my elbow and whispered straight into my brain. 'Don't ever forget that felons have no rights. The system can always find a pretext to send you back to prison. Make a deal with Danavitch's people. If you don't recover the negatives and put them out of circulation with the disk, not even Charles H. Belinsky will be able to save you.'

'Frank has the disk, not me.'

'Then I strongly advise you to work out a deal with him.'

I glanced over my shoulder in the hope of catching sight of Frank in the seating gallery but my parole officer blocked the view.

'The system just cut you a huge break,' she said, as though that might be one of her great regrets in life. 'Use it wisely.'

'You're the one who cut me the break. Maybe I should say thanks.'

Something in what I said cracked the metal in her eyes and before the crack welded over I saw something – regret, pity, I couldn't tell what. 'Maybe you shouldn't,' she said. 'The next day or two be careful.'

Before I could ask why she clipped down the centre aisle and out the door. Douglas had vanished at the verdict. His presence in court didn't make much sense to me and though I couldn't articulate exactly why I dreaded what I didn't know.

Once in the system you don't just walk out, even when that system spits you up. They drove me back to jail in the same van or one just like it. I signed the release forms, waited for those forms to be processed, collected my bag and car keys, asked directions to the police impound yard and was buzzed through one set of bars after another until a door swung open to a concrete walk and a white-hot sky.

The post-industrial streets between the Twin Towers and the impound yard were too inhuman to be walked like a warm-blooded creature. I skittered like a cockroach in the shadow of one burned and boarded hulk of brick after another, past Fords and Chevys stripped of tyres and axle-propped on empty cans of paint, dried ragweed lots festooned with shreds of cardboard box, newspaper, torn shirt-cloth and the inevitable lone rusted shopping cart; I trailed my eyes past squirts of graffiti and gang tags and not once, nowhere did I see another biological creature, not so much as a stray dog until the wheeled aluminium siding that served as the gate to the impound yard squealed open to the burst capillaries and sour-smelling jowls of the attendant. He took my release form and hundred dollars cash and led me through a line-up of cars serving time with their owners.

Not until I saw the Cadillac did I feel free. I wanted to slide behind the wheel, start the engine and drive until I ran out of car or road. A check of the glove box revealed that Harker had been kind or neglectful enough to leave the pepper spray behind. I reached under the dash to the left of the steering column and knew by the emptiness at my fingertips and in my chest that Gabe's original disk was gone. If the system had cut me a break by releasing me I'd use it, but not wisely, not by the system's values.

42

Harry Bendel practised law or a facsimile of it in a squat grey building on that section of Sunset Boulevard where Hollywood dreams faded to one-hour hotel rooms and a quick fix. The building had no doorman or security guard, just a letter-board directory and a set of carpeted stairs worn to the backing. Harry couldn't practise law in a doorman building. A doorman would throw out half his clientele.

In a voice no louder than rustling paper the secretary whispered my name into the phone and told me to please have a seat. The secretary didn't have much to do except block the door to Harry's office and stare at the clock. He excelled at both tasks. I thumbed with some interest through one of the sports magazines on the reception room coffee-table until I noticed the date on the cover had come and gone a year ago. The secretary was not tested by the arrival or departure of any clients and I didn't have to share the couch with anybody. A long and pointed hour later he received his orders and buzzed me through the door.

From behind his desk Harry offered a hand with the sentiment of his delight at seeing me safe and well. He'd been following the investigation of Gabe's murder in the newspaper and when he'd read that another photographer had been killed he'd worried about my safety. I put the Nikon to my eye and ran off three frames of his face cut into strips by the light of the venetian blinds to the side of his desk. The friendly patter ceased. I circled right and shot two frames of his wary, sidelong glance.

'I don't recall giving you permission to photograph me.'

I stepped forward and cut off his forehead, chin and ear to frame an extreme close-up, eyebrows to lips. His expression changed then from wariness to alarm and I shot the transition in four quick frames.

'I'll take the negatives Gabe left with you,' I said, 'and any prints you might have made.'

He turned to the venetian blinds, twisted the plastic rod to trim down the light and looked back over his shoulder. This moment had not been inevitable. Had I not intervened he might have pulled it off. While I waited in the lobby he had prepared strategies to counter what he expected I would demand. Instead of a direct reply he looked at me as though trying to figure what he could get away with. Would I believe a denial of possession? Should he offer to split the money? If he denied at first and then relented would he lose the credibility he needed to make a deal?

'No,' I said.

'No? No to what?'

'No to whatever it is you're thinking.'

'What am I thinking?'

'Doesn't matter. Gabe gave you the negatives and I want them back.'

'Do you know how much they're worth?'

'One point two five million but it's all fool's gold. Nobody lives to collect.'

The breath gusted out of him in a thin stream that ruffled the leaves of the fern on his desk. 'Do you mean one million, two hundred and fifty thousand dollars? How did you arrive at that figure?'

'Somebody sent a proof sheet to Damian Burke and called with a one million dollar price tag. You later delivered a set of prints and a cut-out newsprint note to Stone, Fell and Hughes demanding a quarter million. Different blackmail techniques, different blackmailers. If you can't do the sums in your head, pull out a calculator.'

He took those numbers to his desk and sat down with them, looked at them, said them one more time, then rolled his head back and laughed. I braced the camera against my lap to rewind the film. Photographs crowded the wall behind and to the side of his desk: family portraits, a golfing four-some on a tropical eighteenth green and a half-dozen bleached Kodachrome portraits featuring a massive towhead armoured in football pads and a crimson jersey lettered *USC*. Colour photographs blue as they age. These looked from the late 1960s. After the glamour of his college days, life must have seemed a little disappointing to Harry. 'The best way to get a print is from the negative. You have the negatives. You're blackmailing Finley.'

'And who do you think is blackmailing the movie star?'

'Nobody now. The person who tried was knifed to death and stuffed in the trunk of his car.'

Harry thought like a lawyer and glanced slyly across his jowls. 'Have you talked to the police about this? Have you made an agreement with them? Are you right now wearing a wire?'

'No, no and no.' I lifted the film canister from the camera back and dropped it into my right jacket pocket.

'What makes you suspect I have the negatives?'

I took a fresh box of Kodak, stripped off the cardboard and threaded the film on to the sprockets. Gabe gave Harry the negatives for the same reasons he went to him for a green card. He wanted to go outside the circle of people he knew and could betray him. He chose Harry because he had nothing to do with the tabloid business. And until Gabe died it had been a wise choice. Harry hadn't even bothered to check the negatives until then. After my visit he looked at what Gabe had given him, maybe even with the idea of handing it over to me. When he spotted Danavitch he saw the rainbow. As a lawyer, he knew the town's politics. He'd reason that Danavitch had more to lose than Burke and go after him. But I wasn't going to get into a game of proof with a lawyer. Obfuscation was a standard course they took in law school. We both knew he had them. No explanation needed. 'Why the real-estate company? Why not go to Danavitch directly?'

A gust of air shot through his nose to let me know what he thought of that idea. 'A simple rule in litigation is to look for the deep pockets. Danavitch himself doesn't have that much money.'

'But his financial backers do. You went after them, reasoning they'd keep their mouths shut and pay.'

'Might still work, too. What if I tell you to get lost?'

'Count the bodies, Harry. I'll make one phone call, word will get around and you'll be warming a slab in the morgue within twenty-four hours.'

He groaned as though he couldn't believe I was that big a bitch. 'I'll split it with you. We take both the movie star and the real-estate company.'

'No.' I shut the camera back and rolled through the first couple of frames. 'No doubt in my mind, they'd kill us.'

'By the same reasoning if I give you the negatives you'll be killed.'

'The negatives go from me to publication. When the photos hit the papers the killer won't have any reason to come after you or me.'

'How much will you collect? For the photos?'

'Not a cent.'

His right forefinger wagged disbelief. 'It's your business and I'm no expert but the tabloids would be willing to pay a considerable amount for something like this, or so I've heard.'

'They will,' I admitted.

'Then who are you trying to fool?'

'Nobody. Seventy per cent is already taken so I can't give you more than thirty.' I figured to buy Piña a nice headstone with her share, maybe in the form of a cash gift to her family. If she had any. 'Selling photographs isn't a science so I can't promise any hard numbers but thirty thousand seems about right.'

'Thirty grand won't even buy a car in this town.' Harry picked up the phone, touched one of the extension buttons and told the secretary to lock up for the day.

'Going somewhere?' I asked.

'The negatives are in my home office.' He reached beneath the fern to collect the keys from his desktop. 'Maybe thirty grand won't buy a car but it beats a knife in the gut.'

Judging by the black E-Class Mercedes that rolled out of the parking garage Harry hadn't exaggerated about what thirty grand would or wouldn't buy in Los Angeles. Nothing short of a half-century would have paid the sticker on that car. Through windshield wiper streaks of yard grime I tracked the Mercedes as it slowed and wheeled into the brick drive of Harry's colonial-style home, his arrival greeted by the motorized yip of the garage door. The big E-Class joined a convertible Mercedes roadster already in the garage. Before the garage door shut he pointed vigorously toward the side of the house. I eased into the drive, located the oil spot the

Caddy had left the last time I'd been there and threw the transmission into park low enough to leave a new one.

As I pushed through the side gate I dipped into my right jacket pocket for the canister of pepper spray and came up instead with the canister of film I'd just shot. That brought the first smile to my face in days. What did I expect to do with that, throw it at him? I dropped the film into my left jacket pocket and reached into the right again to pull out the spray. Other than try to blackmail somebody for a quarter of a million dollars Harry hadn't done anything to make me distrust him. The directions read point and shoot. I gripped it with my finger resting atop the nozzle and slid my hand back into my pocket.

Harry didn't make me wait more than a minute. He emerged out the sliding glass door at the rear of his house with a nervous backward glance and hurried step. The thumb and forefinger of his right hand pinched the corner of a letter-sized envelope and his left hand dangled free at his side. I didn't see a weapon but he was big enough not to need one. I kept my hand on the canister of pepper spray in my jacket pocket and stepped up to meet him half-way. He tapped the envelope against his side. The script at the line of address read *Burns* in a hand other than Gabe's.

'How soon before I'll see any money for this?'

'My agent will contact you. The cheques will have to be cut and then clear the bank, so a couple of weeks at least.'

He shook the envelope with short, crisp strokes of his wrist and sucked in his breath. 'You sure you don't want to – '

'No. You play games with killers, they'll kill you.'

He slapped the envelope into my palm. 'Why do I feel like crying?'

I slipped it into my left pocket just as the sliding glass door behind Harry jerked open. A thin blonde in crisply pressed tennis shorts and blouse stepped on to the patio and at the end of her lightly tanned arm she held a chrome-plated pearl-handled automatic. Judging by the size of the bore pointed at my chest I guessed .32 calibre. She shook the gun like a finger and said as though I needed more warning, 'I'm a member of the Beverly Hills Gun Club so don't think I don't know how to use this.'

Having shot a few people myself, I knew not to move when a woman pointed a gun at me. 'Harry, what's going on?'

Harry had enough sense not to step between me and the gun. That he held both palms up in terrified surrender did not reassure me. 'Baby, calm down, I struck a deal. There's no reason for this display of temper.'

'You struck a deal? A big enough deal to meet the mortgage on the house, you moron? How about the credit card debt and the back payments on the Mercedes?'

'Everybody has cash-flow problems, baby.'

'Everybody has cash. We only have problems. Give me the film.'

My fingers still clutched the envelope in my jacket pocket. The urge to pull it out was only strengthened by the sharp vertical shake she gave the pistol. She asked for the film, so I'd give her the film. 'It's in this pocket, OK?' My fingers slipped from the envelope to the canister beside it. Maybe she'd shoot me, maybe not. I pulled my hand out of my pocket, showed her the canister of film and slowly bent at the knees. 'I'm going to drop it right here on the patio, very carefully so you don't think I'm going to try anything. I have no desire to get shot over this.' I set the film canister on to a square of brick and cautiously straightened. 'I'm going to take three or four steps back now so you can come up and get it. You'll have lots of room, I won't be anywhere near you.'

She flicked the barrel of the gun, a gesture I interpreted to mean I should go ahead. I raised my hands and took four long strides back. She let the gun dip when she stepped forward to pick up the film. I was gone down the side yard before she saw me move, half the distance between the corner and the gate covered by the time she yelped at me to stop. The brick walk made easy running and fear of a bullet pumped my motor with pure adrenalin. She yelped again, this time in rage at understanding the trick. I slammed the gate shut and sprinted for the car. I had no idea I could run that fast, couldn't stop in time to grab the handle and had to double back to jerk open the door. I didn't waste the motion needed to shut it. The key stuck the ignition and at the first catch of pistons I hit reverse and floored the accelerator. The door swung shut with the momentum shift when I stomped the brake to throw the transmission into drive. The Caddy was too old and fat to smoke tyres but they sure let out a scream; I screamed too when I ran the first stop sign and nearly broadsided a Lexus. Then I laughed, long and loud. No way they could get a Mercedes out of the garage fast enough to follow me and I was too far gone for a bullet.

Over the steering wheel I shook a four-frame strip of negative from Harry's envelope. Held up to the fading light, the images corresponded to the digital ones I'd seen on disk. I knew a film lab in Hollywood open until midnight. They'd bitch about the rush but they'd duplicate the negatives that night if I backed my request with pocket cash. Without a loop and light table nobody would know the difference. I stashed the negatives in my pocket and picked up the cell phone to call Brenda.

'Where you calling from?' She asked.

'My car.'

'On the cell phone?

When I realized the mistake a curse served as my answer.

'They stick an ice pick through your frontal lobes while you were in the Twin Towers? A cell phone leaves a record.'

'If you and Raul want to back out, I understand.'

'What's the timing?'

'Now.'

She cupped the phone with her palm. I heard muffled voices in Spanish though not clearly enough to make out the meaning. 'Raul wants to know if you still got the photographs you talked about.'

'Even better. I have the negatives in my pocket.'

'Give us two hours then. It's rush hour.'

The road we agreed upon as the meeting point traversed the ridge across the ravine from Burke's estate. We planned to scout the terrain that night and go in the next day. I'd call Burke and Earl to a meeting at a public place ninety miles down the coast in San Diego. Brenda and Raul would have four, five hours to get in, find the tape of Gabe's murder and get out. When I met Burke, I'd give him the duplicate negatives, tell him, live and let live. That would mess with his mind but he wouldn't realize my true angle until the police came knocking on his lumber. Just about the time his lawyer bailed him out the dog photos would hit the newsstands.

At the insistence of local homeowners, a six-foot chain-link fence had been constructed at the border to Griffith Park to discourage people from parking on the street and hiking up into the hills but an enterprising birdwatcher had clipped through the links a dozen feet to the downhill side of the road. I pushed through the brush and skated on loose rock until I gained an unobstructed view of the back of the estate, its marble columns glowing beneath a neon-red sky. The scrub-brush hillside sloped sharply into the ravine and then up to the estate grounds. The safest route would be from the ravine, bypassing the video surveillance and possible alarms at the gate, but the brush and angle of descent might make that route impassable. I climbed up to the car, opened the trunk and propped the lid to my suitcase open with the tyre iron. A big 740-series BMW rolled up beside the Caddy just as I shrugged a jet-black sweater over my head. The sunset reflected in the passenger window slid down to Barry Scanlon from Crash Foto behind the wheel and his chagrined question, 'What are you doing up here?'

I bent over the rear fender to see him better. A thin bandage stretched across his cheek, as though he'd cut himself shaving. Though I couldn't read his eyes through the smoked glass of his wrap-around shades, he seemed shocked to see me.

'You know, just hanging out. And you?'

'I need an image of this actress who's getting the Academy Awards buzz. She's supposed to live further up the street.' The forefinger on the hand gripping the steering wheel flicked forward. 'These murders have scared everybody so damn much I can't find anyone to shoot her for me. You want the job?'

'Can't,' I said.

He shifted into reverse and backed the BMW to the curb. I feared the worst when he stepped out with a 35mm camera and telephoto lens strapped around his neck. Barry was a likeable guy but what I had planned wasn't precisely legal and I didn't want him hanging around my turf. 'I haven't had to work in the field for years,' he complained as he walked up. 'I'm not even sure I'll be able to get the exposure right.' He lifted the camera and for a moment I thought he was going to take a picture of me but his hand instead gripped the telephoto lens and gave it a twist. Next he was probably going to ask me what film stock to use. While he prepared to change lenses he said, 'Technology these days moves faster than you can keep track. Did you know that you can buy a signal scanner that locks into the conversation of someone using a cell phone?'

I half-turned to the trunk and closed my suitcase. I didn't want him peeking at my dirty underwear. 'So what?'

'So that's how I know you have the negatives.'

43

Even as the blade stuck the soft flesh below my left collar-bone I couldn't comprehend what happened. The hand fisted above my breast held not a knife but a telephoto lens. Maybe he wasn't really stabbing me. You can't stab someone with a telephoto lens. When you're being murdered you don't know until it's too late and then you still don't understand. My flesh yielded to the blade but not the hilt and the impact knocked me over the bumper and into the trunk. I thrust my right hand forward to fend the next blow but he instead slashed at my legs. I tucked them instinctively and the trunk lid slammed me into darkness.

Only then did I think to scream but my throat closed and the sound came to my ears like the bleat of a goat. The steel bed beneath me trembled and below my hips the trans-mission clunked. I did not properly understand that I was still alive but as the steel bed hummed and swayed I began to feel the pain in my shoulder and the breath leak back into my lungs. The blow had knocked the air out of me. I couldn't scream because I couldn't breathe. I wriggled the fingers of my right hand. If I could move, I could act. My left arm bent at the elbow but didn't lift from the shoulder at all. I reached across my body, felt a wet slick at the centre of a warm pain radiating through my chest and shoulder. I sucked on my finger, tasted blood. He had aimed for the heart but struck too high and I was alive. In the darkness I couldn't judge how quickly I bled but I was not dying, not yet.

If the blade had missed the major arteries I could hang on for some time. He might not know that. He might believe me mortally wounded. He had struck and backed away like a shark. A shark will strike and shake its prey and swim off to wait for it to die. The thrashing agony of a dying creature is dangerous. Better to strike decisively, then wait until the haemorrhage of life weakens resistance and finally stills it. The second attack begins the feed. The other victims had multiple stab wounds. Piña had lived long enough to scratch the paint inside the trunk. When the trunk opened again I'd see the knife. He wouldn't hesitate. He'd jerk open the lid and attack.

I reached toward the right pocket of my jacket for the canister of pepper spray and brushed against the case of the cell phone attached to my belt. I unclipped the phone, brought it up to my face. The dial glowed green under my thumb. I focused on the numbers and touched three of them. Somewhere the circuits of a relay tower hummed with an electronic SOS. The signal clicked and a woman's voice announced I'd reached 911, emergency services.

What did I want? To be saved? Too late for that. 'I've been stabbed and I'm about to be murdered.' To give witness. That was what I wanted. 'I'm locked in the trunk of a gold Cadillac with a blue right fender, up in the Hollywood Hills.'

'Just stay calm and I'll get help to you.' As if she could. 'What's the licence number of the car?'

The silence in my voice matched that of my memory. I couldn't remember. I had never bothered to memorize it. The idea that Scanlon listened even now jolted me momentarily but that was just the fear thinking; his scanner would have remained in the BMW.

'What's your name, honey?'

I knew that one. 'Nina.'

'Do you know the licence plate?'

'A 1976 Cadillac Eldorado. I was stabbed maybe four or five minutes ago. We're still up on the ridge, haven't gone downhill yet.'

'You just hang in there for a moment while I call this out, OK?'

A taped voice announced that the line was recorded. My last testament would become a matter of public record. If I could talk I didn't have to die in vain. 'This is a message for the LAPD.' I took a deep breath, then another. My brain felt itself rapidly filling with sand. 'The man driving the car is Barry Scanlon. He'll stop soon, try to kill me like he killed my husband, killed the others. I don't know how it happened. I thought it was somebody else. How could I be so wrong?' The warmth of the turning axle radiated through the trunk bed. I coughed once, couldn't remember what I'd just said. Too much to explain, too little time. And if I tried they'd just cover it up anyway. Better to forget all and sleep. But if I talked on record someone would listen and that was more chance than I'd earned. 'Look at the photographs on the disk. That's why they beat my husband. Burke and his bodyguard. Talk to Finley, he'll tell you. The voice on the phone – Scanlon. Of course. Gabe's agent. He must have seen the negatives, struck a proof sheet. Tried to blackmail Burke. The scalp collector saw, what? Gabe's murder. Scanlon wanted the negatives. But Gabe lied. He always lied. No negatives, no payoff. In my pocket – ' The trunk bed swayed like the sea, each undulation of road a wave rolling beneath me, each turn like the gentle rocking of a wake. I said, ' – the negatives.' I was floating at sea through a dark starless night, the salt air thick in my throat, spray flicking off the tips of whitecaps to mist my face, drifting off to the lullaby of gulls and a distant crescendo of waves rushing to shore.

'Are you still with me?'

I was warm, floating.

'Can you hear me? Nina!'

I coughed up something wet. The warmth spun away like water down a drain. I shivered with pain and cold. It was the blood. Losing so much of it. Made me cold.

'Speak to me honey. I'm on the phone. Can you hear me?'

'Sleepy,' I said. 'Gotta wake up.'

'That's right. Talk to me.'

Cold. My body shook with cold.

'What's your name?'

'Betty. Help is on the way. You just stay and talk to me now.'

The voice was warm. I held on to it, pulled myself up. I saw a face: concerned, black, beautiful. Beneath me I felt the Cadillac drift to the right as it slowed. 'Thanks. Gotta go now.'

'You got to stay awake. You hear me?

'Sorry. Time's up.'

I dropped the cell phone and felt along the ridge of my suitcase and down the sides to touch cool round metal – the tyre iron that had propped up the lid. I eased on to my side, braced my legs and pushed the suitcase another foot toward the back of the trunk. Each move fired jagged bolts from my shoulder to the back of my brain. Pain was good. Pain was life. The extra foot gave me room to tuck and twist my body a hundred and eighty degrees so my feet rested where my head had been. The right front tyre chaffed against the curb and the car lurched to a stop. I pressed my useless left arm against the back of the tail-lights, so the rise of sheet metal above the rear bumper would shield what I couldn't defend. The hinges of the driver door squeaked and the car shook when the door slammed shut. I cradled the tyre iron in my lap and palmed the pepper spray, then slipped a pair of sunglasses over my eyes and waited. Between the settling creaks of the car, footsteps scuffed on asphalt and keys jangled.

Then my brain tripped the wire that makes me different from most people. I stopped fearing I was going to die and resolved to kill. Rage, once locked so deep I hadn't known it existed, roiled from my belly. I had grown up under my father's hard fists. I absorbed his beatings, and the beatings of my mother, sister and brothers. And with his beatings I absorbed him, his rage. Then he raised his hand once too often and my rage came out, one-two-three, and my rage was bigger, hungrier, fiercer than his. He withered away then like all birth-giving creatures. His rage was mine. I carried his rage like a legacy, a hereditary curse, as much a part of me as my skin, bone, teeth, hair. It had been his father's rage, it had been his rage, and now it was my rage.

The key stuck the latch. The lock turned. The trunk when it popped sprang high and Scanlon swooped low with a six-inch blade. His swing hitched too late when he saw I'd moved. I sucked in my breath and blasted his face with pepper spray. The trajectory of the knife carried through to my leg, the tip slicing through skin and glancing off bone. The spray soaked the lenses of his wrap-around sunglasses but didn't immediately get to his eyes. I dropped the canister and screamed not in fear but rage. He jerked upright and jabbed again but the angle was bad; he hadn't turned his shoulders enough to get his weight behind the thrust. The tyre iron came up in my fist and knocked the knife to stick the trunk at the side of my throat. He cocked back to strike again. I swung the tyre iron and he leaned into it, the metal curve smashing first into his shoulder and carrying through to the side of his head.

Then it was his turn to scream. Then it was his turn to be afraid.

I lurched forward and swung again. The iron bit rib-high into his back, pitched him to hands and knees. I chopped down at his head but missed and the momentum of the blow carried me out of the trunk and on to the pavement. He had a clear killing angle then but he bellowed instead of attacking and ripped at his face. Sunglasses clattered to the asphalt. The pepper spray had mixed with the sweat beading on his forehead and rolled into his eyes. He raked at his eyes and screamed again. I lashed out with the tyre iron and struck bone at the knee but not hard enough to buckle the leg. He flung himself forward, face contorted by blindness. The blade gouged asphalt high and to the side of my head. I kicked and rolled and came up on my knees. He turned with me, grabbed my jacket with his left hand and swung the blade in a long, wide arc. The tyre iron caught him between neck and jaw. The arc of his swing broke at the hinge of his elbow and both hands jerked toward his face. I chopped down again, heard the bullet-loud crack of his wrist bone shattering. The knife skittered on to asphalt and spun blade to grip to blade. He rolled away, screaming, crawling belly to the ground not toward the knife but just away. I swung again and the curve of metal carved a quarter-moon of scalp from his skull. He kicked and lay still but the screaming didn't stop. I turned him on his back. Though he didn't move, though his eyes were vacant and his mouth slack, I heard him scream. I had no mercy in me, held the tyre iron over my head like a stake, thought I'd drive the socket tip through his eye and out the back of his skull.

A rush of clothing knocked me to the ground. The screaming stopped. Between me and the electric-blue sky hovered lips and two absurd slashes of hair. The moustache wagged in speech but I heard nothing. Then I closed my eyes and watched the blue fade to black.

44

The day I pulled the stitch-thread from the wound in my chest I sat on the wide stretch of empty beach beneath Santa Monica's palisade and watched a riptide form. The sand beneath me was moist from the storm the night before and near the horizon the clouds blazed red and gold above a plummeting sun. After a winter storm the tides are always churlish. The storm surge cuts and grooves the ocean floor and when the tide recedes the join between converging currents forms a riptide. The waters roil with sand churned up from the bottom and the colliding tidal energy launches the murky point of the rip through the blue-green sea like a lance. A good rip will hurtle out to sea for miles before its energy wanes.

I was lucky to be free and alive even if I didn't know what to do with either except test them. Gabe had been dead more than a month. Every day his presence grew dimmer. At times I could no longer visualize the simple things: how he walked, his body naked on the bed, the look on his face when he moved to kissed me. I could not animate him to movement or remember sequential images, only stills – a glance, the play of light, a mischievous turn to his lips. That morning I'd thought of him upon waking and remembered not his face but only photographs of it. Memory eventually would fade into the image until nothing else remained. One day many years hence someone might come across his photograph in a junk shop, like an old tintype, and wonder, who is this man? What life did he lead? The history of his being would be nothing more than a likeness, an image disconnected from all memory. I regretted his going but couldn't miss him. I couldn't miss what I never properly had. Maybe that's what I truly missed, the chance to have.

The ambulance had taken me to Los Angeles County USC Medical Center. Equidistant from the killing fields of South Central and East Los Angeles, no better hospital exists for gunshot and knife wound victims. When my parole officer heard I'd been stabbed she kept a vigil in the lobby until I came out of anesthesia. Hers was the first face I saw.

'Do you want me to call your family?' she asked.

'Nobody to call,' I said.

She felt guilty about what happened. Harker had found a homing device behind the rear axle of my car. Release me under tight surveillance, he suggested, and three homicides might be cleared. They had a suspect. My release might draw him out. I'd be safe enough. I was an ex-con. If the killer couldn't go after me he'd just change targets. I was an ex-con, he repeated. Would she rather see someone innocent murdered? So she copped me.

Four more years in prison or a knife in the chest, I'd take a knife in the chest every time. When I told my parole officer she did the right thing by releasing me she replied that considering my criminal record I wasn't the best judge of moral decisions. She didn't mean the remark to be funny but I took it that way.

Harker came to take my statement the next morning, gripping a bouquet of yellow daisies in his fist like a reluctant suitor. I asked him to put the flowers on the table between me and the next woman over. Her arm was broken, her eardrum ruptured, her skull fractured and her jaw dislocated. She was one of five other women in the room. We were all without insurance and indigent.

Harker dropped the flowers into a plastic water pitcher and wiped his hands with a handkerchief from his breast pocket. 'You either have a lot of guts or you're a borderline psychotic,' he said. 'You would have beat that guy to death if I hadn't stopped you.'

'Sorry to hear I didn't,' I said.

'Don't be. You have enough troubles without a coroner's inquest.'

'You charge him yet?'

'Not yet.'

'Why not?'

'He's still in a coma.'

That made up for my disappointment at not killing him.

'We'll hold him on attempted murder – yours – and work back from there. Skin and blood particles were found beneath the nails of Liliana Tutuila and if we get a DNA match he'll fall on that one first, even if she doesn't fit the profile of his first two victims.'

'Why not?'

There was patience in his look, and a little pity, as though it might be the pain medication and not a small brain making me so stupid. 'She wasn't paparazzi.'

'Didn't have to be. She figured out before I did that somebody else was involved in blackmailing Burke. She said as much to me on the phone. Scanlon was listening in on my frequency. It got her killed.' My call to Madame Alex led him straight to Piña. Once he knew her identity, he posed as a journalist and gained her confidence with a bribe. Maybe she figured out then who he was. Maybe she just talked too much. 'It's my fault, her death. I got her involved.'

'That wasn't her face I saw on the disk?'

He asked the question so innocently I nearly answered him straight. 'I take it that means you've actually looked at it.'

'The one in your car? The one that wasn't blank?' He tried to keep the line of his mouth parallel to the ground but the corners lifted away from him. 'That was my first indication that you might only be half crazy. And save your *mea culpa*. Tutuila was a working girl. She involved herself. The second victim, Dave Schuman, I figure was a case of wrong place wrong time.'

'Schuman was a scavenger.'

'Excuse me for asking, but aren't you all?'

'Then he was the tick in our side. He had a reputation for stealing exclusives, even followed Gabe to Las Vegas the day we got married, so I thought he'd tailed him the night the photographs were taken. Why not? It didn't seem like such a stupid conclusion, not then.'

'You thought Schuman was trying to blackmail Damian Burke?'

'Up until the moment Scanlon attacked me. But I didn't think it through, picked the wrong night for him to be watching. Schuman was blackmailing Barry Scanlon, not Burke.'

He laughed at the idea and opened his mouth to say something funny about it but then his eyes locked and he stared straight over my head, thinking it through. 'You're saying he saw the murder.'

'Sure he did. He knew Gabe was working on something. He followed him the night of the murder to see what it was. He watched Burke and his bodyguard drag him out of the house and drive him down the hill. I don't know whether Gabe was part of the blackmail scheme or not but Scanlon followed Burke down the hill and when he found Gabe by the lake he . . .' I didn't want to finish the sentence and Harker didn't need to hear it but something in me had to say it, to finish it. 'He killed him. He stabbed my husband to death. Then he filled his pockets with rocks and rolled him into the lake. Schuman saw it and when he tried to make Scanlon pay was killed for it.'

'Your husband wasn't part of it, Scanlon's extortion attempt.'

I thought he wished to let my dead rest in peace but I was beyond the point where the kindness of a lie gave me any solace. I asked, 'Then how did Scanlon get a proof sheet to send to Burke?'

'Scanlon was his agent. After the night of the party he brought the proof sheet to the agency to talk about publication. Scanlon was the one who proposed blackmailing Burke. Only he refused to call it blackmail. How could it be blackmail if Burke would volunteer to pay to recover the negatives? He'd blackmailed celebrities like this before. The Englishman decided to play along with it but write a story, an exposé. Bad idea. Scanlon found out. That's why he betrayed him. That's why he killed him.'

'Nice theory but I don't believe it.'

'We found handwritten notes in Scanlon's office. The handwriting matches the Englishman's.'

It didn't take me long to put it together. 'He ransacked Gabe's apartment, didn't get the negatives but found the notes.'

'Maybe Scanlon flew into a rage, maybe he planned it out. Either way he had to kill him or be exposed.'

'If he never comes out of the coma we'll never know, will we?'

'You're happy about that, aren't you?'

'That he might lie on a prison hospital bed the next thirty years, a tube down his nose and a catheter jammed up his willy? Yes, I'm very happy about that.'

He shook his head, said, 'You're meaner than some cops I know and I know some mean cops.' He pulled a white envelope from the inside pocket of his sport coat and tossed it on my lap.

I folded back the flap, spilled out what was left of the negatives. The package was a half-dozen frames short of complete. I held the plastic sleeves up to the bedside light. As near as I could tell without a loop, every frame in which Supervisor Danavitch's face appeared had been snipped out. I didn't have to say anything; Harker spoke up after one look.

'I don't want to do this without your consent.'

I slipped the negatives back into the envelope and set it on the bedside table. 'Looks like you already have.'

'He didn't pay for sex. Technically, he didn't break the law.'

'No crime against watching, that right?'

'The actor set him up and you know it.'

'And he's a friend of the department.'

'I'm not asking you for any favours.'

'People who take generally don't. They just take.'

Harker lifted another envelope from the same inside pocket and shook out the enclosed document. Like all court papers this one crammed legal language to the margins. The most important words were prominent enough to read at first glance: Warrant for the arrest of . . .

'Can you read the charges?' Harker held the form up to my face. 'Kidnapping and assault with a deadly weapon. I talked to Mark Finley about the night you spent together on the mountain. I'm sure I can dig up more if I put a little effort into it.'

The warrant was enough to send me back to jail until I reached menopause. At the bottom where the issuing judge's signature was supposed to be affixed the line was blank.

'I didn't make that crack about you being borderline psycho out of nowhere. You scared Finley so much he quit his job, plans to move to Idaho. I'm afraid to think what might have happened to the actor if you decided to take revenge. Instead of three squares a day in the comfort of a hospital bed you'd be back in the Twin Towers, facing conviction on murder one.'

I took the deal.

'You think I'm your enemy but I'm not,' Harker said before he left. 'I understand loss. I know what it is to feel so bad you just want to go out and hurt something, make it hurt as much as you do. I wish I could give you some sage advice about how to deal with it. I can't.'

It took me some time to fully appreciate what a good friend Frank had been. Had he not kept a copy of the disk I'd still be in jail. He complained bitterly about the deal I'd been forced to make with Harker but agreed not to make the disk public. I told him most of what I knew to compensate him for his loss. He published his story the day the photographs hit the newsstands. Libel concerns compelled him to keep the supervisor's name out of it but Burke was an international star. Newspapers from Novosibirsk to Santiago ran the story and the less explicit images. For one week, the talkshows chattered about nothing else. Burke left the country for an extended vacation in France, where they understand these things. Two weeks later, few people remembered what had happened.

My flesh seemed to contract when I first dived into the surf. The rip was so strong I could barely hold my feet to the sand. I dived again and let it take me. The brackish current flowed out to sea swift as a river. The urge to suicide didn't move me. Far from it. I just didn't care. The rage that had sustained me through the years burned me hollow and cold. I had always believed my life would truly begin when I got through the next big thing before me, whatever that thing was. First, the thing was to get through high school and get out of the house, then to get a job, get married, get ahead. In prison, I believed life would begin when I got out. My rage drove me forward, always the engine of my actions. In my youth those who thought they knew me believed I was a good girl; I wasn't. I was full of anger and fear. I drank because I was angry and afraid. I worked hard because I was angry that I'd never been gifted and afraid I never would be. Fury wrenched apart relationships – mother, father, boy-friends – and fear lashed them together again. I hurt people because inside I raged and clung to those same people because I feared being alone. The fear had left me at Gabe's death and the rage at my revenge. Without my rage, I was empty. Nothing filled me up. I bobbed along the surface, an empty bottle.

The palisade as it receded glowed in the golden light of the setting sun and beyond a fringe of palm trees the towers of the city glinted beneath a lavender sky. I kicked a quarter circle to the north to watch the coast mountains split the sea at the Channel Islands and pitch to shore at the tip of the long blue scythe of bay. After the winter rains the mountain flanks rippled fluorescent green and a deep shade of purple.

A foot above the water a flock of pelicans skimmed single file. The inverted angle of their necks balanced enormous beaks. At the edge of the rip they circled and the lead bird rose into the sunset sky with a great flapping of his wings. At the arc of the climb he tucked his wings and the angle of his neck flattened and his beak pierced the water like the tip of an arrow. His tail-feathers disappeared beneath the waves and then a few feet distant his beak popped up, shaking furiously until the caught fish made a lump in his throat going down. One by one the pelicans lanced into the water, shook and swallowed and hurled themselves again at the sky. The sea beneath me was a living thing and so was the sky and I was not apart from it I was a part of it.

Perhaps that was enough.

I turned my body sideways to the shore, the only angle possible to escape a riptide, and began to swim.

Acknowledgements

Many friends and strangers aided my efforts in the writing of this book, and to all of those who helped, named and unnamed, thanks. Christine Toombs, parole officer with California Department of Corrections, patiently explained parole procedures and the nature of the relationship between parole officer and parolee. Anthony Erba, a private lawyer practising in Philadelphia, helped me to understand legal issues and procedures. Beatrice Smith and Bob Sebald provided information about the Department of Corrections and prison regulations. Alex McGregor, Stephen Oxenbury, Pete Dadds and Rupert shared details about their lives as foreign journalists and photographers working in Los Angeles. Others unnamed educated me about life in prison. I'm much indebted to all. Any errors in the text are purely mine.